PRAISE FOR M. L. BUCHMAN

Tom Clancy fans open to a strong female lead will clamor for more.

— *DRONE*, PUBLISHERS WEEKLY

Superb! Miranda is utterly compelling!

— *BOOKLIST*, STARRED REVIEW

Miranda Chase continues to astound and charm.

— BARB M.

Escape Rating: A. Five Stars! OMG just start with *Drone* and be prepared for a fantastic binge-read!

— READING REALITY

The best military thriller I've read in a very long time. Love the female characters.

— *DRONE*, SHELDON MCARTHUR, FOUNDER OF THE MYSTERY BOOKSTORE, LA

A fabulous soaring thriller.

— *Take Over at Midnight*, Midwest Book Review

Meticulously researched, hard-hitting, and suspenseful.

— *Pure Heat*, Publishers Weekly, starred review

Expert technical details abound, as do realistic military missions with superb imagery that will have readers feeling as if they are right there in the midst and on the edges of their seats.

— *Light Up the Night*, RT Reviews, 4 1/2 stars

Buchman has catapulted his way to the top tier of my favorite authors.

— Fresh Fiction

Nonstop action that will keep readers on the edge of their seats.

— *Take Over at Midnight*, Library Journal

M L. Buchman's ability to keep the reader right in the middle of the action is amazing.

— Long and Short Reviews

The only thing you'll ask yourself is, "When does the next one come out?"

The first...of (a) stellar, long-running (military) romantic suspense series.

I knew the books would be good, but I didn't realize how good.

Buchman mixes adrenalin-spiking battles and brusque military jargon with a sensitive approach.

13 times "Top Pick of the Month"

HAVOC

A MIRANDA CHASE POLITICAL TECHNOTHRILLER

M. L. BUCHMAN

Buchman Bookworks

SIGN UP FOR M. L. BUCHMAN'S NEWSLETTER TODAY

and receive:
Release News
Free Short Stories
a Free Book

Get your free book today. Do it now.
free-book.mlbuchman.com

Other works by M. L. Buchman: (* - also in audio)

Other works by M. L. Buchman:

Contemporary Romance (cont)

Love Abroad
Heart of the Cotswolds: England
Path of Love: Cinque Terre, Italy

Where Dreams
Where Dreams are Born
Where Dreams Reside
Where Dreams Are of Christmas*
Where Dreams Unfold
Where Dreams Are Written

Science Fiction / Fantasy

Deities Anonymous
Cookbook from Hell: Reheated
Saviors 101

Single Titles
The Nara Reaction
Monk's Maze
the Me and Elsie Chronicles

Non-Fiction

Strategies for Success
Managing Your Inner Artist/Writer
Estate Planning for Authors*
Character Voice
Narrate and Record Your Own
Audiobook*

Short Story Series by M. L. Buchman:

Romantic Suspense

Delta Force
Th Delta Force Shooters
The Delta Force Warriors

Firehawks
The Firehawks Lookouts
The Firehawks Hotshots
The Firebirds

The Night Stalkers
The Night Stalkers 5D Stories
The Night Stalkers 5E Stories
The Night Stalkers CSAR
The Night Stalkers Wedding Stories

US Coast Guard

White House Protection Force

Contemporary Romance

Eagle Cove

Henderson's Ranch*

Where Dreams

Action-Adventure Thrillers

Dead Chef

Miranda Chase Origin Stories

Science Fiction / Fantasy

Deities Anonymous

Other
The Future Night Stalkers
Single Titles

ABOUT THIS BOOK

When one of their own is threatened—the nation's #1 air-crash investigation team enters a race to survive.

An airliner downed on a Pacific atoll. A CIA covert strike team sent in to "clean it up." An old enemy seeks revenge. This time, the NTSB's autistic air-crash investigator, **Miranda Chase,** *and her team are in the crosshairs. The action races around the globe as US military airbases become shooting galleries and their lives are placed on the line.*

And hidden from sight? A treacherous plan to grab political power and start a new war with Russia in the Middle East. Only Miranda's team stands in their way, if they can survive.

PROLOGUE

Seattle-to-Sydney Direct
600 miles southwest of Hawaii
39,000 feet
Seat 57A

HOLLY DID NOT APPRECIATE THE IRONY OF THE MOMENT.
Not even a little.

She'd been sitting one row from the very rear of the Airbus A330-900neo jet. If she didn't hack off her legs to get away from the muscle spasms soon, it would be a Christmas miracle—too bad it was October.

Tall people were *not* meant to sit in economy on fourteen-hour nonstops. But National Transportation Safety Board investigators also knew better than to sit in the front of airplanes.

Statistically, the rear rows of modern jetliners were marginally enough safer that she couldn't quite bring herself to sit forward, no matter how safe airplane travel in general had become. Far and away the safest form of transport—except when it wasn't.

And her job as a crash investigator was all about when it wasn't.

The very tail of all wide-body jets had a motion that seemed disconnected from the rest of the aircraft, and, at the moment, the vibration was almost as annoying as her legs.

Only six hours into fourteen, for a flight she didn't want to make. It was lucky for whoever wasn't there that the seat beside her remained empty; it was best that her need to vent her frustrations to someone, *anyone*, had no ready target.

Hell, at the moment she'd even vent to Mike, though their parting at the airport hadn't gone smoothly.

Are you sure you don't want me to go with you? And Mike had even insisted on driving her to SeaTac for her flight. As if he somehow *knew* how hard this trip was going to be for her—despite her not telling anyone anything about why she was going. Of course it was Mike, so he'd known even without being told.

Which was almost as annoying as how comforting his presence had been on the drive.

But the *last* thing she wanted was her past touching any part of her present.

It was a completely rank horror-show that she herself had been given no choice.

Then at the curb he'd gotten all clingy, like he was going to miss more than having her in his bed most nights. Like he...*owned?*...some piece of her?

So not her.

She'd already been with him longer than anyone before in her life. Maybe it was time they were done—just to avoid his getting *too* attached. Soon, maybe he'd be wanting more than she was willing to give.

The period of the vibration shifted.

Rather than the slightly annoying slow sway of the airplane's butt—like riding in a big old 1970s station wagon that desperately needed new shocks—it took up a distinct rhythm.

One that accelerated fast.

With a periodicity that, in all her experience, should never happen to any airplane.

She opened her left-side window shade to glare out. Her eyes ached as they adjusted from the dim you-should-be-sleeping-now interior to the glaring dawn over the Central Pacific.

There was the source just at the edge of her view—the Number One engine was shaking visibly.

Shaking hard.

It didn't explode or shatter like an uncontained turbine failure. Those happened in milliseconds; things occurred fast when meter-wide titanium fans shattered at thirteen thousand rpm.

This engine was swaying side-to-side on its mount.

She'd never seen that before. Or read about one doing that. Or even heard of such an event. Holly barely had time to wonder if Miranda ever had.

Three seconds later it broke free of the left wing.

Shit! There was an event she could go a lifetime without witnessing herself.

Just as the engine mount's shear bolts were designed to do, rather than letting the engine destroy the wing, they sheared.

The suddenly disconnected Rolls-Royce Trent 7000

turbine— unburdened from doing its half of dragging the two-hundred-and-fifty-ton twinjet across the ocean—shot forward, then climbed up and over the wing. As it passed safely above the wing, the engine did finally fail. It shattered spectacularly before disappearing aft faster than she could track.

Holly cringed and dug her fingers into the arm rests, but no metal pinged off the main fuselage.

She held a deep breath for maximum blood oxygenation, ready to exhale with the abrupt hull decompression.

But there wasn't one.

No oxygen mask suddenly dangled inches from her face.

Apparently the hull was still intact. The engine failure was directed downward from the inverted engine's top, pummeling the wing with a single loud bang. The well sound-insulated plane muffled it to little more than the noise of retracting landing gear.

Holly's fingers ached as she released the padded armrests, even though it had only been seconds.

She tried to remember the last aircraft she'd heard of suffering a complete breakaway engine loss, but she wasn't Miranda Chase. Her team's IIC—Investigator-in-Charge— carried the entire encyclopedia of aircraft accidents around in her head. It was only one small part of what made Miranda the best IIC in the entire National Transportation Safety Board.

Herself, not so much.

Holly took a slow, deep breath before she dared to look again.

The engine was definitely gone.

She focused on recalling her military training to remain

calm in a crisis—because crisis was just the normal state of operations.

Then she looked down and lost the bit of calm that she'd mustered.

That was definitely the vast emptiness of the world's largest ocean seven long miles below.

She looked over her shoulder at the two flight attendants. Still chatting quietly in their seats.

A glance up the long aisle revealed that most people were asleep, except for a few diehards watching movies. It was seven a.m. back in the flight's origin city of Seattle— after a one a.m. departure; sensible people *were* asleep just the way any airlines wished their passengers to be. Always. She was surprised they didn't just drug the coffee and be done with it.

The aisles were empty, and there was no splash of light from any other open window shade revealing the pile-driver sunrise pounding in her window.

She knew that from the angle of the cockpit it would be impossible for the pilots to check the engine visually. However, their instruments would certainly be reporting the loss with several catastrophic tones. Trained pilots would now be ensuring the integrity of the Number Two Engine.

But someone should be coming out to look out a window that could actually see the engine. Or at least a flight attendant should have been asked by the pilots to inspect it for them if they were too busy with alarms.

She would count to ten.

Holly made it to five before she punched the call button.

One of the flight attendants behind her, a male, reluctantly unbuckled and came up to her seat.

"You really should keep the shade down, miss. Others are

all catchin' a bit of shut-eye." While she enjoyed the Aussie accent—it was a real relief after spending the last year in the US—she had other priorities.

"I didn't want to alarm anyone, but you just lost an engine." She kept her voice down and her tone even.

The attendant hadn't started out looking friendly and now was looking less so. "I'm sure the pilots have everything well in hand."

Holly grabbed the attendant's pretty two-tone tie by the back strap, used her thumb to slide the knot tighter to make sure she had his full attention, then dragged him across the empty seat beside her and her lap to mash his face up against the window.

His choked-off squeak of alarm sounded ridiculous coming from a guy, especially an Aussie.

"We've lost a bloody engine, mate. See?" She thumped his face against the plastic a few times to make her point.

"Don't move!"

Holly looked up and into the muzzle of a Glock 19, the new Gen5, which she'd been meaning to check out. An air marshal must have been sitting in row 56 directly in front of her. He now knelt on his seat and had aimed his sidearm at her over the seat back.

Her former training as an operator in the Australian Special Air Service Regiment kicked in.

The air marshal held it one-handed, and with his finger outside the trigger guard. He was making it too easy.

Keeping one hand firmly on the flight attendant's tie, she swung her other hand up from where the marshal wouldn't be able to see it over the seatback. Catching the barrel in the Y-shape between her extended thumb and hand, she grabbed on and rotated it upward away from her face, forcing his finger to slip completely off the trigger guard and below the weapon.

If he'd been using a two-handed hold, she'd need a different, more difficult technique, but he didn't even get that right.

Continuing the motion, she peeled the gun completely out of his hand.

Then Holly tossed it in the air just enough to flip her hold from barrel to handgrip and jammed the barrel up his nose.

Her finger was inside the trigger guard.

"You! By law, air marshals are required to flash their badge and give a warning before wielding a sidearm. So you're in serious trouble there, mate. Now sit down and behave unless you want your brains to finish the flight with a free upgrade to First Class."

He made a tiny nod of acknowledgement—about as big as could be made with a 9 mm pistol rammed up one nostril.

She hit the magazine release, dropping it on the back of the flight attendant still pinned across her knees. He flinched and gagged a bit.

Racking the slide back against the edge of her folded tray table, Holly saw no round in the chamber. He hadn't been a real threat at all. She pulled the trigger on the empty chamber, tugged the paired slide release levers midway down the barrel, nudged the slide against the tray table again, and, with a quick shake, the gun fell into pieces.

The air marshal started to move, but not the right motion to turn and sit.

She dropped the rest of the parts on her temporary tray table built from the choking flight attendant's back—she eased up his tie a bit—and grabbed the air marshal's windpipe with her free hand. Holly pinched hard enough that he wouldn't make a sound that could alarm other passengers.

"And if you reach for your bloody baton, you wanker, I'm going to use your own handcuffs on you and leave you face down in the thunder box." Not an airline toilet in the world didn't reek after the first six hours of a flight.

She shoved him away, gathered up the Glock parts from the flight attendant's back, then hauled him off her lap.

"You! Call the bloody cockpit and tell them they've lost the Number One engine." She glanced out the window and saw it was even worse than she'd expected. "And that the wing isn't looking so pearla either."

———

First Officer Quint Dermott slid into the empty seat next to the golden-blonde staring out the window. She was a serious treat. If she had the face to go with that hair and body, she'd be a stunner.

If this was an airport bar, he'd think some thoughts. But they'd just carked a bloody engine in the middle of the Pacific Ocean. If the flight attendant hadn't been freaking, he sure as hell wouldn't be here—it was hard to spook one that much.

"I'm the copilot. What seems to be the issue here?"

"Well, mate. I'd say you're the one having a serious issue." She didn't bother turning to face him as she spoke. Her Strine was so broad it was like being home.

"Fair dinkum?" Quint could have a good time calming this passenger down, not that she looked upset. Long blondes with legs to match and who spoke like they were from the heart of the Outback were something he hadn't run into in far too long. Maybe *never* a Sheila of this quality. Too bad he had to hustle back to the cockpit.

Twice he'd been blocked from the left side of the aircraft by some doddering fool getting out of the seat, so he'd just hustled down the right side without getting the outside view he wanted to check the engine's status. They'd hit the fire bottle, but there were no readings at all, which they should have from even a crippled engine.

She waved out the window.

This wasn't the best angle to see the engine but it was better than nothing. He leaned in. Close enough to see the wing out her window and feel—his heart skip the next three beats.

An ES—Engine Separation. *Shit!* No wonder there were no readings coming back to the cockpit.

"I'm seeing some serious flexion at rib number nine," her accent slid away as she continued at a volume barely louder than a cozy whisper in his ear. "Directly above the engine pylon is where it seems to be doing the worst of it. You're already getting enough buckling in top panels eleven through fifteen that I think the rear spar is FUBAR as well."

"Uh, where?"

She pointed.

He leaned in again. He was a pilot, not a mechanic, so how in the world would he know which skin panel was which? But practically lying in her lap, he could see what she was talking about. There was a crinkle in the aluminum skin directly above where the engine had been. Like a fist had punched down on it from above—a damn big fist. Fucked Up Beyond All Recovery was a depressingly accurate assessment.

"You'll also want to switch off any cross-tank transfer pumps or that leak is going to empty the plane of fuel faster than a possum up a gum tree."

Now that she'd pointed it out, he could see the dribble, okay, the fair gush of petrol going the wrong way.

"Oh, one more thing." She dumped the parts of a handgun into his lap, then reached forward and patted the head of the man seated in front of her.

He cringed as if he'd just been whacked by a hammer—a ruddy farrier's one. For shoeing Budweiser Clydesdales.

"I didn't really want to give that back to your air marshal. He seems inclined to want to shoot me."

"Happen much?"

"Not anymore." She offered a luminous smile.

"How—"

No time for finding out how she knew any of that.

"You—"

Nor how she'd disarmed an air marshal.

"ATSB structural specialist on loan to the NTSB," she answered his first question at least.

On the Australian *and* the Yanks' Transportation Safety Boards? That explained a hell of a lot.

Definitely time to get back to report to the captain.

"You're with me." He shoved to his feet.

Or tried to.

She hooked onto his belt and used it to slam him back into the seat before he was half out of it.

"What?"

"Don't want to scare the B&S unless you're into a dog's breakfast," and her broad Strine was back.

He looked up the long aisles.

A Bachelor and Spinsters Ball was a common dance

party in rural Australia—a fun and typically very big gathering. Maybe not as many as were presently on the plane but on a good night...maybe. It wasn't only singles who came out for a B&S Ball dance.

And a dog's breakfast was always a proper mess.

Righto, he'd leave the passengers to their quiet sleep and free-movie pacifiers.

He did his best to smile at the blonde and rose as normally as he could.

She smiled back like she hadn't a care in the world.

———

"DANI. IT'S ME. I HAVE A TAGALONG," HE LOOKED AT THE pieces of the air marshal's gun that he'd carried up the aisle. "I'm the one with the weapon. We're good as Vegemite."

He ignored the blonde's snort of laughter.

It was today's agreed-on safe word. Without it, Captain Dani Evers wouldn't have opened the door.

There was a sharp snap as the cockpit door's three heavy bolts unlocked.

He swung it open and flinched when he saw the captain's sidearm aimed to just behind him. Quint hadn't known that Dani was one of the thirty percent of airline pilots who now flew armed. He showed her the gun parts, not that he had a clue how to put them together, then moved for his copilot's seat and dropped them into a cup holder.

Dani lowered her aim just enough to center on the blonde's chest as soon as he was out of the way.

"Clean as if I showered just last Thursday." The blonde didn't flinch. Instead, she did a slow turn with her hands out, like she was a runway model for airplane disasters, then shut the door behind them.

"Who is she and why is she in my cockpit? And how bad off is my engine?"

"Bad. Gone."

"Explain."

He just waved a hand at the woman.

She sat in the jump seat located just behind and to the left of his own righthand seat. She slipped on a headset, then propped her feet up on the end of the central radio console that ran between his and Dani's positions as if she was kicking back at home to view a program on the telly.

Dani offered the blonde one of her patented Looks of Death.

The feet went away. Experience had taught him that Dani Evers' Look of Death could scorch a pushy guy in a pub right down into a puddle on the beer-stained floor. He could almost feel the blonde shrug as if it was no big deal.

However, in keeping with her stated background, she launched into her observations, explaining the status to Dani in a way that was detailed, concise, and rattled off like the professional she claimed to be.

Quint buckled in and cut the fuel flow to the left wing.

Dani looked at him in question when she described the damage to the wing.

He nodded that it looked exactly as bad as the assessment made it sound.

Dani's semi-eyeroll was her version of a violent curse—not something you did when the cockpit voice recorder was listening. It was one of the many reasons he liked flying with Captain Dani Evers. No games; there was never any question about what she was thinking.

He watched the fuel gauges for a minute to make sure the flow had stopped, and tried not to feel incompetent just listening to the passenger.

"You've got an ETOPS-330 rating on this jet," she reminded them as she finished her analysis. "Three hundred and thirty minutes of Extended Operations flying time on a single engine. All that right ripper ability won't be doing you a spec of good if the wing comes a cropper first."

"We're eighty minutes past Hawaii," Quint checked the charts. Then glanced back at the blonde.

She was staring at the Escape Rope cubby beside the overhead breaker panel. There was one on each side so that, in the event of a crash blocking the cockpit door, he and Dani could open a side window and descend safely.

It had always been an academic bit of knowledge from training—maybe not anymore.

After a long study, she turned back to him.

"I might just be chucking a wobbly," she was perhaps the least berserk person he'd ever seen, "but I don't think you have reaching-Hawaii kind of time. And eighty minutes past Hawaii means that Howland Island is the next nearest watering hole, two hours the other way—that's if you want to be landing on a deserted sandy beach and curling up in a watery sleepout with Amelia Earhart. Howland's the place she never reached in the end. Leaves you but one squat to plant your tush." She stopped, not telling him where, of course.

Quint had to search around a bit until he found Johnston Atoll. The island was abandoned and the runway closed, which was why it hadn't shown up right away as an alternate field. It was less than twenty minutes away. It would take them that long to descend seven miles—unless they lost the wing, then it would be much faster. More like ninety seconds, which wouldn't end well.

Technically, Johnston wasn't available for any kind of landing. But nine thousand feet of decommissioned US military-grade runway compared with crashing into the ocean when their wing fell off wasn't a contest for him. He'd argue with the Yanks' FAA *after* he'd survived. Better, he'd let Dani do it; she was the Captain after all.

"How sure are you?" Dani asked as Quint put Johnston on the center screen, then flipped the radio to the satellite frequency for their airline's emergency mechanic.

"Personally, I'm surprised we're still aloft." The blonde recrossed her legs the other way as if she had nothing better to do. He did notice that despite her apparent ease, she'd put on the jump seat's full five-point seat harness: lap belt, shoulders, and the crotch belt from the front edge of the cushion to the central clasp that any mere tourist would have missed.

"Who the hell are you?" Quint felt as if he should know. But even thinking about her being in a totally unexpected place, he couldn't account for her.

"Sergeant Holly Harper, retired from the Oz Special Air Service Regiment. At your service, mate. Wondered when you were going to ask."

Quint could only stare at her.

Couldn't even blink.

SASR were the elite special operators of the entire Australian military. Which explained why she was so calm in a crisis.

What it didn't explain was...*Holly Harper?*

"Christ. I thought you were dead."

"Close a few times, maybe more than a few, but not yet. Why were you thinking that?"

It would take far too long to explain.

He turned to Captain Evers.

"We're going down, Dani. We need to get on the ground fast."

Because if there was anyone who knew about surviving, it was Holly Harper.

1

"OKAY IF I PLACE A CALL?" HOLLY PULLED OUT HER PHONE.

"You'd need a sat phone from here to—" Dani glanced back.

Holly waggled her satellite phone at her.

"Sure, go ahead." Then she turned to the copilot. "Quint, plot me a course to Johnston. Then get a call in to operations and find out what a minimum stress descent looks like—make it a quick one."

"Roger that."

Holly dialed, then studied the back of the first officer's head while it rang.

Quint? Quint *Dermott?* That actually fit. He'd been a skinny kid of twelve when she was a still-gawky sixteen-year-old who'd left town after being thrown out by her parents. He'd certainly shaped up very nicely—all handsome, broad-shouldered, and Australian.

"This is Miranda Chase. This is actually her, not a recording of her."

"Hey, her." Holly could feel herself relaxing, even if

Miranda was three thousand miles away in Seattle, it made Holly feel better just to hear her voice.

"Where are you? Passing over Johnston Atoll? Can you see it? I've always wanted to go there."

"Funny you should mention that. I expect that I'll be seeing it real soon now—up close and personal like." Then she explained their situation.

"The runway is not authorized for use. Not even for emergency landings."

"Good, they can come arrest me if we survive. Warm cell, three squares a day, bolted solidly to *terra firma*—I could get down with that. Besides, that's part of the fun of an emergency, you get to break all sorts of rules."

"I was never particularly good at breaking rules. Are you with the pilots?" Holly could hear the fast rush of computer keys.

"Yes."

"Speakerphone." Miranda was also never one for the niceties of conversation.

She continued as soon as Holly had switched over and called for Dani and Quint's attention.

"Temperature at Johnston Island Airport is eighty degrees; winds are east-northeast at seventeen so you'll be landing on Runway 23 with an elevation of two meters above mean sea level. Barometer is currently 29.96. Visibility is reported at ten miles in light haze." She continued with their best rate of descent for minimum wing-loading stress, proceeded to tell them what landing configuration to select right down to flaps and airspeed, and might have told them every detail of the approach if Holly had let her.

"If I don't die, Miranda, I'll give you a shout on the mobile to let you know."

"I'll get the team in motion." Because, of course, Miranda would want to investigate the cause of the crash, whether or not they died. "If it's going to be a water landing, call me and we'll mobilize the Coast Guard."

Which was surprisingly thoughtful for Miranda. Holly knew that Miranda's ASD—autism spectrum disorder—made it extremely hard for her to think about people.

"Though I wouldn't hold out much hope for recovering the aircraft if it does go into the ocean. The abyssal plain comes within a few kilometers of the atoll and is principally below the four-thousand-meter mark. Recovery from those depths is exceedingly difficult."

So much for thoughtful. Thoughtful about the plane anyway. Miranda's parents had died in the 1996 crash of TWA 800, which was recovered from a hundred and thirty feet of water just off Long Island, New York—not thirteen thousand feet off a remote Pacific atoll. She'd have been sure to remain very well-educated on the complexities of deep-water recovery operations.

"That's an extremely unlikely type of double event, breakaway and then an uncontained turbine failure in the same engine. If anything, the opposite would be more typical, but an ES is an exceedingly rare event. That's remarkably interesting. It is difficult without a more recent inspection of the skin buckling, but based on your initial description..." there was another sharp rattle of a computer keyboard. "Models are projecting a nineteen percent chance of losing the wing on gear-down and an eighty-two-point-five percent chance of losing the wing during the landing."

"Thanks. I'll hopefully be in touch soon, Miranda."

"Okay. Bye." And she was gone.

"Who the hell was that?" Dani snapped out, but Holly

noticed that she was flying exactly on the profile Miranda had recommended.

"She's the NTSB's top air-crash investigator." Holly considered what a lame statement that was to describe her. "She's...unusual. But she's also rarely wrong."

Miranda, despite all her oddities, was also her friend.

It was going to really suck if she herself died, because neither she nor Miranda had a whole lot of those.

2

Miranda called Mike as she hurried from the house, across the meadow, and up the grass runway to Spieden Island's hangar. She didn't like breaking the law, but the urgency was high enough that she was willing to drive one-handed while using her cell phone. It was an oversight that she hadn't set up the island's golf cart with a hands-free system.

The data said that the law should have been written to prohibit *all* phone usage while driving, even hands-free, but that had proved to be too unpopular a choice for vote-minded representatives in Washington, DC. Safety bowing to consumer convenience was a trend she'd witnessed all too often in how the FAA's decision-making process selected which of her own recommendations to implement and which to ignore.

And now she was a contributing factor to one of the most dangerous problems that the NTSB's surface transportation teams were always struggling to correct.

The fact that she owned the island and was the only person presently here perhaps diminished the risk.

While waiting for Mike to answer, she navigated along the dirt track over the half-mile from her house to her aircraft hangar. The local deer were very calm when she was the only one here, and she had to wait for a family of them to graze across the track in front of her.

"Hi, Miranda. What's up? Do we have a launch?"

"Holly is on a flight to Sydney, currently over Johnston Atoll in the South Pacific."

"Right. I knew that. I've been following her with a flight tracker. What's Johnston Atoll?"

Miranda considered the priority of answering the question...and chose not to. Holly would congratulate her on proper selection of information organization. However, the "where" was indeed pertinent.

"It's *where*," she emphasized for clarity that she was amending his question, "her plane will be crashing in approximately nineteen minutes. Or near there if the damaged wing falls off before they arrive at Johnston. I estimate that she has a sixty-two percent overall chance of survival."

The deer remained grazing in the middle of the track. As much as she hated to do it, she beeped the golf cart's horn. They looked at her in some surprise, but moved aside and she was able to continue toward the hangar. She was most of the way there before Mike responded.

"Would you mind repeating that?" His voice was so soft that she could barely hear it over the swishing of the tall grass against the underside of the golf cart. She really needed to get out the tractor and mow the runway soon.

"Yes." She hated repeating herself. Mike knew that, but

she did it for him. "Holly is on a flight to Sydney, currently over Johnston Atoll in the South Pacific. It's *where* her plane will be crashing in approximately nineteen minutes. Or near there if the damaged wing falls off before they arrive at Johnston. I estimate that she has a sixty-two percent overall chance of survival."

"Holly. Crashing. South Pacific. I'm...going to need...moment."

Miranda wondered at that. It wasn't a difficult concept. Unless this was one of those interpersonal things that she never understood. Mike took care of those for her. But he wasn't making much sense at the moment.

Perhaps it was because he and Holly had been lovers for most of a year now. Would that be a significant factor? His stuttered reaction said yes.

"Is Andi there?"

"Uh-huh."

When nothing happened, she decided that she had to be extremely specific. "Please hand the phone to her."

"Uh-huh."

For seven more seconds nothing happened, then there was a shuffling sound.

"Miranda, what did you say to Mike? He's gone white as a sheet."

She decided that her third repetition wasn't actually repeating herself if a new person was involved.

"I said, 'Holly is on a flight to Sydney, currently over Johnston Atoll in the South Pacific.' Then I told him, 'It's *where*,'" she did her best to match her earlier emphasis for exactitude, "her plane will be crashing in approximately nineteen minutes. Or near there if the damaged wing falls off before they arrive at Johnston. I estimate that she has a sixty-two percent overall chance of survival.' That percentage is only a first-order approximation; I should have mentioned that. Then he asked me to repeat it and I told him the same thing again, also without the first-order approximation amendment."

"Okay, Miranda. I'll try to fix it. You need to think about how important Holly is to us all, but especially to Mike. You could have found a better way to say that."

"But she *does* have a sixty-two percent chance of survival. That's a good thing."

"The fact that she's in a pending plane crash and has a thirty-eight percent chance of dying is a bad one."

"Oh, I get that now." At least enough to state that she did. But... "No, I don't. Can you explain it to me?" She'd carefully used as positive an explanation as the data allowed. She always started with the positive once a period of A/B testing had revealed that it made for a much more efficient and effective interview than when she started with a negative—even when the negative was far more factually supported.

"Later. Let's get moving."

"Oh, right." Miranda had parked at the hangar but become too involved in the conversation to continue with what she'd been doing. Driving and phone conversations were *not* a good combination. "I'll be at the Tacoma Narrows airport in twenty minutes. Call Jon. We're going to need a longer-range jet than either of mine to fly there."

"He's your boyfriend. Shouldn't you be the one calling him?"

"That will only delay my flight to you." Miranda unlocked the hangar door and pressed the garage opener. She concentrated on keeping in motion, which made it harder to follow the phone call.

"And he may not wish to use a military asset for a civilian crash."

"Remind him that Johnston Atoll, closed or not, is still a military property."

"Okay, I'll twist his arm for you."

"Why would you do that? I'm not certified to fly any current military jets. We'll need both of his arms intact."

"It's a saying, Miranda. It means that I'll take care of it as soon as I can get Mike and the others moving. Are you sure that you don't want to call him?"

Miranda thought a moment. Their last conversations had been...uncomfortable. Jon kept asking for things she didn't understand; like he was the one in control and her opinion was damaged to begin with. She knew that. She was the one who was autistic after all, not him. But she still had them and—

"I'll take that as a no," Andi spoke up.

"No what?"

"No, you don't want to call Jon."

Miranda considered the time factor and the annoyance factor. Weighed separately either would be acceptable. Compounded? "No, I don't."

"Okay. I'm on it. Now go," and Andi hung up.

Miranda realized that she'd come to a stop again. Cell phones really were dangerous.

She hung up, pocketed the phone, and did the preflight inspection on her Korean War era F-86 Sabrejet. It was only as she was rotating aloft that she remembered the hat sitting on the mantle over her ocean-cobble fireplace.

Holly had given each member of their NTSB team a bright yellow baseball hat from her beloved Australian women's national soccer team, the Matildas. She was quite insistent that they all wore them to every site investigation. They had the added advantage, except when hard hats were required, of making the other members of her team easy to locate at a site investigation.

Miranda must remember to ask if it was still technically a baseball hat if it touted a soccer team, which being Australian was actually called a football team.

Instead of being further distracted by that thought, Miranda wondered if there was some deeper meaning in the fact that she'd left it behind.

Not one she understood.

Besides, hats were replaceable.

Holly wasn't.

Oh! *That* would explain why Mike was upset at the possibility of her dying.

Now that she'd followed the thought full circle, she aimed the jet south and pushed up to the sea-level limit of just under seven hundred miles an hour. From the San Juan Islands, she was now less than eight minutes to Tacoma Narrows airport.

3

HOLLY WOULD HAVE PREFERRED TO NOT OVERHEAR QUINT briefing the cabin crew over the intercom. The words were quite unnerving: *possible water landing, probable hard landing, wing loss might mean that the exits over the port wing would become unavailable, fuselage, break up...*

She'd be happier if she was still in her back row seat, still asleep—which she'd never been and wouldn't last another thirty seconds anyway. Right now, the flight crew were scrambling to get all the passengers ready and in their brace positions.

While the passenger area was probably a land of mayhem and panic, the cockpit was a quiet refuge. The two pilots discussing emergency checklists and rates of descent as if they were chatting quietly over crumpets and tea. Maybe it was worth giving up her tail-section seat to not be a part of whatever was happening back there.

Quint was doing a respectable job of not giving in to his nerves. But Miranda would like Dani Evers' nerves—in this crisis, she didn't give a single sign that she even had any. At the moment she was pure pilot, and Holly appreciated that.

They'd descended from thirty-nine thousand feet to fifteen thou, and they still had two wings.

She really should message the others. That's what many of the passengers would be doing, or trying to. Not a lot of cell reception in the middle of the Pacific Ocean. Her sat phone could reach Mike easily enough.

But she had no idea what to say to him.

Besides, her training had long ago taught her that the only direction to look during a crisis was ahead.

Still. A short message—

"Holly, could you go look and see just how bad off the wing is?"

"Oh sure, Quint."

She appreciated the interruption as an excuse to tuck the phone away unused.

"You've just kicked the entire cabin into full alert. No worries. I'll just mosey my civilian ass out of your secure cockpit. If some wuss packing a death wish like it was his best mate busts in, you can deal with that. Then I'll just make a point of staring out at the wing with stark fear on my mug. Should I return the air marshal's Glock while I'm about it or just shoot any passengers who really are chucking a wobbly?" If Quint had unnerved her with his instructions to the cabin crew, it seemed only fair turnabout to tease him some.

"You never were one for following orders."

"Not on *your* bloody crew, mate." Actually, she'd been damn good at doing precisely that, in a way. Eleven years in the military had taught her how to follow orders. Of course, Special Operations Forces was more about making up the rules as they were needed—not exactly the land of conformists. "Besides, will knowing if we're all about to die change any of your choices?"

"She's got you there, Quint. Let's stay focused." Whether Dani was ordering herself or Quint wasn't clear in her tone.

Holly soon wished she had taken the offer of strolling through the panicked crowd; at least it would be something to focus on other than how small Johnston Island Airport looked. In the middle of Johnston Atoll, which was four tiny islands and a ring of submerged coral, was the biggest of the four islands that broke the ocean's surface. And Johnston Island was a runway...and not much more. A pinprick in a wide blue ocean that made it seem far smaller than the numbers said it was.

The coral ring outlining the atoll was mostly submerged. The lagoon was a tropical blue but outside the ring it was the blue-black of the Pacific depths. She knew it would get bigger fast, but for all her flying, she'd never approached a runway in an airliner. The fit seemed very unlikely from the air.

Why did Miranda have to remind her of quite how deep that dark blue was? It was a depth from which Malaysia Airlines Flight 370 was never recovered, or even found.

Three other tiny islands were all that dotted the ten- by twenty-kilometer lagoon. Johnston Island itself was emphasized by a too-geometric semidarkness around its perimeter. The runway must have been built on dredgings from the lagoon's reef. That would explain the island's nearly perfect rectangular shape and only being a little longer than the runway that stretched along the whole centerline of its surface.

Sterile cockpit rules during essential operations—like

not crashing—meant she couldn't even distract herself with some easy banter.

She unbuckled long enough to peek out the left-hand windows. The outer wing section, which was all she could see from up here in the cockpit, was flexing a lot in the last stages of the descent. Crossing to the other side, she couldn't tell if the intact right wing was better or worse.

Patience.

It was one of the hardest skills she'd ever learned in the SASR—one of the hardest for all grunts to learn. There were times when the only real option was to park your hind end and wait. So she parked it and buckled back in. It could be days, waiting for a target to pass within range of a lookout or a sniper hole. Weeks and occasionally months could go by between deployments. Of course, the intensity of the constant training required to remain at peak performance had filled those times reasonably well. As had the easy access to a watering hole for a nice frothy pint or three afterward.

Five thousand feet.

Dani and Quint were doing pilot jabber.

"Descent rate fifteen hundred feet-per-minute."

"Flaps One."

"Speed Two-zero-zero."

"Range twelve miles. On planned glide slope."

"Three minutes down." Assuming the wing lasted three more minutes.

She noticed that the landing gear was still up. Miranda's warning that lowering the gear might put too much stress on the wing was being listened to.

Once Quint had called their operations department, it had taken them almost ten minutes to confirm what

Miranda had known off the top of her head. At least if she herself was going to die, it would be based on the best advice that Miranda could give. It was just bloody awkward that the landing gear was attached to the wing itself, rather than the body.

The best-chance strategy of surviving a crash was remarkably counterintuitive to her.

The Special Air Service Regiment's training had taught her to maximize body flexibility. The way to take a hard blow in hand-to-hand combat was to stay loose—absorbing the blow with motion rather than resisting it.

Parachute training was about absorbing the shock with soft knees, then flexing into a roll onto thigh, butt, and shoulder to absorb the impact in stages.

In a crash, the rule was to line up your body and brace hard. The chances of a snapped neck dropped dramatically if she aligned her head with her shoulders and spinal cord, and she tightened her muscles to keep it there. Back injury protection was augmented by no twists in the spine at time of impact. Bracing as hard as possible at the moment of maximum force made it less likely to sustain any torsion or compression injuries.

"Descending at fifteen hundred fpm."

"Flaps Two."

"Speed One-seven-five."

"Range eight miles. On planned glide slope."

"Two minutes down."

Each word they said, she followed from instrument to instrument. At Dani's call for "Flaps Two", Quint pulled back on the large black lever in the horizontal console close by where Holly had braced her feet again.

She jerked them to the floor and hoped neither pilot noticed.

Of course they were rather busy.

Dani's partial turn and half smile said that Holly had been caught red-footed.

The runway looked impossibly narrow from the front seat of the jetliner. To the south, there was a taxiway and airplane parking area. To the north, there were plenty of footprints of buildings that had once served the island but only one building of any size remained—a lone blockhouse of heavy concrete.

"Flaps Three."

"Are you sure about that?" Quint asked with his hand on the lever. "More flaps increases wing stress."

Damn it! Holly should have kept Miranda on the phone.

"Belay that," Dani stated in a perfectly chill pilot way.

"Speed One-fiver-zero."

"Range four miles. On planned glide slope."

At two miles Dani ordered, "Gear down."

Quint rested his hand on the gear lever at the center of the console above the throttles. It had a black handle shaped like two side-by-side tires. With impressively little hesitation, Quint then moved it down as if Miranda hadn't predicted it to be the most dangerous moment prior to the landing itself.

There was a dull whir and grind—more felt through the soles of her feet on the deck than through her ears.

With a distinct thud, they locked into place and the three down-pointing green arrows directly above the lever lit brightly.

Nobody moved for a full five seconds.

Quint's voice sounded thin and breathless as he managed, "Gear down and locked."

"Confirmed," Dani sounded little better off.

For all her vaunted confidence in her ability to handle anything, Holly wasn't sure she could have spoken, even if called on to do so.

"Okay," Dani nodded to herself. "Okay. Set Auto-Brake to low. We need to minimize stress on the port wing. We'll depend as much as possible on the starboard engine reverser. Quint, you ride that carefully. Don't spin us off the runway."

"Roger that. Thirty seconds."

Johnston Island, which had looked so small moments ago, now dominated the forward view. The pavement, so narrow from above, now looked comfortingly wide and safe.

"One mile. Three hundred feet. Speed steady at one-four-zero," Quint read off.

"Half mile. One hundred."

In her estimation they were going to crash hard into the front end of the runway. She wanted to shout "Too low! Too low!" but kept her mouth shut.

"Flaps Three. Do it now."

Quint didn't hesitate.

Holly braced while wishing for her seat back in the tail.

The additional flaps gave the plane extra lift, making it seem to float the rest of the way to the runway threshold.

The wing held and Dani kissed them down onto the first X painted broadly across the pavement—declaring the runway wasn't a legal runway anymore—so smoothly that Holly barely felt it.

4

MIRANDA WAITED A VERY FRUSTRATING TWENTY MINUTES *AFTER* stowing her jet in her hangar at Tacoma Narrows Airport. She had covered the ninety-eight miles far faster than Jon was taking to cover ten.

By the time she'd finished with the jet, three of the members of her normal investigation team had arrived and gathered in the office to wait.

She'd stayed outside despite the light rain—staring at the sky to the east. She could *see* JBLM's airspace from here, including Jon's terribly belated takeoff into it.

The fourth member, Mike Munroe, her human resources specialist, had waited with her...sort of. Without saying a word, he had paced back and forth in the rain with such jarring steps that she barely recognized him.

Finally, a slim C-21A Learjet had slipped into the sky above Joint Base Lewis McChord and turned in their direction.

Three long minutes later, he landed here at TNA and taxied over to her hangar. The others came out with their site investigation packs and personal go bags just as he eased to a halt.

"Miranda," Jon called out as he descended the steps of the US Air Force C-21A Learjet. "I'm not your personal taxi service. You're lucky I was local. I was teaching an advanced incident investigation class at JBLM next door."

Major Jon Swift was a member of the US Air Force Accident Investigation Board. However, the idea of him teaching anything past an intermediate class was a disconcerting concept. He simply wasn't that good at it. After all, he'd missed Taz Cortez's *not* dying in a crash he'd investigated—there had only been *thirteen* people who had died in that military incident—yet he hadn't reported her body as unaccounted for. Even in a fiery civilian crash involving hundreds, all bodies were eventually accounted for and most remains were identified.

"The crash is on an ex-military base on what is still US government restricted-access land." It should be obvious why they needed a military pilot. And it required no profound knowledge to conclude that her team's little Cessna Citation M2 bizjet didn't have the reach to cross the Pacific.

"That doesn't mean that it was necessary to call my uncle." Jon's uncle, the Chairman of the Joint Chiefs of Staff, often helped Miranda when a crucial military investigation was being blockaded or interfered with.

Miranda glanced at Andi who smiled happily.

"When Jon refused, I took the liberty of unleashing Taz."

"I'm not your fucking dog," Taz growled, surprisingly like one. But she was smiling and Andi didn't appear to be worried, so perhaps it was okay.

Taz was the newest member of their team, and Miranda

understood her even less than she comprehended the mannerisms of her other team members—or most people.

"Christ, you two are a pain!" Jon also sounded...angry? Growling, but without Taz's smile probably meant angry. She still wasn't sure of Taz's emotion.

Miranda took a quick peek at her autism reference notebook. Taz's face did match happy, but her tone...? She wasn't ready to consider the concept of a tone communicating a different emotion from an expression. That seemed terribly complex. She didn't even make a note for future reference before tucking her notebook away.

However, Miranda couldn't agree with Jon's assessment that Taz and Andi were both a "pain." She'd found them each immensely helpful on crash investigations or she wouldn't have included them on her team.

Taz ignored Jon. "I didn't have the chairman's number, so I took the liberty of calling his wife. General Elizabeth Gray was actually the one who got Jon's Air Force ass moving."

Andi and Taz smiled at each other. They were both shorter than Miranda's five-four. But, despite Andi being of Chinese descent and Taz of Mexican, their smiles were nearly identical for reasons that eluded Miranda—even without any tonal elements to confuse matters.

Jon just groaned.

"Why are we wasting time? They should have landed twenty-two minutes ago." Mike grabbed her arm, clutching it hard. "Have you heard from her yet?" It was the first words he'd spoken aloud since arriving at the airport.

Miranda checked both her phone and her satellite phone. "Not yet. Let's go."

Mike looked as if Holly had just punched him in the gut —even though she wasn't here.

And seeing his posture—and a quick glance at his face— she finally understood. It was the way she'd felt when her parents had gone down in TWA 800, when the 747 had exploded off Long Island, New York. She'd been thirteen, but her insides had felt just how Mike looked.

She turned to Andi, "I get it now."

Andi glanced at Mike, then nodded.

Mike and Jeremy climbed aboard the little jet.

"Aren't you forgetting something?" Jon stopped her on the first of the three steps ascending into the gray US Air Force C-21A Learjet.

Miranda couldn't think of what.

"Sure, Jon." Andi pushed Miranda to continue aboard. "Thanks, Jon, for not making Taz and me come over to Joint Base Lewis-McChord to kick your ass in person to get you moving."

Miranda wouldn't have phrased it quite that way, but the statement was accurate.

"Yes, thank you for that, Jon. That would have taken far more time than it already has."

Then she ducked low enough to enter the plane and turned for the rear to join the others.

It was only after she sat down that she realized her lover had probably wanted a hug of greeting. Even during an emergency? Apparently yes. She jotted down an entry in her personal notebook under the Relationships heading.

5

THE LANDING OF THE AIRBUS A330-900NEO UNFOLDED WITH a movie-like slow motion feel—even more painfully drawn out than watching Engine One destroy itself and the wing.

At least that's how it appeared to Holly as the adrenaline surge slowed her perception of time.

It began with Captain Dani Evers' landing, so perfectly smooth that it didn't seem real. Only the screech of the tires accelerating from zero to a hundred and forty knots indicated they were in contact with the runway.

Keeping an eye out the left window, Holly could just see the left-side wingtip continue down to the ground, spark, then flop onto the ground. Not breaking free, it dragged at that side of the plane.

"Reversers on Engine Two full!" Dani and Quint shouted out in near perfect harmony, trying to slow the right side with the engine enough to match the drag from the broken left wing.

The roar was so loud that Holly's ears popped.

"One-twenty."

"One-ten."

Holly braced as hard as she could. For once, she truly didn't appreciate Miranda's assessment of a plane's airworthiness. Her eighty-two-point-five percent chance of wing failure on landing had just paid out.

How—

Of course! In flight, the wing was flexing upward with lift. The undamaged bottom skin of the wing had remained under tension. But as soon as that lift was lost on landing, the damaged upper surface couldn't hold the wing's weight aloft.

Gods, but Miranda was so good. Holly should have figured that out, but Miranda simply knew it.

But even though she probably knew, Miranda hadn't said what might happen next.

Holly had seen enough accidents to have a very vivid imagination at this particular instant.

At one hundred knots, the left landing gear let go. The left wing and landing gear broke away and skidded to a halt. The left side of the jet's fuselage lurched sickeningly down onto the runway. The sudden drag of two hundred and nine feet of aircraft hitting the runway twisted it sideways on the pavement.

However, the momentum of two hundred tons of plane and fuel, twenty-five tons of passengers and baggage, and twenty-five more tons of cargo—all still moving at ninety-three knots, a hundred and seven miles an hour—was not to be denied.

If the landing gear had held, they might have been sent careening sideways across the rough side field into the ocean, but the struts weren't designed to withstand a force at ninety degrees—to the side—as the plane twisted.

Both the nose gear and the remaining right-side main gear buckled, then tore away at the lateral force.

The aircraft, now sliding fully sideways to the direction of travel, began to roll.

When the right wing slapped down onto the runway, the fuselage's momentum was still far too great to be stopped so easily.

The wing acted as a lever of resistance.

It didn't give.

Yet the fuselage had to roll.

It initially sheared in two places.

Immediately ahead of Row 20, at the slight weak spot due to the emergency exits directly in front of the wing, the hull's structure gave way. At the center of the destroyed cross section, the forward economy-class galley shattered, spraying meal containers and soda cans in every direction.

The occupants of Row 20, Seats D, E, and F, were severely burned by the spray from the shattered coffee machine. They didn't survive long enough to care when a fully loaded drinks cart slammed into them and caved in their chests.

Seat 20F gave way under the massive blow, and its seatback crushed the occupant in Seat 21F.

Aft of the wing—in the wide gap between rows 41 and 42 —the fuselage sheared again, utterly destroying the four mid-cabin lavatories. Passengers for five rows both fore and aft were sprayed with ten gallons of high-pressure toilet disinfectant, staining them bright blue.

With the shearing of the fore and aft sections of the fuselage, the wing pinned the middle section of the fuselage in place. But the plane's momentum was far from spent.

As of this moment, only the four unfortunates killed by the errant drinks cart had died.

The next several tenths of a second vastly increased the death count.

As the wing and midsection slid more and more slowly along the runway, problems were multiplying beneath the wing.

The remaining Rolls-Royce Trent 7000 engine under the right wing was being driven into the runway's surface and ground upon by the fuselage section. The angle of the wing pressing down directly on the engine stopped the shear bolts from breaking the still-running engine safely away.

At the moment of landing gear failure, First Officer Quint Dermott's head had been thrown against the cockpit side window hard enough that he lost his grip of the Engine Two throttle.

The seven-ton Rolls-Royce Trent 7000 remained spinning at full power.

The abuse ultimately bent the housing enough to strike the titanium alloy fan blades of the high-pressure section of the engine—spinning at over twelve-thousand rpm.

Because Captain Dani Evers had decided to trust Miranda's estimation of pending failure and had chosen to dump all of the fuel except what was needed for the landing, there was a fire at the wing, but no explosion. No overflash of incandescent heat shot into the passenger cabin.

It didn't matter. As the engine shattered, shrapnel plowed upward through the containment shield, then the fuselage. The most fortunate of the passengers in the starboard and center seats—who had paid for an upgrade to the more spacious midsection accommodations of Enhanced-Economy—died instantly.

Most of the rest of the midsection passengers died long before help reached them.

The forward section of the fuselage, including the cockpit—which had sheared at the galley section—rolled over the sand and clump grass parallel to the edge of the runway. Like an eighteen-foot-diameter rolling pin that was seventy feet long, it flattened coconut palms and hedge cactus for the length of an entire hundred-and-twenty-yard soccer pitch. After rolling six and a half times, it finally came to rest completely upside down.

The tail section didn't fare as well after it broke free from the midsection. It flopped and flailed like a landed fish twice around—breaking fifteen people's necks with the force of the battering—before the sturdy horizontal stabilizers and tail fin held the very aftmost section in place despite the remaining momentum.

This caused the rear fuselage and tail section to shear once more.

The tail section remained right side up at only a slight angle. The two stewards seated in the aftmost portion of the tail section—including the one with the sore throat from where the passenger in Seat 57A had choked him with his own tie—blinked at the tropical sunrise that hammered down on them through where the rest of the plane had been.

The rest of the rear fuselage continued rolling down the runway. The lavatory waste tanks, built into the below-decks cargo space along the shear line, were under half full. They fractured. A hundred and eight gallons of blue-immersed human waste sprayed the last six rows of seats.

In Row 56, the soaked air marshal experienced three

more rolls before his section of the fuselage came to a stop. Hanging sideways, high in the air, he vomited with spin-induced vertigo, splashing the waste-coated occupants of seats C through J in his row.

The rear galley and Row 57, including Holly's former seat, had been shredded.

6

No slashes on the wall carving out the endless line of days.

Or rather nights.

No passage of daylight told the time here.

She was merely Guest Seven.

Guest!

Her prison, her *cell* was below ground. It had a coolly moist atmosphere that didn't fit with an above-ground sunbaked blockhouse.

Here it was the nights that counted.

Trained to never sleep more than four hours at a time, each night stretched on forever. Hell began when the sliver of light under her cell door went out, plunging the common area into darkness. No more well-muffled sounds slipping in with the light. Silence.

It was the CIA's luxury prison: for prisoners so high profile that the Americans chose not to try them, because that could go public. Or execute them, which was against their oh-so-cute laws—but too dangerous to be roaming the world either.

If that was intended as a compliment, she wasn't feeling it.

For a time, she'd thought they might be sliding days on her—sleep-cycle inversion, random time changes, and the like. It was a common interrogation technique implemented by an artificially fast cycling of days with a combination of lights and drugs. The lack of REM sleep drove individuals to desperation in a matter of days.

She had used it herself on foreign agents any number of times, back when she still had a life as a Russian Zaslon operative. It could make even the innocent beg to confess within days—it didn't matter to what.

She'd been here a year.

But everything felt normal, just boringly mundane.

They weren't interrogating her. Maybe they were hoping she'd simply rot away.

Not when there was a chance of getting back at them.

By day, she had an allotted ninety minutes in the common area—an exercise room and not much else. Her time slot shifted from day to day, but not too annoyingly. Off the one hall, there were nine locked doors besides her own. The only other entrance to the common area was from a set of stairs leading up to a door that belonged in a bank vault. Above it was a small red "Exit" sign that was seriously, seriously, *seriously* annoying.

Nothing else.

Her room was comfortable.

A good bed, high-grade sheets, comfortable chairs, even a treadmill when she'd asked for one. It let her maintain her condition with a minimum of three hours of running a day.

Because there *had* to be a chance of escape.

Electronic books, music, television including the news, regular meals... The high frequency of tropical ingredients was the sole indication of where this prison lay. Unless that too was a trick.

She could scroll the news feed, but send no messages. Communicate with no one except "The Host" if there was a problem—like she needed a new pair of jeans—and that only electronically.

Except for the phone.

How many times had she smashed that phone?

Each time it was simply replaced while she was out in the common area—by two armed guards in full US military combat gear to watch her while the fully-kitted technician worked. They moved with all the precision of Special Operations.

With her training, she *might* get past them...but that vault door was a major problem. They never came through it if she was even touching the lowest step of the stairs. It always thudded shut before they descended from the upper platform.

The landline phone had no way to dial. She picked it up, and it auto-dialed her handler. That the handler was the Director of the CIA was again a compliment she could do without. Clarissa Fucking Reese never lost her cool. Never failed to answer until the time she'd called Clarissa precisely every three minutes for twenty-four hours straight.

After that, the technician installed a timer. She could only place one call a week after that.

No interrogation by Clarissa, they just...talked. World politics, power, men, and not much else. Neither of them cared about much else.

As it was her only outside contact, she'd learned to protect that.

At least until three weeks ago.

When her phone rang for the first time, it had nearly given her a heart attack. She didn't even know it could do that.

Then the world had changed.

No identity on either side.

Simply a male voice, *Interested in making a deal?*

What kind of deal? Can you get me out of here?

Not likely. But I know what you are, if not who. I need some of your contacts, and your knowledge of field craft.

I have a price.

Name it.

I need to erase some people—with extreme prejudice. She wanted them dead, dead, very painfully *dead.*

I too need someone removed.

She thought it over quickly. *That* had been her specialty out in the real world.

Over the next two minutes, she sketched out the bare bones of a plan that she'd been formulating for an entire year.

No problem.

She'd resisted the urge to scream with delight, do a happy dance, or offer to fuck him blind.

I want to add one more name to your list, he'd suggested, and told her who.

I have no problem with working that in.

I'll be in touch, then he'd been gone. But true to his word, he'd called the next night.

She'd fully reworked her plan, and they reviewed the details for hours.

Whoever he was, he was sharp. A power player with deep-level political savvy that placed him in either Moscow or the American capital.

By the end of the call, they had an agreement.

Now, I need someone able to pull it off.

Did you hear about the August 2nd parade through the streets of Moscow?

The man snorted out a laugh.

An entire class of sixty young bucks from the FSB Academy—internal security, like the American FBI—had piled into fourteen black Mercedes Geländewagen luxury SUVs and then raced through the city, shooting selfies at every chance. It had blown their usability as secret agents. The entire class had been shipped out to the wilderness of the Kamchatka Peninsula, their instructors demoted or forced to resign.

They were exactly the sort of renegades that her new "friend" needed.

She gave him the contact information.

She'd worry about getting out of here later.

For now? Today was finally the day her revenge began.

Today was judgement day for NTSB investigator Holly Harper.

7

HOLLY HUNG UPSIDE DOWN FROM THE CEILING THAT HAD ONCE been the deck. Out the forward windscreen, the view offered some three meters of white sand. Nothing remained visible out any of the side windows. One escape window was immersed in the sand, the other in the center of a very prickly looking hedge cactus.

"Well, this must be Australian football rules. Too rough to be Association Footy." Holly really would prefer to be in a soccer stadium seat at the moment. Ideally with a Four'N Twenty meat pie burning one hand and a twenty-five-ounce oil can of Foster's lager cooling the other.

"Let's not go out that way."

Quint looked at his window, then back at her. "Seems like a half-decent suggestion."

Very carefully, she tested her limbs.

Flexing her toes, she could feel them move inside her boots, which was a good sign about the integrity of her spine. Joint by joint she worked her way up until she cricked her neck just far enough to make its usual pop. The only thing that hurt was her fingers, from how tightly they'd been gripping the chair arms.

"Rugby would be my guess by the beating we just took," Quint grunted. Then he released his seatbelt and collapsed onto the cockpit's ceiling. "You still with us, Dani?"

"Most of me, anyway. But I think my clean flying record didn't survive." She made much less work of getting out of her seat than he had.

Holly had forgotten the kind of graveyard humor that kicked in when a mission had come too close to offing everyone on the team, but they'd all survived. For the moment, this disaster was three people wide and one inverted cockpit long and tall.

Holly propped a hand on the ceiling, found her balance, then released the seatbelt. She turned it into a handstand, then lowered herself to the ceiling and rolled into a cross-legged sitting position.

"Show-off," Quint muttered. Then went to open the cockpit door. Even once he managed to disengage the safety bolts, it didn't budge. "Something must have been bent."

"Like your entire airplane?"

"Yep. Something like that."

A small debris field lay at the low point, which was the curve of the cockpit's ceiling. Water bottles, a flight case, some miscellaneous paperwork, and the butt of the air marshal's handgun sticking out from under a sneaker. She scrabbled around for the slide and magazine, slapped the weapon together, then jammed it into the back of her waistband and pulled her shirt over it. It wasn't the sort of thing to leave lying around. She'd have to remember to give it back to the marshal...if he'd survived—and promised not to go pointing it at her again.

In the process, she found Dani's gun, which Holly handed to her, and a Snickers bar. When neither Dani or Quint wanted it, she tore it open and bit off a chunk.

"Never know when you'll have time to eat again," she mumbled at them around a full mouth. It was the old Spec Ops rule: the best place to store food and water was in your body.

Quint eyed her, snagged an energy bar from the ceiling turned into a floor, broke it in two, and handed half to Dani.

Holly stood up and opened the floor hatch, now overhead. Grabbing the rungs of the steel ladder that normally descended down into the avionics bay under the cockpit, she dragged herself hand-over-hand up it.

"Christ on a crutch but I'm out of shape."

"Your shape looks just fine to me."

She offered him a snort of mockery. What did he know? It shouldn't be this hard to haul herself upward just using handholds; she was woefully out of training. Of course, she wasn't Spec Ops anymore, which meant she didn't train five to ten hours every day, minimum.

Maybe she could blame it on Mike. He wasn't a runner, but he was amazingly comfortable to lie against during quiet mornings. Taz *was* a runner. Holly had started running with her, at least on occasion. She promised herself, now that she was alive, that she'd start getting up in time to join her...at least more often.

The avionics bay was a dark, cramped space. All of the airplane's computers were stored here, as well as the escape hatch at the bottom, now the top, of the plane.

She helped Dani up.

While Quint was struggling to join them, Holly located the QAR. The Quick Access Recorder was mounted in the rack of backup gear. In addition to the main computers, there were two complete redundant systems.

But only one QAR.

She flipped open the cover to extract the drive.

"Hey!" Dani shouted at her in protest. "Don't go messing with my plane."

"NTSB, remember? My plane now. Besides, Miranda is going to want the data from this as well as the black boxes."

"Didn't you say she was in Seattle?"

Holly looked at her watch. "Twenty-five minutes since I called. Under twenty from her island to the airport office—including the eight-minute flight in her personal 1958 F-86 Sabrejet. I'll bet you a hundred that she's already aloft and headed our way."

"Australian or US dollars?" Dani released the now-overhead belly escape hatch. "We're about halfway through the flight, you need to be specific."

"Australian. I'm just a poor crash investigator, not some globe-trotting glamorous pilot who just crashed a three-hundred-million-dollar jet. I'll bet you another fifty that you're going to kick back, pour a frothy, and let someone else pick up the tab for that. Which is okay. This is just me, but I personally think we're at the end of this flight."

"Johnston Atoll means we're still on US soil. It means we play with US money." Dani slithered up and out.

Quint waved for Holly to go next, "I send all my vast riches home to my aging, sick mother."

"How *is* your mum? Still making the best roo-burgers in the Northern Territory?"

"Ah! Leave it up to you to remember food at a time like this. She's fine actually. And she'll be twice as glad to know her boy is alive."

Holly tried not to grimace. Her own parents had certainly not given a shit if she herself lived or died.

Holly grabbed on to the edges of the hatch as Quint put his hands around her waist to lift her up. "Don't be getting any ideas there, bloke."

"Too late on that one, you grew up into one fine Sheila." He eased her effortlessly aloft into the thick tropical air. It might be only eighty degrees, but Miranda hadn't mentioned anything about the jillion percent humidity.

Quint Dermott, globe-trotting pilot, grown up so pretty and strong. He was an interesting flash from her past. A past she'd done a fair job of ignoring until just five days ago.

Holly crawled the rest of the way out, then turned to help Quint.

She didn't complete the gesture.

They were six meters up in the air on top of the inverted nose section. It gave them a clear view of the entire airfield.

And the scene was ugly.

The left wing lay pancaked near the very beginning of the runway like a dead fish.

Then the snapped-off landing gear lined up like three fallen dominoes.

The four round sections of the fuselage were scattered across the runway like chopped-off chunks of a banger. Bangers and mash described the crash site all too well.

Theirs was by far the longest intact section and lay completely upside-down.

Another long chunk that must be the rear fuselage lay sideways about fifty meters back along the runway.

The tail section remained upright, though each fin had been folded over badly from doing at least one roll.

The midsection, still marginally attached to the second,

right-side wing, had sunlight shining through a hundred ominous holes that shouldn't be there. The wing hadn't lost all of its fuel. It burned brightly enough to be easily seen even in full sunlight.

The first passengers from their own section were staggering out into the open. Some battered, some bloody, and some...blue.

Nobody was moving around outside the midsection.

At least there weren't many bodies that had made a hard landing on the tarmac personally. But it was definitely time to see how many would never get out of their seats on their own.

In unison, the three of them slid down off the nose of the aircraft and went to help the injured.

8

"WHY HAVEN'T WE HEARD FROM THEM YET?" MIKE HAD slipped into a state that Miranda could only label comatose-without-the-coma for the Learjet's climb to cruising altitude. All the life had drained from his face and he slumped in his seat like...some metaphor she'd never think of.

The five of them were sitting in the aft section of the passenger cabin. She, Andi, and Taz were all so slight that they fit comfortably across the three back seats. Jeremy and Mike rode backward facing them. Up ahead, Jon and an Air Force copilot flew the plane. The engine was a steady pitch now—she'd always found the Garrett turbofans an interesting counterpoint to the deeper tones of most jet engines.

Miranda recalled Andi's admonishment to be gentle with Mike. Though she knew the scenario was unlikely, she began with the most positive possibility she could imagine.

"Perhaps she's busy. Even if they landed successfully— there was a seventeen-point-five percent chance of that," she felt it was only honest to add, "—panicked passengers can take time to deplane and settle."

Mike checked his watch. "They would have landed half an hour ago."

Miranda considered how best to discuss, in a positive manner, the next-most likely scenario: wing departure from the airframe upon landing without losing the associated landing gear. Before she could come up with anything, Andi pointed at her chest.

"Why don't you try calling her?"

Miranda looked down. Her satellite phone was in her breast pocket where she'd tucked it prior to departing her island. "Oh."

She pulled it out, synced it to the Learjet's system, and placed the call. She held it up to her ear until Andi gestured for her to place it on speaker.

On the fourth ring, even Miranda could feel the tension in the silence that had enveloped the others.

There was a loud click that could be the switching to voice mail. Or—

"Hey, her." Holly answered brightly. "Sorry, my hands were full."

"What's the condition of the plane?"

Holly just laughed. "First, tell Mike that I'm fine."

Miranda turned to Mike, "She says she's fine."

"I heard." Mike wiped at his face, several times, then spoke up. "Good to hear your voice, Holly. Real damn good." His voice cracked badly.

"Aww! Now don't go all mushy on me."

"Not gonna happen," he sounded more like his normal self. "Just glad you're not dead."

"Me, too. I'm fine but we've got a bit of a mess here. You

called it, Miranda. Left wing failed on landing, from flight to dragging. It sheared fully, and we lost the left landing gear at a hundred knots. About two hundred and forty cast and crew on the manifest. But no big fire, so we're down by only thirty-four so far, though there are still a few in their seats we haven't accounted for yet."

"Oh! I didn't think about that. We'll call Hickam Air Force Base on Oahu and—"

Taz was shaking her head.

"Just a moment, Holly. What is it, Taz?"

"I already got them moving for you. Hickam was busy in a major training exercise. Rather than breaking that up, I called the Coast Guard's commandant. Once I convinced him that I was still alive, and he was nice enough to pretend that he was happy to hear that, the admiral was very quick to send a pair of C-130J Super Hercules." Taz's smile must indicate something more than simple pleasure at a job well done, but Miranda couldn't think what that might be.

Perhaps something to do with her returning from the dead after being declared dead for six months?

Or maybe it was related to when she was nicknamed "The Taser" for being three-star General JJ Martinez's right-hand hatchet person. For a woman not quite five feet tall, the former Air Force colonel was certainly effective working with the military.

Taz leaned in closer to the phone. "The Coast Guard should be on-site in under three hours, Holly. We're about two hours behind them—lost a half hour courtesy of when Major Jon Swift changed his name to Major PIA—oh, hi, Major."

Miranda looked up at where Jon stood hunched beneath

the low ceiling between Jeremy's and Mike's seats. "Why did you change your name?"

Jon just glared at her.

"PIA, Pain-in-the-ass," Andi whispered in her ear. "A joke."

"Oh," she wasn't much better at jokes than at metaphors.

Jon still wore a down-frown—unhappy face—despite Andi's claim that it was a joke.

Taz continued talking before he could comment. "We'll be further delayed by a refueling stop in Hawaii because Jon requisitioned a lame-ass C-21A Learjet instead of something useful like a C-37B Gulfstream 550 that could actually get us there direct. The Coast Guard is bringing medical and temporary shelter supplies. It will take them at least two round trips to evacuate everyone. Their main concern is whether there's enough runway?"

"I doubt if we used the first thousand feet. Leaves them most of two miles. Just tell those blighters to hurry. We've got some badly injured and the rest of the natives are getting antsy."

"I'll let them know." Taz picked up one of the airplane's built-in phones to call the Coast Guard.

"Um, Holly?" Miranda didn't like to contradict her, but something wasn't right. "There *are* no natives on Johnston Atoll. As far as I'm aware, there never have been."

"I was talking about the crash survivors, Miranda. They live here, for the moment."

"Oh, right. I suppose they do. Can you actually be said to live somewhere if you haven't at least spent a night there?"

"Not a time to worry about such details, Miranda."

"Okay." She pulled out her personal notebook and made an entry to ask about that later.

"What does Johnston look like?" Jeremy called out.

"Like a tropical island that someone paved over."

"Oh. Is that all?" He looked sad or disappointed. Miranda had still found no reliable way to delineate the two.

"Why? What's it supposed to look like?"

Taz slapped a hand over Jeremy's mouth before he could continue. "What do you know about Johnston Island?"

Jeremy did have a tendency to respond to succinct questions with long answers, which Miranda never minded, but also, based on Taz's action, must not be appropriate at the moment.

"Other than it just saved our asses? Not much."

Taz uncovered Jeremy's mouth, "Short answer only. Okay?"

"Okay," Jeremy nodded fiercely. "You don't want to let people wander off. There were several failed nuclear rocket tests there in the early '60s, so the soil is contaminated with plutonium. Also, at the end of Vietnam, they unloaded over two million gallons of Agent Orange there. The Army built a massive incinerator plant to torch it, but a lot leaked out of the barrels first, into the ground and the lagoon."

"Just peachy. Any other good news?"

"Don't go swimming. The way they dealt with most of the soil pollution from the failed nuke tests was to shove it into the lagoon. Then they dredged it back onto the island to extend the runway again, bringing it back onto the site." He turned back to Taz. "Was that short enough?"

She kissed him on the cheek, which he seemed to think meant yes. There were far too many forms of unspoken communication occurring today.

"Crikey!" Holly groaned. "And I thought the Chinese were slobs down on the Spratly Islands. You Yanks really are not worth the trouble. Okay, I'll keep these bludgers corralled."

"Holly," Miranda spoke up when it sounded as if Taz was done, "could you secure the QAR and the recorders?"

"Already done."

"Thank you, Holly. Also, keep everyone away from the left wing. I want to inspect that myself. I have encountered both a breakaway engine loss and an uncontained fan failure, but never both together. I really wish we could recover the engine."

"It went walkabout out in the middle of the deep blue. We're never going to see that again. The flight recorder should be able to pin it down to a smallish area, but I can't imagine anyone will go after that needle in a haystack."

"I suppose not. And Holly..." Miranda wasn't sure if it was appropriate or not, but she felt it was something she should say, "...I'm glad you're alive."

"Me, too. Miranda. Me, too." Then she hung up.

9

"That all sounded mighty cozy," Quint finished tucking a complimentary blanket over the corpse they'd just set down when the call came in.

With a big marker, he wrote the body's seat number on a page torn out of an inflight magazine and tucked it into their pocket. They'd set up a temporary morgue out of sight of the rest of the passengers, behind the shattered midsection of the fuselage—which conveniently included the majority of the fatalities. It also had the advantage of being downwind of the best shade, which lay in the shadows of the fore and aft sections that had rolled farther down the runway.

"Just Miranda checking in." And Holly had to rub a hand over her face for a moment to shake off how good Miranda's last statement had felt. As good as belonging to her SASR team? Better.

"Checking in that her plane crash is all in one piece, so to speak? Or at least in one place." Quint added a rough laugh that chopped off quickly as he looked down at the temporary morgue spread around their feet.

"Yeah, that's definitely her." It was so *completely* Miranda that it felt as if she was already here, which also felt better than anything should.

"And who's Mike? You settle down?"

"Shit, no! Not this side of the end of the world, mate!"

"Easy, Holly. But first thing you did was make sure he knew you were still moving around on your own two pins."

She had, hadn't she.

And he'd sounded....maybe too damn happy?

"Just shaggin' the boy on occasion is all." She winced inside even as she waved a dismissive hand.

Quint muttered something that might have been, "Lucky tosser."

"I haven't lost my mind, Quint. You?" Because she needed an *immediate* subject change. She had never been tied down and never wanted to be. She wasn't the kind of gal with a puppy dog, point-seven of a child, and a classy urban-core condo for two. Mike was the same. That's why it worked between them. He was just her fuck-buddy...he *had* to be just that and no more. Even if he knew more about her than anyone ever had, even her brother. Even if he *had* offered to come with her on this trip to hell. Even— Please, someone tell her that she hadn't lost her mind. She didn't belong to anybody but herself.

"I tried the marriage gig," Quint stared down at the rows of blanket-covered bodies. "Didn't stick. No kids, so we were able to walk away friends...mostly."

He looked sad about that, so she changed the subject again by leaving the morgue area. Even hauling the final few dead out of the midsection was better than dissecting the corpses of their past sex lives.

The tropical sun hammered down on her head the

moment they were out of the shade. Only an hour or so after sunrise and the heat already had a palpable weight to it.

Most of the passengers, and the triage area for the wounded, were still hunkered down in the shade of the two longer sections.

The air marshal sat with the others doused by the waste tanks, in the narrow shade of the tail section—downwind and off to the side. They'd been cleaned and disinfected, but they were still rank.

The stewards had found a job to keep some of the antsier passengers busy. They were digging through the overhead bins and the lower hold, queuing up the luggage beside the plane.

Holly spotted her own pack and snagged it.

Yanking on the lightweight vest with NTSB emblazoned across the back made her feel almost half normal. A lone inspector among the shattered wreckage. When she pulled out a Matildas hat, Quint recognized it immediately and offered a friendly bark of laughter.

"Got me a Socceroos cap somewhere about," Quint nodded toward the sprawl of luggage.

"My team could whip those little boys' butts blindfolded."

"Not a chance, girlie. We're talking the men's national team."

"I'm talking the *women's* national team. Go on. Find your Socceroos hat and I'll take you down one-on-one just to prove my point."

Quint's grin went sideways. "Tempting me, Holly. Seriously tempting me."

Given their circumstances, it *did* sound good. Forget about the mess here in a man's arms. It never worked, but it always *sounded* good. Forget about Mike's attachment while she was at it. She couldn't ever again risk someone depending on her.

She hadn't moved this many dead bodies since—

Shoving that thought away was the only way to deal with it.

It didn't go away, of course.

Since crawling down into the canyon to retrieve the bodies of her SASR team was the single worst thing she'd ever done—other than the minor mistake of killing her big brother. Stevie was the last person she'd ever loved, or ever would.

10

HIS PHONE RANG ONCE.

He waited.

When it rang again, he answered because he was alone.

"The plane survived the crash," his key analyst informed him with no wasted greeting.

"Where?"

"Nothing place in the middle of the Pacific, Johnston Atoll."

"I'll fix it," he hung up.

Damn Guest Seven and her FSB renegades. The damned Russians had utterly screwed up. They hadn't even managed to kill one goddamn airplane.

He stared out the window.

Johnston Atoll. A thousand miles from anywhere.

His father had served there, died from Agent Orange poisoning while cleaning up the massive stockpile stored on the island after Vietnam. No government acknowledgement of course.

That had been his father's battle. Military service always had a high body count.

No one died sitting in their office chair. Or not often. He tried not to remember the day that an airliner had flown into the World Trade Center towers—and the side of the Pentagon. Far too close.

He had different battles to fight.

Quickly coding out a set of top-security orders, he sent them through a masked and misreported channel set up by another of Guest Seven's contacts.

Then he turned his attention to the east where the next step would soon be aloft.

Not far east, just a few miles away—in the heart of Washington, DC.

11

"WELL, THAT'S A HUGE FREAKING RELIEF." QUINT WATCHED the pair of white-and-orange C-130J Super Hercules as they lifted into the heat-shimmered sky above Johnston Atoll. The first load, which included all the surviving passengers and wounded, were heading for the nearest land—Hawaii.

Dani had insisted on the brutal task of tending the wounded. She was now aloft as well—sticking at their sides until the end. Only he and Holly remained with the dead and the shattered airplane.

"Your captain is slick."

"Dani's the best. Taught me a hell of a lot about what it means to be a pilot."

"That bit with the alcohol was priceless. Wish I had pictures of the passengers' faces."

They shared a laugh. "They were fit to crack the shits." Quint had helped her pour all of the tiny airplane bottles of alcohol into a big tub as disinfectant for the wounded and the sewage stained. When some of the passengers had wanted to drink from it anyway, Dani had "accidentally" dropped a stained cloth in the tub. The fact that it was stained with a bit of harmless grease rather than blood didn't matter, everyone eased off.

"Never hooked up with her?"

"Happily married, two kids. Like goofy happy."

"Hard to imagine Captain Dani Evers being goofy."

"She's got it in her, until she gets within a kilometer of her plane. She's also an urban gal. Loves being in Sydney. I'm still out in Tennant Creek."

"Shit, you *are* from the GAFA."

"Yep! A proud son of the Great Australian Fuck All. Just like you." Because if ever there was a woman who'd belonged in the Never of the Outback, it was Holly Harper.

Holly's grimace said volumes that he couldn't quite read but none of them looked good.

To give her some space, Quint watched the Coast Guard planes—injured, crew, and the surviving passengers (with their precious luggage)—until they became just white dots against a blue sky, then disappeared. The best news was that the injured were now the USCG doctors' problems; they'd lost three more before the cavalry had arrived. One of the stews was an EMT, but it just hadn't been enough for some of the worst cases. He'd seen each loss hit Dani like a hammer blow as she helped them move the victim to the morgue.

"Well, *now,* that's a huge freaking relief!" Holly said with a huge sigh. She must have been watching for the same moment. It was like a weight gone into the sky.

All that remained on the island now were the cargo that would probably never reach Australia except for a few mail bags, the dead, Holly, and himself. The Coasties had tried to get them both onboard, too. Neither of them had felt right leaving the morgue they'd spent so much time in.

The quiet practically echoed. The wind was soft and steady, sweeping across the island with little interference. The highest points were the section of fuselage and the concrete bunker at the far end of the island. Now that the people and planes were gone, the calls of the seabirds were the loudest sound. A great frigatebird spread its nearly three-meter-wide wings to soar above the flocks of white terns. It almost felt... peaceful. As long as he didn't look at the shattered airplane.

"Five hours until they get back. Let's..." he didn't know what, "...go for a walk. Get away from this mess for a moment."

"Works for me," Holly shouldered a small bag marked NTSB.

He decided not to ask why.

Instead of heading for the long walk down to the other end of the runway or through the few shady trees along the north side of the runway, she headed for the left wing near their landing point. It lay baking on the gray-black pavement, shimmering with the heat. Now the bag made sense.

"I thought tropical islands were supposed to be a romantic spot to go with a hot number."

"What? Are you still twelve?"

"Turn thirty next week. But, damn, woman, you grew up eight kinds of fine. At some point I'll get the shakes about not being dead out in the middle of the South Pacific thanks to you. But there be miles of beach here that could have our names on it." He tried to make it light, but...

He glanced again at the lines of blanket-shrouded

corpses and shuddered. Whatever dose of macho that hadn't let him beg off when Holly suggested a morgue area, it had barely sustained him. Though their old adventures in the Outback had hardened him some—life was fragile out there —it hadn't prepared him for people who had died aboard his flight. Another Dani lesson: every crew member had to take possession of each flight as if it was their very own.

"All alone on a radioactive tropical desert island with a 'hot number' and fifty-three corpses doesn't quite ring the chimes, does it, Quint?"

He could only shake his head.

"They're dead. Past caring."

He knew her better than that. He'd been with her when they brought the battered remains of her brother's pickup truck back in. Never found much more of him than a sneaker—even that was dingo-chewed almost past recognition.

He'd seen Holly's agony. He knew she felt it, even if she didn't show it.

Then she'd been gone. Dead as far as anyone knew. Word was she ate her knife, but he'd never been able to fit that with the wild girl he'd known.

When they reached the wing, still more or less intact, Holly pulled out a camera and squatted to photograph the break point.

Personally, he felt almost as ill looking at the mangled remains of his airplane's wing as he had when handling the dead. So freaking close to...

"Can't believe we're not dead. I owe you a life, Holly Harper."

Holly had stopped moving, just staring at the shredded remains of structure, wires, fuel lines, and what all. She hung her head and didn't move at all.

"What? Did you find something?" He squatted down beside her.

She shook her head.

"What? Aren't you glad to be alive?"

She nodded.

"Choking on an emu, Holl? Spit it out 'cause there's no way to swallow it."

She nodded again, then shook her head, then looked at him from almost kissing close.

She'd told him not to have thoughts about being with her, but he'd had those since they'd been a pack of about twenty kids who went into the bush, as the deep Outback was called. Mostly aboriginal kids from families that still kept some of the old skills of tracking and survival in the bush. Any chance they had would find them headed out into the Barkly Tablelands with little more than a knife, a canteen, and a swag roll of a blanket.

Holly and Stevie had been the only white kids other than himself.

And now that he thought about it, he remembered how he'd become a member of the gang at just twelve years old—following his first major crush...Holly Harper.

Six months later, Stevie and then Holly were dead and buried just a week apart.

Or so he'd thought.

"What did happen to you?"

Holly shook her head. Not like she was refusing to answer, more like a bluey cattle dog trying to shake off the flies after a hard day's herding.

She slowly came back to life.

"You do *not* owe me a life. I don't want that. Never again,

Quint. *Never!*" She hit him hard enough that he tumbled onto his butt and rolled a lot of the way into a backward somersault before stopping.

"Shit, Holl. What did they do to you?" Quint rubbed his shoulder. Christ but she had a punch. It definitely hurt worse than all of the bangs and scrapes from the crash combined.

She shoved to her feet and moved along the hundred-foot length of wing lying right-side up and surprisingly intact on the black-tarred surface.

He found his feet and followed, at what he hoped was a safe distance.

"They threw me out for killing my brother."

"Who? Your parents? For...*what?* But that doesn't make any sense."

"It was my fault he died. I did something stupid when he told me not to. Drove his ute, his pickup, into a running wash. We got swept off the track into that massive arroyo close by the bridge on the Stuart Highway. He got me to the bridge deck. I had hold of him..." she held out her hand into space as if striving to hold him across the width of the wide wing, "...but the current was too strong. He was dragging me in; we both knew it. He let go to save my life, and Stevie dropped down into that raging river." She dropped the hand to her side.

"Shit." Quint knew the place. Dry as a bone, often for years at a time. Then there'd be a dumper of rain somewhere out in the desert. In hours the canyon, eighteen meters deep and half a kilometer across, would fill as a monster river appeared from nowhere. Two days later, it would again be as dry as a drover's dog.

"After they tossed me, I stuck out my thumb. Hit Three

Ways and took a right turn to Mt. Isa. Lied about my age for some waitressing jobs while I finished high school. Went Army, then SASR. Now I'm here."

Once more, she returned her attention to her camera and worked down the length of the wing on one side and back up on the other.

12

THERE WERE TIMES HOLLY WISHED SHE WAS MIRANDA. THEN she could compartmentalize and focus on what she was doing to the exclusion of all else.

Maybe being autistic gave a real-world advantage beyond being an air-crash genius. For all the screwed-up problems she had, Miranda seemed to have a real peace when she was working on a plane wreck. Like Dani when she was flying— except Miranda had no goofy side.

All Holly could think about was that she herself had killed everyone she cared about: her brother, her team. And she'd come so close to getting Miranda's team killed by a Russian Zaslon operative that it still gave her nightmares a year later. It had taken everything she'd had to capture one of the SVR's—Russian Foreign Intelligence Service's—elite assassins and saboteurs.

And now Quint was stirring those memories back up hard.

Deep breath!

No wuckin' furries.

Just—

"What are we looking at?" Quint leaned in close.

"I thought you were a pilot. It's called an airplane wing."

"Huh! I guess dumb old me didn't recognize it lying there on the ground. Isn't it supposed to be attached to a plane or something?" He made a such a show of looking around that she finally caught up with what he was doing.

"Getting me to laugh at the moment might be a hard yakka, but I appreciate the thought."

"Anything for you, Holl." And he said it like he meant it. "Not just for old times' sake either. You were always... special...to me."

When she looked up at him, he was studying the ground by his feet pretty hard. He definitely wasn't the gawky twelve-year-old tagalong that she remembered, always there every time she turned around. Always...

"Okay. That's really sweet, Quint. And just a touch ridiculous given our current circumstances."

He shrugged a maybe, then pointed at the wing while aiming a pretty nice half smile at her. "So, assuming—for just a moment, I'm trusting you on this for old times' sake and all—that this is indeed an airplane wing, what can you tell me about it?"

"It's long. It's heavy."

"I'll avoid the obvious crude joke here."

That almost did get her to laugh. "You wanker."

"Caught!" Then his smile faded. "Seriously, Holl?"

"Well, Miranda would hate me jumping to conclusions without detailed forensic analysis..."

"Thankfully, she's not here then. Saves her baking her brain in this sun, too." He flicked the brim of the green-and-yellow Socceroos hat he'd dug out of his gear.

"...but, looking at this cracking in the two ribs and the rear spar..." She pointed a flashlight into the guts of the wing's structure, exposed by the break. The large frames that supported the structure and shape of the wing had severe cracks in the lower two-thirds of each element. He might be a pilot but he must be able to see how bad it was.

"We...uh..." Yeah, his choking voice said that he could see it.

"...should *not* have remained in flight. About the only thing holding this wing on was the skin." She flicked a finger against an upraised corner and it twonged. It wasn't much thicker than the tin on a box of mints.

The high whine of a turbine engine on idle for landing had her looking aloft.

Four engines.

Big ones!

She was looking straight up at the underside of a jet so big and so low that it appeared to blot out the entire expanse of the tropical blue sky. It was the second largest airplane in the American military, a C-17 Globemaster III, and it came down to land farther along the runway.

"Holy shit! When your Miranda calls for help, she does it up big."

Holly watched it carefully as it slowed, then trundled onto the taxiway, before returning slowly toward the crash site. It didn't *feel* like Miranda's style... Though Holly couldn't even begin to count the number of times she'd underestimated Miranda in the year since she'd joined her team. Not because she thought so little of her, but because Miranda kept exceeding each new level of expectation that Holly could have of her.

The airplane was almost back to them when she heard the high whine of near-idling jet engines a second time.

This time she looked up into the belly of the long needle-shape of a twin-engine Air Force C-21A Learjet. Except for the long wings, two of the Lears would fit easily nose-to-tail inside a C-17's cargo bay.

"No," she told Quint, who was also looking skyward. "That's Miranda. The big jet, that's...something else."

Not even waiting for the Learjet to land, the big jet turned back onto the active runway with its stern facing the crash.

The unexpected move had the slim Learjet roaring to life with an aborted landing, then circling once more to land farther down the field.

13

BY THE TIME HOLLY AND QUINT HAD SPRINTED BACK THROUGH the heat, the big doors at the rear of the C-17 split horizontally and folded, one half swung up into the fuselage and the longer, lower half of the sloping rear underbelly swung down to become the cargo ramp. A group of men came down the ramp.

She grabbed Quint's elbow as he went to move forward.

"What?"

Holly just shook her head and kept watching.

Six of them.

Moving like a trio of two-man rifle teams.

They didn't move past the end of the ramp, instead stopping at the end of the slope, moving to either side, and facing outward.

Guards.

Rifles were slung over their backs, sidearms were holstered, and they had fighting knives strapped to their thighs. Beards, dark sunglasses, black bill hats, and the standard black t-shirt, jeans, and boots of military.

Like recognized like. By the way they moved and stood, they were Special Operations Forces.

Except they weren't.

Their gear didn't match by more than just personal taste. A Spec Ops warrior might choose one knife or another, but a fighting unit needed to be able to exchange ammo during a firefight, so their armament always matched.

They did all wear the same rifle—M4 carbines with EOTech scopes.

But the sidearms were a crazy mashup. Two wore the Glocks favored by Delta, three the Sig Sauer P226 favored by SEALs, and a completely incongruous Desert Eagle. A Deagle was so big and heavy that it was often called a hand cannon, and it only looked right in hands the size of Arnold Schwarzenegger's. Its owner was no Arnold.

Holly would wager twenty-to-one against her last dollar that he'd have the ego to match his sidearm, not his size.

Mr. Tiny-dick Deagle was the only one who wore a double-holstered shoulder rig, though it took her a moment to recognize the bright yellow handgrip of the second weapon. It was almost enough to make her smile—almost.

They weren't Spec Ops; they were *former* Spec Ops. Which meant hired mercenaries or—

A deep roar sounded inside the shadowy cavern of the C-17. A cloud of black smoke puffed out the open cargo door and then a deep grinding sound that was amplified ten-fold by the funnel of the cargo bay.

"Do they have a dragon in there?" Quint had to raise his voice and repeat the question.

"Construction machinery," she knew the sound.

"Maybe they want to clear the runway?"

Miranda's Learjet came around a second time.

Not a single one of the guards looked up as it slid by low over the C-17's towering T-tail and landed on the closed runway of Johnston Island.

"That," she nodded toward the guards, "is no construction crew."

14

Miranda stepped off the C-21A Learjet and into the crash scene.

Every time it was a visceral shock, like when she finally got home to the island after a hard investigation. This—so different from the rest of her life—was where she belonged.

Most airplane crash sites were curiously serene places by the time the NTSB investigation team arrived. The plane was done crashing. The people were already evacuated. The area was often cordoned off or so obscurely remote that there were few gawkers. She'd always enjoyed the peace of approaching a wreck in a slow, logical fashion.

She and her team could approach it, study the weather, the environment, the debris field, and finally the crash itself with an orderly, rational methodology.

Plovers and boobies dodged around the black great frigatebirds that soared lazily on the midday thermals rising off the sun-heated runway. The breeze, as noted on the weather station that she'd reported to Holly, remained steady out of the east-northeast.

The crash lay strewn upon a perfect tableau of a closed runway on an unpopulated island. No airport officials would try to hurry her investigation along so that they could reopen the runway.

She could already see the impact of force dynamics that must have occurred to spread the pieces across the field in such a pattern. That was a rather startling observation. Even a year ago, she couldn't have looked at that until she'd mapped the outer ring of debris and the debris field itself. She must remember to tell Mike about this.

She turned to look at him, but he wasn't at her side. Instead, he was heading over to where Holly stood, looking like a man who needed to run—but couldn't.

But that's where all common sense stopped.

Parked in front of the wreck, so close that the four big engines' backwash must have disturbed whole sections of the wreckage, was a monstrous C-17 Globemaster III belching smoke like her woodstove when the chimney was blocked.

A man stood near Holly along with six armed guards nearby. No one else was around.

Even as she watched, a sunshine-yellow Cat 313 excavator lumbered down the ramp. Seventeen tons of excavator riding on twin steel treads that were each eighteen inches wide and twelve feet long. With its twenty-foot boom arm folded in half and tucked flat in front of it, the excavator almost looked like a child's toy as it emerged from the great maw of the C-17's loading door that was twice its width and half again its height.

There was a mesmerized stillness as it clanked its way onto the pavement, unfolding its arm as it proceeded forward.

Not a scratch on its paint, not a spec of mud on its tracks. This was a brand-new machine off the showroom floor.

At the end of the boom there was a tined bucket with an opposing gripper called a thumb.

If the operator was good, that would be a great help. That gentle grip could lift or turn over heavy parts as needed, for her inspection.

Mike had stumbled to a halt halfway to Holly. The rest of her team was gathered around her.

The excavator drove up to the tail section with the armed ground assistants walking along either side. She hadn't seen armed construction workers before, but she had little experience with them.

The excavator stopped just a few feet short of the tail section and began reaching out its long arm with the steely jaw wide open.

That wasn't right.

She hadn't inspected anything yet.

Miranda hurried toward Holly.

15

Holly wasn't sure where to look. Too many things were happening too fast.

Time to cut down on the variables.

"Quint. Get the hell out of sight. Get way back. Fast! Behind some cover, I don't care what. Just—away."

"Why, Holl? What's going on?"

She turned and grabbed him by the open lapels of his shirt. Then yanked him in until they were nose-to-nose. His eyes weren't wide in panic, no rapid breathing; he just didn't understand what was about to happen.

"Snap to. Think like your plane just crashed. Emergency evac!" She shouted the last just inches from his face.

He blinked at her once more in surprise, glanced at the armed mercenaries over her shoulder...and finally his eyes shot wide. "You *know* them?"

"Their type. Seriously bad news. Move. Now!"

"Uh, right. Right!" He turned and practically plowed into Mike, who was rushing toward her.

"Take Mike with you. Both of you. Get to safety... wherever that is on this godforsaken island."

Mike sidestepped Quint. "Holly? What are you talking about? They're just—" She didn't have time to deal with waking Mike up to what was happening. Civilians could be a real pain in the ass.

She cut him off with a rabbit jab to the gut.

The air whooshed out of him.

"Mike, since when did you turn stupid? This is me. Holly. That over there? That's something unbelievably bad. Go. *Now!*"

To his credit, he didn't say anything before getting in gear. Of course, she'd hit him a little harder than she'd intended, and he might not be *able* to say anything.

There was a scream like death close behind her.

She spun around, fully triggered. All of her Special Operations Forces training slammed into top gear—with no idea what had just happened.

Bad shit coming! Deal with it! Now!

Her training was screaming at her.

In the few second she'd been dealing with Quint and Mike, the other four members of the team had come up behind her.

The excavator by the tail had reached out its bucket, clamping it almost lovingly around the butt of the rudder still sticking up from the tail section. Then the hydraulic thumb swung down to take a vise grip. With a firm grasp—and a deafening roar of diesel power—it tore, twisted, then crushed the rudder down into the tail section.

The scream hadn't been rending metal.

Wrong tone.

It had been...Miranda. "My plane! Holly, make them stop what they're doing to my plane."

The excavator's claw disengaged, grabbed a section of elevator—the flat side-section of the tail assembly—and folded it into the fuselage as well. They were folding up the wreckage into a small ball for transport.

That's when Holly figured out exactly *where* they were working.

The mounts for the two black boxes—the Cockpit Voice Recorder and the Flight Data Recorder—were at the epicenter of the excavator's destruction. It was working to hide something. Something that they didn't want found.

Thankfully the CVR and FDR were safely tucked away in her big flight bag—safe for now at least.

"Jeremy," she grabbed his shoulder and shook him hard enough to make sure she had his attention. "Follow Mike. Take Miranda to safety."

All safety being relative at the moment.

"And protect this with your life." She pulled out the drive for the cockpit's Quick Access Recorder and stuffed it down the front of his pants for good measure.

She grabbed Miranda's phone, then gave them both a hard shove that would force them to either fall or run.

Arm-in-arm, they ran.

Holly plugged in a headset pair of earbuds so that she'd have both hands free.

As she was dialing, Major Jon Swift, who must have finished with shutting down the Learjet, walked past. Fucking oblivious, he headed straight toward the guard team's leader, Captain Tiny-dick Deagle.

"Excuse me. I'm Major Swift of the US Air Force Accident Investigation Board. What do you think you're doing?" She could barely hear him over the roar of the straining excavator as it continued its work of folding the tail section into the smallest possible volume.

She looked at the last two members of the team as they came up to her.

Andi Wu was five-two of American Chinese, but she'd been a top Spec Ops helo pilot before PTSD had slammed her out of the service. Taz Cortez topped out at four-eleven of pissed-at-the-world Latina. Being forcibly retired Air Force after decades in the Pentagon might have meant she was useless, except Holly had seen the street fighter in her.

They were both good.

"Either of you armed?"

Two headshakes. Meaning they had their fighting knives —with which they were both lethal—but no firearms.

"My left and right. Three paces out."

She had planned on calling Miranda's pal, Four-star General Drake Nason, the Chairman of the Joint Chiefs of Staff. He'd fixed any number of military problems for them. Of course, they'd solved several international crises for him. That's why she'd grabbed Miranda's phone, none of them had his direct number except her.

A glance at the military cleanup team had her selecting a different number.

She hit Call and tucked the phone into a vest pocket.

In a line, she, Andi, and Taz walked toward the leader. It was like a Charlie's Angels movie that was suddenly far too real.

As they drew closer, Major Swift must have finally pissed off Captain Wankasaurus one time too many.

She wished she was standing behind Captain W. From there she'd be able to see how hard Jon's eyes were crossing as they struggled to focus on the darkness of the Desert Eagle's .50 cal barrel, hovering close by the bridge of his nose. Holly knew that a half-inch hole-of-death made you feel as if you *should* be able to see the bullet that was going to kill you, but you never could.

The phone started to ring over her earbuds.

Jon stumbled and collapsed backward onto the pavement.

Holly stepped over him.

Captain W. took one look at Holly, Andi, and Taz, then holstered his weapon, crossed his arms, and grinned.

Another ring.

"Now what do we have here? The Babe Squad?"

"Oh, yeah, honey. That's exactly what we are." She stopped way too close, well inside his personal space where an unknown should never be allowed.

"You got a problem I can help you with?"

"Oh, man, can you ever."

A third ring.

There was a loud click as the phone was answered. "Hello, Miranda. What are you up to today?"

"Hi, Clarissa. Holly here." She kept her voice smooth and sweet.

"Oh fuck!"

"Aw, I thought you'd be pleased to hear from me." The chances of CIA Director Clarissa Reese welcoming a call from her even *after* Hell froze over were awe-inspiringly low. Before then? Not a chance.

"Don't make me laugh. What do you want?"

"Could you hold please?"

Captain Wankasaurus was apparently done inspecting

Holly's breasts. He looked up to see what was going on with the whole phone thing.

The moment that he tipped his head to try and peer at the earbud hidden by her hair, Holly swung her arms upward. At the last instant, she crossed them at the wrists.

She yanked both weapons from Captain W.'s shoulder harness before he could even flinch. The monster Deagle hand cannon from his left holster landed into her crossed-over left hand, and the other weapon into her right.

Uncrossing her arms fast, she launched his weapons to either side.

In her peripheral vision, she could see that Andi and Taz had both made clean catches of the weapons she'd thrown. She'd just pray that they had her flanks.

At the full reach of her toss, Holly gave her wrist the extra snap to release the drop blade she'd restrapped to her forearm the moment she'd reached her checked luggage.

After making sure that Captain W. could see it, she rammed its point up into the flesh under his chin, drawing a slow trickle of blood. He went up on his toes and she followed him up with the knife.

Like finally recognized like.

Snapped out of mental stereotypes, he stayed perched on his toes. He knew as a Special Operations Forces soldier that if he came down, her hand wouldn't move and he'd be ramming the knife into his own brain.

With her other hand, she pulled the air marshal's Glock out of her back waistband—she'd honestly forgotten to return it when he'd gone out in the first wave, it just felt so natural there.

Due to changes in the grip design—they'd finally

removed the damned finger ridges—it had a feel she wasn't used to.

She fired three shots over Captain W.'s shoulder—close enough to his ear to really hurt.

The first went astray.

The next two found their targets.

They'd lightened the trigger pull a little, too, which was nice.

Then to be sure, she fired a fourth.

16

THE SHOTS RANG SO LOUDLY—HARD ENOUGH TO HURT HER EAR over the phone—that they made Clarissa jump to her feet.

"What the hell is going on there?" Clarissa glared at the gathering around the conference table in her office, daring a single department head to question her breaking the no-calls-during-meetings rule.

There were very few numbers she'd answer during a meeting, but she'd learned to always answer Miranda's calls. Miranda's calls were always high stakes. That Holly was the one actually on the phone only escalated the severity.

Besides, Holly Harper was simply too goddamn dangerous to ignore.

"Just a sec more. I need to see if this wally is really as stupid as he seems. My wager? If I carve my way in to check, I won't find a brain at all."

Clarissa made no apologies to her staff. It was better to keep them on edge; it made them far more likely to make revealing mistakes of their own.

"So, Captain Wankasaurus, who sent you?" Clarissa wondered who the hell Holly was speaking to.

There was a grunt of pain, but no words that the phone could pick up.

"Now would be a good time to talk."

A whispered, "Bitch!"

Holly made a resigned-sounding sigh, followed almost immediately by a squeal of agony—though the agony was definitely male.

It was a sound Clarissa knew well from when she'd been a baby agent running a CIA Black Site in Afghanistan. This Captain Wankasaurus person had just been kneed in the balls so hard that he wouldn't be speaking for several minutes.

"Maybe I'll carve him open later, to test my theory," Holly continued calmly, "my wager stands."

"What are you talking about? What's going on?"

Holly sighed. "We have a crash of a civilian airliner on a remote Pacific atoll. We managed to survive it—most of us. Then a six-man team swooped in to do a little cleanup. Too well-equipped to be militia; too arrogant to still be in Special Operations. Made me think of you, Clarissa. So, why are you running a mercenary team to... No. Oh, fuck *me!*"

"What is it?"

"Andi, Taz," Holly shouted loud enough to make Clarissa's ear ring again. "Be careful how you secure the bastards. Assume the worst and you'll still miss half."

That said something worse than mercenaries.

Holly's voice shifted from unfriendly to full snarl. "Why did you fly in an SOG team to destroy one of Miranda's crash sites before she could inspect it? You'd better have a damn good reason for me not to hunt you down and cut your heart out. Do you even have one?"

"I don't—didn't." Miranda's team was something Clarissa kept a trace on, and last night's report still had them in Washington State. But they must have launched to a crash site since then. Certainly nothing she'd launch a CIA Special Operations Group—SOG—squad to deal with. "How well-equipped?"

"They arrived in a C-17 Globemaster III with a shiny new Cat excavator for destroying the downed Airbus passenger jet, on less than five hours notice."

That sounded like the kind of muscle the SOG could swing on short notice. They were the CIA's extreme forces team. They were the enforcement arm of the Special Activities Center. SAC handled undermining foreign governments, assassinations, insurrections, and other particularly delicate missions. A six-man team was a major asset; that many together could take down an ISIS leader *and* his entire compound.

"I'm—" then she remembered that she had an audience at her conference table, "—I'm unclear about the origin of that at this time."

"Well, Clarissa, if you didn't send these muckabouts, then who did? And if this goes where I think it's going, then you've got a major problem. I'm starting to think seriously that this plane crash wasn't an accident. Which means that very, very soon you've got all the joys and blame for fifty-three dead US and Australian citizens landing on your desk. Along with a botched cover-up operation, I might add."

"I, uh, appreciate the notification." And if she ever did go after Holly herself, she'd remember to send more than a six-man team. How in the world had she taken down a whole

SOG squad herself? Nobody was that good, were they? Though she'd called out to Andi and Taz, they weren't warriors. No question it had been Holly versus six.

"Notification? Shit! I called to give you warning to start running so that I could have some fun hunting your ass. Not this time, I guess." Holly utterly cheerful tone and Outback-thick Strine accent completely belied her words. "Well, if you could make sure that we're not about to get a cover-up missile dropping down on our noggins, that would be half decent."

"Okay. I'll look into that. Thanks for the call." Clarissa hung up and stared out her top-floor office window in the New Headquarters Building while she counted slowly to ten —twice.

There, just six miles away down the Potomac, lay the heart of power, Washington, DC.

There also, beneath the towering Capitol Dome peeking above the trees, sat the Gang of Eight. The majority and minority leaders of both houses of Congress and both houses' intelligence committees. They were *supposed* to be notified of any covert operations—notified *by her.*

And, except on a few *very* quiet occasions, it required a Presidential finding to mobilize an SOG team.

Not this time.

Was it really an SOG team?

If anyone would know the difference, it would be Holly.

Clarissa turned back to the waiting group of ten department-level directors: one for each of the six continents, plus the directors of the Russia, Middle East, and China desks. The Deputy Director/CIA made ten.

Careful to give no sign, she returned to the table.

"I'm sorry for the interruption. We were discussing the threat matrix emerging in Costa Rica?"

As the Latin America director returned to her report, Clarissa watched the table.

Every department head was here. No one with less clearance physically *could* authorize an SOG team launch. The order had come from this table.

And one of them had just tried to kill Holly Harper.

The question was who hated Holly that much?

No, the real question was who had given orders to the Special Operations Group without clearing it through the President, the Gang of Eight, and most importantly *her* first?

That's where the true threat lay.

17

HOLLY KNELT ON THE SOG LEADER'S SOLAR PLEXUS TO guarantee he wouldn't be getting his breath back anytime soon. She frisked him, came up with two hidden carries, a garrote wire for cutting someone's throat, several knives, a radio...and a set of zip ties. She bound his hands to the belt behind his back, then surveyed the situation.

Andi and Taz had done well.

They each had a knife at a guard's throat and were covering the two other guards with their captured weapons. The excavator driver was wisely remaining in his little glass cab.

Holly made quick work of disarming and cuffing each one in turn.

"I saw the goddamn last-second arm cross," Taz grumbled at her as Holly tied the last guard's wrists and ankles.

"I don't know what you're talking about," Holly managed to say it with a straight face, though even after a lifetime of being an Aussie, it was a hard pull.

"I ought to shoot *you* with this goddamn thing," Taz waggled the Taser 7 CQ at her.

"It seemed fitting; you were called The Taser for nineteen years inside the Pentagon, after all. At least it's the newest model."

Taz merely growled.

With the SOG team disarmed and secured, she looked up at the Cat 313 excavator.

Her first shot had only scuffed the paint on the excavator's arm near the high first joint.

The next two had punctured the pair of hydraulic hoses controlling the bucket and thumb. Driven at six hundred pounds per square inch—forty-one times atmospheric pressure—the red, high-pressure hydraulic oil had fountained forth as the bucket and thumb clunked to uselessness.

With the fourth shot, she'd punctured the excavators' fuel tank.

Unlike the movies, getting shot in the tank didn't make a vehicle explode, but it did make it leak. A sheen of shimmering diesel fuel spread across the runway around the base of the excavator.

She waved her sidearm to get the excavator's operator on the move. He didn't climb down—he leapt and sprinted away. No obvious weapon, he *was* just the operator. But he kept running, as if there was somewhere to go on a desert island in the middle of the South Pacific. Maybe he'd figure it out when he hit the ocean.

Holly skipped a couple of shots off the machine's big metal treads. The bullet fragments would be topping eight hundred degrees centigrade. The flashpoint of warm diesel was below sixty and didn't resist much. The third one ignited the fuel vapor rising off the hot runway. As diesel continued to stream from the tank, the excavator was slowly enveloped in a ball of flame.

She yanked Captain Wankasaurus to his feet, nudged him up to the edge of the fire. By a firm fistful of his shirt collar, she held him forward off his center of balance over the edge of the flames.

"Now, unless you want to go for a swim, mate. Tell me who cut your orders."

"It doesn't. Work like that." His fight to breathe despite the heat kept his sentences short. His panic made his few words almost unintelligibly fast. "We get orders. It has a verifiable code. We go."

"What were the orders?"

"Right pocket."

"I'm not gonna jostle your balls for you, you prick."

"Shirt."

She fished into his right shirt pocket, then tossed him to the ground.

As soon as she read the orders, she wished she'd thrown him into the flames rather than into the clear.

Johnston Atoll. A330-900neo. Destroy in order: Tail section, cockpit, left wing. Load. Discard debris from C-17 during return flight over deep Pacific. All speed.

Shit.

All speed?

That phrase had a lot of implications in Special Operations and none of them good. It had been no coincidence that the SOG cleanup operation had landed within minutes of the last civilian departing the island on the Coast Guard planes. Their timing was far too good. And the cleanup criteria, in order, would destroy: the flight recorders, the QAR recorder, and the damaged wing. Damaged...or sabotaged?

She kicked him in the gut.

"You sabotage a passenger airliner, asshole?"

He groaned and shook his head.

Holly cocked back a foot to ram his balls into his throat by the direct internal route.

"Not our op. Just cleanup. Only know. What's on that sheet." He grunted it out in such a tone of desperation that she was inclined to believe him.

Instead of castrating him by force of impact, she put her boot on his hip and shoved to roll him away from the building fire.

"And what about us?" She waved toward Quint and the rest of Miranda's team slowly coming out of hiding.

His "Are you stupid?" look answered that one. Any witnesses would have exited the C-17 along with the key sections of the crushed airliner.

She couldn't even find the energy to put a boot to his gut, instead shoving his hip hard enough to roll him farther from the flames.

"We okay, Holl?" Quint had come back to stand beside her now that things were quiet. Or quieter.

"It seems that someone didn't like your plane." She photographed the note and sent the image to Clarissa before tucking it away.

Holly tried not to take it personally.

Even with the CIA's involvement.

But the itch between her shoulder blades said maybe she should.

18

THE COLLINS AEROSPACE CARGO WINCH USED BY THE C-17 HAD a rating of seventy-five hundred pounds. Thankfully, it didn't have to lift the destroyed seventeen-ton Cat excavator into its cargo bay. It hadn't burned long because she'd shot it high in the tank. Most of the fuel stayed safe inside the machine.

Holly watched as the C-17's loadmasters used it to tug the excavator aboard, rolling on its own two treads. The cleats flashed light and dark as first the fire-soot-stained sides showed, then the tops that had only been heated until the pretty yellow paint job had peeled.

"Bets on whether they paid for the insurance rider on that?" Quint was the first to speak as they watched it being dragged aboard.

"Quarter million either in taxpayer dollars or upped insurance premiums. Either way, we pay," Holly shrugged. Not her concern.

"Not this boyo. I'm from Oz. This one's your shout."

"I'm not buying a round of pints for a pub. Tell you what,

Quint. I'll pay for the Cat if you pay your half of the airplane you just trashed."

"Ouch!" Quint tossed up his hands, declaring no deal.

"Cheapskate."

They grinned at each other. She'd forgotten how much harder it was to communicate with Americans. They never quite followed an Aussie's sense of humor. Of course, neither did folks from some of the Big Smokes like Sydney or Melbourne. In those kind of places it was hard to tell you were even still in Oz.

Once the excavator was back aboard and the loadmasters were hurrying around with chains to anchor it in place, Holly trooped the SOG team aboard. With more zip ties, she had Andi and Taz strap them to the notoriously uncomfortable fold-down seats near the tail of the plane. Every third seat, so that they had no chance of helping each other.

The lead pilot had come down from the cockpit tucked up in the nose of the plane.

"What the hell are you doing that for?"

"Are you Air Force or SAC Air Branch?"

"I'm not authorized to discuss—"

Holly pulled out her NTSB CAC card and handed it over. The Common Access Card had her name, face, a verifiable chip and barcode, and her clearance level—Miranda's entire team was Top Secret or better. Between the Chairman of the Joint Chiefs and the President, they'd made sure that the whole team's clearance was *much* better.

He studied it for a moment but didn't bother scanning it. He had been standing at the head of his plane's ramp, watching when she'd taken down a six-man SOG squad. He knew enough to not doubt that she was for real.

Of course, it never should have really worked, except for most Spec Ops operators' tendency to still underestimate women. It was better not to think about how close she'd just come to having all three of them killed. With her, Andi, and Taz down, the rest of the team really might have wound up in the deep ocean.

SOG-level operators were lethal, even tied up as they presently were—they also had the morals of a cowbird laying her eggs in another's nest to raise.

He handed her card back. "I'm Air Force, ma'am. I was told that the CIA's Air Branch had no pilots available in the area on such short notice."

"Okay, do yourself a favor. These jokers had clearance to dump the debris of a downed civilian airliner."

His face darkened as he caught the active form of the verb; downed meant sabotaged or shot.

"*With* instructions to dump key parts, like the flight recorders, midocean. It wouldn't surprise me if there wasn't a secondary order to dump your crew along with them. I'll arrange for someone to meet you at your destination. My advice, if one of them gets loose, shoot him."

The lieutenant colonel looked thoughtful for a moment. "We'll be back at Travis in just under six hours."

"I'll make sure someone is waiting."

"Thanks for the advice, ma'am. I appreciate it." He hooked a thumb at the scorched CAT excavator. "What am I supposed to do with that thing?"

"You could do worse than dumping *that* in the middle of the ocean. And not a tear would be shed in this world or the next if these six just happened to be tied to it at the time."

"Don't tempt me, ma'am. Don't even tempt me." He offered a salute and turned back to his crew.

Within minutes of her deplaning, the C-17 Globemaster III fired off its four monster Pratt & Whitney engines. Then it launched back into the sky so fast that it was clear the lieutenant colonel wanted to be anywhere but here. It didn't even use half the runway before it was aloft. Now that was a sweet cargo plane.

She turned to Andi and Taz. "Appreciate you having my back."

"Next time the Chinese chick gets the Taser and I get the Deagle," Taz's tone said that she was still as cross as a frog in a sock.

Andi made a show of tucking the big gun, which she'd kept, in her back waistband. Holly noted that Taz had kept Captain Wankasaurus' Taser as well, its flat nose holstering neatly into her jeans' back pocket. They'd dumped the rest of the arsenal that they'd stripped off the SOGs with the C-17's crew.

"A big gun like the Deagle would just knock you on your ass," Holly kept teasing Taz. She still didn't have a handle on the woman.

"Just try me, Holly. I dare you."

She knew that wouldn't be the best idea. When she *did* run with Taz in the mornings, much to her chagrin, Taz could dust her every time.

19

"Is it safe to start my investigation now?" Miranda couldn't look away from the dismal wreckage of the plane's tail section. Extracting any information from that area was going to be much harder than necessary.

"Cheer up, Miranda," Holly nudged her elbow against Miranda's shoulder. Miranda had noted previously that their six-inch height difference made it so that shoulder-to-shoulder bumps didn't really work. "I've got the recorders stashed over in my kit bag."

"Oh. That's good news."

Jeremy had come up beside her.

Holly leaned over and rapped her knuckles against Jeremy's crotch. There was a metallic clank, even as Jeremy stumbled back.

Miranda was fairly sure that it was from surprise rather than pain.

"And there's your QAR. You can take it out of your pants now. Just the drive please, leave the rest of it tucked away for Taz."

"The rest of it..." Then Miranda stopped herself. Oh, Taz was staying in Jeremy's room at the team house in Gig Harbor. Why Holly was talking about their sexual relationship at the same time as the airplane's Quick Access Recorder was beyond her.

"Jeremy, could you take a look at that?"

He pulled it out of his pants, made a show of wiping it on his shirt, then stared at it intently without saying anything.

Holly burst out laughing and punched him hard enough on the arm to send him reeling into Mike, who just propped him back upright.

"I meant with a computer," Miranda was surprised she had to clarify her wishes.

"I..." Jeremy stammered, then blushed. "I only meant... I was going to..." Then he shook himself. "I'll take care of it, Miranda. The first thing is the left engine breakaway, right? I'll look at everything about the whole left wing, but I'll focus on that because an event like that hasn't happened since—"

"Jeremy," Holly cut him off. "Also see if you can get any information regarding last-minute changes to the engine while we were still on the ground. We were half an hour late for takeoff. Quint, was that for engine service?" He'd remained in the background of the group.

"Um, yeah. We had a light on the Blue Loop for Engine One hydraulics. But engineering cleaned it up right quick."

"I'll just bet they did, mate."

Miranda sighed. "You think someone sabotaged Engine One." Holly might have a suspicious mind, but that was part of what Miranda depended on her for.

Jeremy hurried off to fetch his gear bag from the parked Learjet. Taz went with him.

Miranda turned to the crash.

Was there any point?

She hadn't even begun the investigation. Hadn't recorded the weather. There wasn't anything *to* map about the terrain. The edges of the debris field were scattered down a thousand feet of runway but had already been altered by the destructive excavator, the fire that had destroyed it, and now the pounding blowback from the departing C-17's four Pratt & Whitney forty-thousand-foot-pound-thrust engines.

They'd had to back the aircraft up very close to the excavator to load it. That had placed the engines' exhaust practically in the wreck on departure. The exhaust had blasted a wide area with fifty-mile-an-hour winds and a much wider area with thirty-plus.

"Just once..." she whispered to herself.

"Just once what?" Andi stood close beside her. Everyone else had drifted away to other tasks.

"Just once I'd like to investigate a crash where no human failings were involved. No human errors, attacks, mis-designs, laziness, sabotage, foolishness, outsider interference—"

"You're repeating yourself, Miranda."

"—pilot errors, mechanics errors, manufacturing errors—"

"If that were the case, there wouldn't be many crashes for us to investigate."

"I know!" The words felt as if they were ripped out of her chest. "That's my point. How am I supposed to do a proper investigation when I already have reason to believe that the plane was sabotaged? How am I supposed to start to understand what's happening when it has nothing to do with the machinery and everything to do with people?"

"I hear you, Miranda." Andi rested a hand on her shoulder. That, at least, was steadying.

Steadying? It was the only thing keeping her from flying apart.

"But I think that if we just—"

"Hell, of a mess, huh?" Jon stepped up beside her and wrapped an arm around her shoulders, knocking Andi's hand aside.

Miranda could only look at him aghast.

She twisted out from under his arm.

"*Hell...of...a...mess?* That's your *professional* assessment as a United States Air Force major of the Accident Investigation Board? *Hell of a mess?*"

"Well, it is. I mean, just look at it. Chunks of torn-up fuselage scattered everywhere like dropped toys. And all the shredding along the edges. If that isn't a mess, I don't know what is."

Miranda *hated* looking at the crash before the debris.

Jon knew that!

And the debris field before locating its perimeter. And that before the outer spheres of influence of terrain and weather had been assessed.

That *his* delay had denied her the opportunity to inspect the tail section of the crashed A330-900neo *before* that excavator had destroyed it.

That all of those hundreds of hours she'd invested in discussing crash investigation methodology with him was being passed on to unsuspecting AIB students, with who knew how many errors and omissions.

The only thing Jon seemed to really care about was them in bed together. Somehow, sex, aircraft, investigations, military protocols, and excavators had all been dumped into a single massive cauldron and stirred like...like...like a whole lot of things mixed up together in a massive cauldron.

Everything was a jumble—and she couldn't hold it inside. Couldn't keep it organized in her head, her chest, her body.

Unable to control it, manage it, contain it, she let it out in the only way she knew how.

Just as when she'd seen the excavator tearing into her wreck—wantonly destroyed potentially valuable evidence— she let all of the rage, anger, and confusion out in a single blast.

She screamed her agony out into the world.

20

CLARISSA REMAINED AT THE HEAD OF THE CONFERENCE TABLE after the meeting ended and everyone else had dispersed. Through the glass tabletop, she could see her Kate Spade ankle boots.

She wasn't given to tantrums, had never understood them. Her way forward had always been achieved by calm, cool thinking.

At the moment, though, she wanted to kick the table's legs with her Kate Spade boots until her feet were in bloody shreds.

Not a single one of her department heads had offered any hint of having circumvented her authority and mobilized an SOG team. Thank God they hadn't lost the C-17 plane, too; that would be almost impossible to explain.

She needed more information to figure out who was after her job but couldn't think of how to begin.

A message beeped into her phone.

It was a photograph of an SOG team. They looked... ragged. Heads bowed and hands clearly bound behind their backs—probably a first among SOG outside of resistance training. Holly had really done them in. But—

It had taken her a moment to spot why they looked so disheveled. They'd been stripped of their weapons. Empty holsters, untucked shirts, torn open pockets and seams. Whoever had cleaned them out—Holly—knew exactly what to look for.

The caption on the last image, the six operators tied to airplane seats to either side of a charred excavator, was very brief: *Travis AFB. 6 hours.*

She sent the six face images to Kurt Grice, then dialed his number.

As always, the head of the Special Operations Group answered her call immediately. They'd first worked together in Afghanistan when he was still just a 75th Ranger. As far as she could tell, he was a complete and total eunuch in every way. He wasn't tempted by men or women, by drink or drugs; he wasn't even a glory hound. Kurt Grice was simply a warrior to the core.

She'd never been able to discover what made him tick, but over the years they'd been *extremely useful* to each other.

Long before she'd been made CIA Director, she'd convinced Clark to place him in charge of SOG operations.

"Go ahead." His standard greeting.

"I just sent you six images. Please confirm they're your people."

There was a pause. "They're mine."

"Did you dispatch them this morning?"

"Per order. Coming to you."

She glanced at the terse words of the order, noted that the authorization code was in the right format. It matched the first image that Holly had sent her half an hour ago.

Clarissa forwarded it to her two pet hackers, Harry and Heidi, with a quick note: *Find out who sent this. Don't let anyone catch you looking.*

She turned her attention back to Kurt. "They botched an operation that I didn't order. They're arriving at Travis Air Force Base in six hours and you'll need to have a cleanup team in place."

"That *you* didn't order," Kurt made it a flat statement.

"Yes. As of this moment, all SOG orders must be verified by me and me alone."

"Not even the deputy director?"

Clarissa pictured Pamela Rosewater. Ever so slightly plump and a little motherly, like she was a cliché of herself. Clarissa knew that behind that cheerful exterior lay a very keen mind, but it was never one she'd doubted. Still...

"Not even her."

"Roger."

"And Kurt?"

"Yes?"

"Make that *in person.*"

"No mistakes," he acknowledged and was gone.

A message pinged back from The Hacker Twins as she typically referred to Harry and Heidi, the two heads of her Cyber Security and Cyber Attack Divisions.

You did. Per encrypted tracking record.

She'd issued the order?

When she found out who was setting her up, they were going to die.

Slowly.

Painfully.

And she was going to take care of it personally.

21

MIRANDA'S SCREAM SEEMED TO ECHO ACROSS THE FATHOMLESS blue arc of sky over Johnston Atoll.

This time when Holly spun looking for the source, she had the Glock up. The safety, integral in the trigger, was depressed and she'd taken up half of the pressure to fire the first round.

Andi was curled up on the pavement with both arms clasped over her head.

Miranda was bent over, clutching herself tightly as she unleashed another ear-piercing gut-wrencher.

Jon came within milliseconds of being shot in the face.

"What the hell did you do to them?" Holly jammed the gun into her front waistband rather than the rear one for faster access as she hurried up to them.

No one answered.

Holly tried to wrap her arms around Miranda. For her trouble, Miranda almost crotched her with a flailing bunched fist.

Mike knelt beside Andi, who was staying in a tight protective ball.

Taz surfaced next with her new Taser drawn. Jeremy and Quint were close behind, but Taz stopped them before they got closer.

"What the hell did you do, Jon?"

"Nothing. I swear. Nothing. I just—" he waved a hand toward the wreck. "I said something and she went into crazy-spastic-woman meltdown."

"What. Did. You. *Say?*" Holly reconsidered her split-second decision to *not* shoot Jon. At least in the arm or leg.

"I didn't say...anything." He honestly didn't know. He also didn't think his last statement was damnation enough.

Miranda had dropped down to sit beside the curled-up Andi. Miranda's head was down, and her arms were wrapped around her knees as she rocked and rocked and rocked. She was mumbling something over and over.

Holly squatted close to hear. It took several incredibly fast repetitions before she got the hang of Miranda's words as she rocked.

"Hell of a mess. Hell of a mess. Hell of a mess."

She glanced at Mike still hovering over Andi. His headshake said that she was in full PTSD lockdown—Miranda's scream had tripped some internal trigger hard.

Holly pushed to her feet and scanned the situation.

One shattered plane, fifty-three corpses, a desert island, eight people—nine with the other Air Force pilot apparently napping inside the Learjet.

"Hell of mess?" She focused on Jon.

He waved toward the wreck. "Well, it is. That's all I said. Why'd *that* make her go all freak?"

It took everything Holly had not to take the bastard down right then and there. Jon was always trying to make Miranda be more "normal." Some of it had stuck, some just wasn't there.

Miranda liked him and he was kind to her, which were the only reasons Holly had put up with him. Triggering a full-on Miranda meltdown, like Holly had never seen, was beyond the limit.

Jon squatted down close in front of Miranda. "Hey there, you. What's going on in that head of yours?"

Miranda reacted faster than Holly could. Her slap was hard enough to slam Jon's head aside.

"What the *fuck* is wrong with you this time?"

Mike lunged from where he still knelt by Andi.

But this time Taz was fastest.

There was a loud pop of not-quite gunfire over Holly's left shoulder. Twin Taser electrodes shot into Jon's upper shoulder—one of the most effective locations with an electroshock weapon. Fifty thousand volts of electricity delivered two-point-one milliamps of current into his nervous system. All of his muscles spasmed at once, and he collapsed helplessly to the runway.

Holly looked back along the two wires that had passed within a foot of her left ear to face Taz.

"Glad you know how to aim that thing."

"No big loss if I missed. The 7 CQ has a double cartridge. I could have fried you both."

"Gee thanks. Still rather I gave *you* the Deagle?"

Taz shrugged a maybe not. "Now what?"

Holly resisted the urge to tell Taz to zap Jon again. Then she spotted the other Air Force pilot approaching cautiously from the C-21A Learjet.

That definitely gave her an idea.

22

"I'M NOTICING THAT WE'RE DOING A WHOLE LOT OF STANDING here and watching planes leaving without us being on them." Quint noted that the pretty little Learjet had departed even faster than the massive C-17 Globemaster III.

"It is becoming a thing, isn't it?" Holly nudged his shoulder. "Thanks for the help."

"Piss-easy. He weighed less than a wallaroo." At Holly's signal, Quint had tossed the still twitching Major Jon Swift over his shoulders in a fireman's carry and dumped him in one of the Lear's passenger seats.

"Still. Owe you."

"Shit, woman. Still owe you a life even if you don't want to hear nothing about it. Anyway, got me a question." He had about a thousand. Starting with just what was up with Miranda and Andi? A third of the NTSB team was out of commission without anyone touching either woman. And now they'd shipped out the Air Force AIB investigator still twitching from the Taser charge.

"Fire away."

"We're on a desert island." He left it as a simple statement.

"Uh-huh," she was still watching the disappearing dot of the Learjet, like she was wishing it to be gone even faster.

"Eight hundred miles to Hawaii."

"'Bout the size of it."

"I'm noticing that the only plane here on this desert island of ours isn't going anywhere this side of next Christmas." He waved at the wreckage of his A330-900.

"Yep." Holly agreed easily.

"Knowing all that..." he drew it out to tease her, "...you're still thinking kicking them aloft was a clever idea?"

"Bloody righto, mate." Holly shot him the kind of smile that could fry a man's brain.

"Okay. Just wanted to make sure I had my facts straight."

She leaned in and kissed him on the cheek. "Smack on!" Then she headed back to check on her teammates.

Christ, the woman was killing him.

23

WHEN MIRANDA FINALLY LIMPED HER WAY BACK, IT WAS JUST her and Holly.

A shredded engine cowling had been propped up against a pair of seats to act as a sunshade.

She felt...shredded.

"Where is everyone?" Her voice croaked.

Holly handed her a warm can of soda. "Sorry, all of the ice has long since melted."

"Thank you."

"They're doing the accident investigation. You saved a lot of lives today, Miranda."

"It doesn't look that way." She could see the lined-up bodies beneath their blankets.

"Almost one-eighty more would be dead without your help. Me included, which I wouldn't have enjoyed one bit. You called it exactly. We lost the wing out past the missing engine on touchdown, but the landing gear survived until we were down to a hundred knots."

"Oh, that explains the breakup pattern." She'd

expected significantly more damage than she'd seen on their two flyovers before landing. "A twenty-nine-point-five percent reduction in speed from one hundred and forty-two knots best landing speed to one hundred would have a commensurate reduction in the translational momentum force of two-point-six-nine kilogram-meters-per-second."

Then she closed her eyes before she dared ask the next question.

"Where's Jon?" She remembered yelling at him. Or being yelled at by him. Or maybe both?

"Halfway back to Hawaii by now."

"Halfway to—"

"Well, first you slapped him. How's your hand?"

She flexed it experimentally. "Sore."

"It was a good one. Then Taz zapped him hard with her new toy. I figured his best chance of survival was shipping him out."

"On our only airplane?"

"Well, it was either that or I was going to have to shoot him with something much worse than a Taser the moment he opened his mouth again. Seriously, Miranda. I hate to intrude, but why the hell are...were...you with him?"

Miranda listened to the wind for a minute. She could hear the voices of the rest of the team investigating the wreck, with the occasional bang of metal as a piece of wreckage was shifted aside.

"Jeremy's leading?"

Holly nodded.

"That's okay then." He was skilled enough that it was time he took the lead on at least a partial investigation. A good next step in his training.

She also tried listening to her own feelings. They were less obvious.

She tugged out her personal notebook and flipped to the emoticon pages that Mike had given her. She scanned each of the round faces until she found the one that best fit what she was feeling and read the label.

Then she turned it to Holly and pointed.

The little face was wiping its brow and huffing a breath out of a rounded mouth.

"Relieved," Holly read aloud softly.

Miranda nodded.

"Good. I wouldn't want to upset you, but it was all I could think to do at the time. Why were you with him so long?"

"I'm autistic. I don't like change. Jon was nice to me. And it was nice to have him in my bed. But he isn't particularly good at his job and he was always—" she shrugged because she didn't have the words.

"Pushing you to be someone other than who you were?" Holly offered.

"Yes. That's it. He really wanted a neurotypical girlfriend, not an autistic mess."

"No, Miranda, don't go there. This one's on him. Besides, he's gone for now. Up to you whether or not you ever invite him back."

Miranda really didn't like change. Now that she knew she was relieved that he was gone, she didn't want to change that either. She just shook her head.

"Feel up to looking at that left wing?"

"Yes. That sounds good. Very, very good."

Holly rose to her feet, then offered Miranda a hand.

Once clear of the cowling, Miranda could see the team and a man she didn't recognize.

"Who's he?"

"Quint Dermott, first officer of the crashed plane," Holly explained. "From my old hometown, if you can believe the world is that small."

"It's only twenty-four thousand, nine hundred and one miles around. Four of the eight planets are significantly larger and only three smaller."

Holly smiled. "It still seemed unlikely, running into him on a crashing plane."

"Well, I think it's nice. Andi's missing."

"Your scream—"

"I screamed?"

Holly's shudder didn't appear faked. "Like you were dying."

Miranda wondered if maybe a part of her had been; she felt...lighter. And a little light-headed from the soda; it had been caffeinated.

"Anyway, Andi's PTSD got caught in the side blast. She's up, but shaky. Decided that she wanted to sit with the dead. Keep them company until the Coast Guard came back for them."

"And for us."

"And for us."

Miranda offered a half wave when Andi looked up. It felt as if every one of her muscles was being stretched to the limit by even that.

Andi's return wave appeared much the same.

Holly offered her a sideways grin and thickened her accent. "Let's go see that wing before these bums take all the glory."

"It's not about glory..." Miranda started, then gave up.

Holly's smile said that she already knew that and was just teasing.

Miranda knew that she'd never learn. But she didn't miss not feeling Jon's eye roll somewhere over her shoulder.

"I forgot my hat." She was the only one of the team not wearing the yellow Matilda's ball cap of Holly's favorite soccer team. It had made Andi easy to spot among all of the blanketed corpses.

"Quint had some spare ones with the airline's logo. We'll get you one of those so that you don't scorch."

"But I'll be different. Will I still be on the team?"

Holly rose to her feet then offered Miranda a hand to help her up.

"Miranda, you *are* the team." They turned shoulder to elbow and began walking toward the left wing.

She didn't understand how one person could also be a team; those were different categories—individual versus group. But Holly sounded so certain, that Miranda decided it was better not to contradict her.

24

CLARISSA WAITED UNTIL NINE P.M. AND MOST OF THE SENIOR staff had gone home before dropping in on the Hacker Twins. It was something she'd taken to doing a couple times a week. If someone was watching for her reactions to their hijacking an SOG team, it wouldn't stand out.

Harry was practically nose to his screen, his fingers prowling about his keyboard in brief bursts that appeared to be afterthoughts while the rest of his body was frozen in place. Except for an ever-present slice of pizza, his workstation was as immaculate as ever.

Heidi, the queen of kitsch, had her feet up on her desk with her keyboard in her lap. Her workstation was heavily adorned with witch paraphernalia. Wizard Boy and Witchy Lady were their hacker handles, so it was appropriate—just ridiculous.

When she nodded toward Harry in question, Heidi explained.

"He's chasing a hole in a Finnish firewall. Thinks it might

be an old back door that will let him slip past the Russian defenses."

"Okay." Clarissa had no idea why and really didn't care tonight. She knew that when he was in this state, they could do anything except zap more pizza and he'd never notice.

Heidi, on the other hand, was always chatty. And she became even chattier when she was on the attack. Since she was head of Cyber Security, she was more typically building and testing code, but Clarissa had been around to see it happen a few times.

For the hundredth time, she considered asking if that same pattern held true when the couple was having geek sex. But some things were perhaps better left as a mystery.

Clark was out of town again, doing his vice-presidential dance at an Alaskan wildfire this time. So she took a slice of pizza from the nearest box—triple pepperoni, Harry had clearly placed the last order—and zapped it for a minute in the microwave before sitting across from Heidi.

"So, what do you have for me?" She began peeling off the pepperoni with every intention of setting at least three-quarters of it aside.

"Some raisins?" Heidi leaned over to fish a box out of her lower desk drawer.

"Ha. Ha. Ha." She hadn't even cleared off one whole layer when she ate a piece of the pepperoni. It wasn't that pale-red pressed stuff; it was dark, New York deli grade sliced paper thin. She began putting pieces back on despite the pending grease load.

"Oh, you mean how did your account issue an illegal order to the Special Operation Group without *you* ever issuing it?"

"Yes," Clarissa sighed. "That." She'd learned not to mess

with Heidi's little games or Heidi would take her down convoluted paths of logic just because she enjoyed being contrary.

"I did look into that a bit." Heidi began eating from the box of raisins.

It damn well better be her Number One priority!

"And?" Heidi could be just as much of a pain in the ass as Clarissa knew she herself was. She rather liked that about Heidi, but wouldn't admit it.

"The engine departed company from the airplane at ten a.m. our time this morning, about eleven hours ago."

"Civilian, right?"

"An Airbus A330-900neo. Two hundred and forty passengers and crew including the cockpit. So, at eighty percent of capacity. They were six hours into the flight when they lost the engine. They managed to crash land on a nowhere spot called Johnston Island Airport, which is unsurprisingly on Johnston Island, one of the four islands of Johnston Atoll, which has an utterly fascinating history—"

"That if you tell me about right now, you'll be eating those raisins through your nose as I ram them up there with a sharpened pencil."

"But I'll leave that out for now as I rather like my nose the way it is," Heidi didn't miss a beat. "Still. Look it up. A lot of weird Air Force history out there. The B-29 *Enola Gay* refueled there crossing the Pacific. Nuclear rockets, too. Bad ones. The kind that blow up on launch and pollute the shit out of everything. Just saying." She kept eating her raisins. "Approximately ten minutes after the crash, the captain called her head office with the information that they'd crashed and had some survivors, number unknown."

"When did the order go out to the SOG?"

"Not until twenty minutes after that."

"Okay, a bit slow off the mark but—"

"They received their launch orders *precisely...*" Heidi took such joy in cutting her off that Clarissa started looking for a sharp pencil, "...one minute after one Holly Harper completed her second satellite phone call of the morning to the NTSB's lead crash investigator, Miranda Chase. Her first call was approximately five minutes after the loss of the engine. Both calls were unencrypted, and because you added her to the watch list, we captured both conversations. The first was all about the damage and not crashing. During the second call, she revealed that most of the passengers had survived a hard landing on Johnston Atoll. We also heard that Miranda's team was already en route to the crash site, along with the US Coast Guard, also mobilized by Miranda's team."

Clarissa decided that letting Heidi ramble a bit in her explanations had its merits.

"So, I've been building up a timeline of what happened because we left Coincidenceville way back somewhere in the deep ocean. Within fifteen minutes of the US Coast Guard forces departing, the SOG team arrived. The USCG reported that they left two survivors on the island. Probably awaiting Miranda Chase's arrival."

"One of them being Holly Harper."

Heidi nodded. "And Chase's plane did arrive within minutes after that. It's unclear what happened, but approximately forty minutes later, the C-17 departed with a destroyed quarter-million-dollar excavator—which, by the way, an SOG communique issued by Group Commander Kurt Grice had them eject into the ocean, *sans* parachute."

Done with her raisins, Heidi began fooling with her

necklace. The round medallion was actually three concentric rings and a tiny hourglass at the center. She gave it a flick and the inner rings spun in different directions.

"Poof, gone like it never existed. Kurt Grice also did *not* authorize the C-17's crew to untie the six-man SOG team for the entire return flight. Bet they are some kinda pissed. They'll be back at Travis Air Force Base in just a few minutes. Which provides our sole piece of actually possible coincidence. That is less than two minutes from when the second flight of the Coast Guard's pair of C-130J Super Hercules out of Hawaii are expected back at Johnston Atoll to complete the evacuation of the dead and the cargo. Chase's team have their own plane."

"Busy day."

"Hmmm," Heidi agreed.

Clarissa managed to wait three heartbeats before she couldn't stand it anymore. "And the order that I didn't send?"

"Oh, that."

"Yes, that."

"Hmmm," this time Heidi's noise was more thoughtful than agreeable.

"Heidi..." Clarissa fought to not grind her teeth.

"Well, it was definitely sent with your ID and authorization, but the IP address is a little squirrely. There's a double-layer mask that—"

"There it is!" Harry shouted so loudly that Clarissa bit her own tongue instead of her pizza slice. "Man, that's so weird."

"So weird?"

"Your order—"

"It *wasn't* my order!"

"Uh-huh," Harry nodded, still distracted by his screen. "Your order—"

Clarissa sighed.

"—came through the Finnish back door."

"From Russia?"

"Into Russia."

"How did those goddamn bastards—"

"But," Harry dropped back in his chair and picked up his own slice of pizza, "it's ultimately all just a pass-through."

"From *where?*" Maybe she'd threaten to cut off his pizza budget.

"Here."

"What?"

"The signal didn't hit any of our servers, or we'd have seen it. Instead, it picked up a low-security trunk line out in Bethesda. Masking itself as a signal originating here, it—"

"Harry, cut to the chase or I'm going to fucking ruin your life."

"It originated in Bethesda..."

"That does it, I'm going to cut off your pizza allowance."

Harry ignored her. "From there it traveled low security with a CIA IP signature. Bounced through a mash-up of old routing equipment Iceland-Finland-Russia. It reappeared at the Russian military airbase at Tiyas, Syria. The next hop should have been impossible, and I almost lost the back path there. It entered our system at our al-Tanf Garrison in southern Syria, definitely have to plug that hole; I sent their IT guy a note on which physical cable to yank—probably left over from when the Syrians occupied the base. After picking up the CIA secure link there, it shuffled down to Diego Garcia, then pounded back into our system as an order originating from you."

"Diego Garcia?" Clarissa could barely manage a whisper.

"You know, that weird little island that the US and the UK grabbed to make a military service base out in the middle of the Indian Ocean. A totally bizarro choice for a server to bounce off. Like I said, weird."

"Very strange, also," Heidi offered in a sing-song voice like a fake Indian accent.

"Mm. Strange indeed," Harry said back in the same fake voice like they were quoting movie lines at each other.

Normally that made her nuts, but at the moment she didn't care.

Several of her picked-off-then-replaced pepperoni slices had dropped onto her new Yves Saint Laurent mulberry satin blouse. The stain was going to show forever. And she didn't care about that either.

A false order.

Framing *her*.

That she cared about a great deal.

She could only think of one thing that connected her, the Russians, and Diego Garcia.

Weird? Strange?

No.

It was absolute worst-case scenario.

Somehow, Guest Seven had reached out from down inside her hole.

There was no way to predict where the next blow would be coming from.

25

HE SAT IN THE DARKNESS OF HIS PARKED CAR, LISTENING TO the soft fall of rain patter on his roof.

It was a pity about the SOG team failure, but the back door Guest Seven's contact had prepared for him in advance had just paid its first dividends.

He hadn't intended to use it until later in the operation, but a few more pointing fingers never hurt.

Wouldn't hurt him, at least. They were going to be very painful to someone else though.

He sipped his coffee as he sat in the Dunkin' Donuts parking lot at the northwest corner of Andrews Air Force Base.

Not the rich brew of Jerusalem or the sweet-and-cardamom of the Turks, but it was sufficient to the moment.

He'd—

There!

Taking off from Andrews. The US Air Force C-40B was headed aloft. He tracked the converted 737 up into the night sky.

There, it turned east and headed out over the Atlantic.

He resisted the urge to wave goodbye, just in case someone was watching him.

Except for a refueling stop, he would be the last person to see any of them alive.

26

It was four hours after "night" had fallen outside her cell.

Thankfully, they didn't cut off the television feed. Instead, they fed her an unending supply of American prime time. Endlessly insipid shows and movies with an unseemly number of advertisements. Didn't Americans have lives?

The only thing she could ever stand to watch was CNN. It was so skewed to American news and American points of view and American "ideals" that it was almost unwatchable. At least they didn't do the BBC: *Oh dear, we're so very understated about everything distasteful.* The Americans were at least blunt about their pitch.

But three a.m. offered few other options.

So it was CNN.

Presidential this. Congress that. Another murder in the streets. Even strolling through southwest Moscow's Bitsevski Park during the Chessboard Killer's years of rampage was less dangerous than the news made out every American city to be.

She'd actually hit the off button when a fading image caught her attention.

The five-second restart on the television felt like five years.

It was a crashed plane, spread across an island atoll runway.

We're just now getting reports from a terrible airplane crash on Johnston Atoll in the South Pacific. It rises alone from the ocean depths a thousand miles southwest of Hawaii.

She bolted upright in bed.

Not lost in the middle of the Pacific.

No! No! No! This couldn't be right.

As you can see, the damage was extreme.

Not enough! It wasn't shattered across the runway in a hundred thousand tiny pieces. The fuselage had broken into four neat sections.

It lies only eight hundred miles from where Amelia Earhart's plane was lost near Howland Island.

Like who gave a fuck. That was forever ago.

These images are from survivors' cell phones, recently uploaded upon their safe return to Hawaii aboard US Coast Guard C-130J Hercules airplanes.

Survivors was wrong. It *had* to be wrong.

Fifty-three are reported dead, with a hundred and eighty-seven survivors including the entire flight crew.

Please let The Bitch be one of the fifty-three.

The cause remains unknown, however—

Even as she watched, there was a fresh clip of a woman wearing a vest with a bright yellow NTSB logo on the back.

—a crash investigator was on the flight and is already studying the wreckage.

And then the image zoomed in.

Tall, shapely, gold-blonde hair just past her jawline—shorter than the last time she'd seen The Bitch—but no doubting who it was.

She heaved the remote control at the screen.

It just bounced harmlessly to the carpet.

Impossibly, Holly Harper was still alive.

She glared at the phone, but it didn't ring. Her unknown contact had to know that Harper was still alive—*and he wasn't calling her!*

If she ever caught up with the man, he was going on her goddamn personal kill list.

She'd offered to fuck him for his help in offing Holly.

For sixteen years, her father had taught her what it meant to serve Mother Russia.

For another eighteen she'd studied. Army, Spetsnaz Special Operations, and her last decade for the SVR foreign intelligence bureau's lethal action arm—Zaslon. She'd been stuck in this cage for a year, waiting.

Well she was done with waiting.

She was thirty-four and one of most highly refined killing machines ever created. She was goddamn Elayne Kasprak!

Fuck the bastard on the phone?

She'd goddamn fuck him to death!

But. She. Was. Still. Stuck. In. This. Fucking. HOLE!

Elayne screamed her fury at the unyielding walls.

27

By the time the pair of US Coast Guard C-130J Super Hercules returned to Johnston Atoll, Holly felt as if she was going to shatter.

With no sleep on the plane, she was already thirty-six hours awake with no end in sight.

On one hand, Quint was being Aussie-subtle about his interest in her—about as obvious as a dingo-dog's balls. It was...flattering, she supposed.

On the other hand, Mike was neither oblivious to Quint's interest nor subtle in his own need for reassurance that...

Hell if she knew what.

That she was alive?

Couldn't he just see that for himself and be satisfied?

She'd finally sent Taz to sit with Andi because who knew what the PTSD attack had done to her. Andi had refused to leave her vigil over the dead or give up the damned Deagle sidearm, which was almost as big as she was. If it looked right in Schwarzenegger's hand, in Andi's it looked like she was toting around a howitzer.

Miranda appeared to be fine, but Holly had stayed close just in case. If she never heard another scream like that one again, it would be a lifetime and a half too soon. The last time she'd heard one like it, she herself had been sixteen years old, clinging to the steel bridge deck on the Stuart Highway and watching her brother be sucked under for the last time.

The only one she wasn't having to worry about was Jeremy—other than possible sunstroke as he had returned to the wreck again and again to verify what he'd found on the QAR.

The USCG planes landed, and for just a moment, it seemed like a bad replay of the SOG team's arrival.

As the rear ramp of the first Hercules lowered, there was a thudding roar of machinery from deep inside the plane. No fireteams of guards came down the ramp. Instead, a midsize D4 bulldozer trundled out into the sunlight.

About two seconds before she pulled out the air marshal's Glock and shot the dozer, the operator cycled it down to an idle.

He climbed off and strolled over to them. "I've been asked to clear the runway, ma'am. Anything you need preserved before I start?"

That was a welcome change. She took her hand off the Glock.

"The first ten feet of the left wing," Miranda pointed. "The fat end, not the pointy one."

"That's it?"

"Yes, we've recorded everything else. If you could turn it over for inspection, that would be helpful."

"We have instructions to get a move on. Bird sanctuary and all. Is it okay if I go ahead and just load it on the plane?

They can always use the hoist to flip it in there. You'll have a long flight back to check it out."

"Yes, thank you." Miranda sounded perfectly normal whenever she was talking about airplanes.

"I'm on it." He spun up the machine and trundled it over to the tail section that had been mangled by the excavator. With an expert nudge, he began shoving it toward the side of the runway.

A small rotary-brush sweeper mounted on the front of a Bobcat came out the C-130J's shadowed cargo bay and was soon sweeping bits and pieces ahead of it.

The second Coast Guard plane had landed near the temporary morgue. A team armed with litters began loading the bodies into bags and carting them aboard.

Taz and Andi remained at attention as an honor guard until the last of them were aboard.

The dozer operator broke off the last ten feet of the wing by the simple expedient of driving over it widthwise repeatedly in a steel-tracked, thirty-thousand-pound machine. After shoving the main section of the wing onto the sandy verge, he made quick work with a few chains to raise the remaining piece just a foot into the air.

Before he drove it onto the plane, Holly and Miranda lay on the ground a moment to look at the underside.

"Just like you said, Miranda. The skin held it together. I thought the spar and rib damage would be too great to survive the descent. Figured I'd bought it this time."

"I was most careful in calculating the odds I told you earlier. It was my considered assessment that it would hold. You have to remember to think about the in-plane tensional strength of the wing skin material. It has poor shear strength and worse compression resistance, but it's the old trick of you can't tear a sheet of paper in two by pulling outward at either end."

"That's a metaphor, Miranda." Holly couldn't help smiling.

"No, it's an quantifiable analogy."

"Either way, I look forward to inspecting the bottom of this more closely."

"The engine mount never should have failed like that. Something is wrong here." Miranda practically crawled under the suspended wing section.

"Aside from the fact that it crashed?" Holly tugged her back out.

"Yes, aside from that. Note the frame member bending in the engine pylon? That's most unusual."

Holly stared at it more carefully—without crawling into harm's way. The bend was unusual. As if it had been slammed by a huge lateral force that wasn't explained by the angle the plane had hit the runway.

She did rap her knuckles on the wing's aluminum skin. It ponged sharply. Nothing wrong with this side of it.

They stood and waved the dozer away. "My old job was always about leveraging the weakness, not analyzing the strength."

Miranda nodded. "I know. Mindsets are like in-plane tensional strength, they are very hard to break. It's like why I stayed with Jon; I couldn't pull it apart until it completely sheared."

"Now *that* is a metaphor."

Miranda blinked in surprise, then smiled brightly. "I got one!"

They high-fived.

Then Holly turned and practically impaled herself on the nose of an airplane.

It must have landed and taxied while she and Miranda had been buffered by the steady roar of the bulldozer. She'd heard the whine of the turbojet engines, but hadn't thought much of it. It had already been a day of too many sensations.

The high whine seemed to cut through the air louder than the dozer now banging its way up the C-130J's cargo ramp with their chunk of wing. It actually felt as if the whine was the stripping of gears inside her own head.

Miranda, of course, had probably heard it when it was still twenty miles out and only thinking about landing. She certainly hadn't flinched at finding it close behind them.

Holly stared at the nose of a sleek Gulfstream G650 painted in the same cheery colors as her own flight had been —before it crashed.

Turbine engines.

The twin Rolls-Royce engines slowly wound down and the whine began to fade.

Perfect—more people for her to keep alive on a desert island.

As a distraction, Holly tried to get the stress diagram to form in her thoughts; structural issues were her specialty after all. She felt drugged by the heat and people. The air was so thick she couldn't breathe properly.

"Before it sheared..." she turned to Miranda. The morning seemed so long ago but there'd been something important. "Yes, there was a vibration. Hard enough in Seat 57A to be very annoying."

"That wasn't picked up by the QAR." Jeremy pulled out his tablet. "Can you describe the exact sequence of events so that I can try to match them up? We should really have Mike here. After all, interviews are his thing."

Before Holly could stop him, Jeremy yelled out for Mike. Quint, then Andi and Taz followed until they were all gathered around her as the Gulfstream finally finished winding down.

She didn't need a goddamn flock of gawkers. She needed—

28

"Quint Dermott," the airline's president shook his hand the moment he stepped off his business jet and out into the sunshine. "Thank you for saving as many as you did."

Quint had never even met Eli Jackson before, yet the president gripped his hand like they were old drinking buddies.

"Uh, did what I could, Mr. Jackson. But it was mostly Captain Dani Evers' doing, sir. As I recall, I spent most of the time just trying not to piss myself." He had to shout a bit as the dozer was now nudging the aft chunk of circular fuselage into a lazy banging roll across the runway.

Eli looked down at Quint's pants, raised a questioning eyebrow, and offered a flash of his famous smile. He appeared in a lot of the airline's ads as well as being the CEO. His two-day-old beard looked hip. When Quint had tried it, both Dani and Mum had voted him off the island.

"Dries up fast in the tropical heat," Quint brushed at the front of his pants and explained with the straight tone of Aussie humor.

"Good man!" Eli pumped his hand one more time, then released his grip and thumped the side of a fist on Quint's shoulder. "I reached Dani just as they were landing in Hawaii. She says you kept your head way better than she did."

"Sorry, sir. That's an outright whopper. She flew dead cool and kissed the sweetest landing you ever saw. She saved a lot of lives with how she put us down, sir. All I did was take over some of the cleanup afterward." He nodded toward the morgue flight where they were loading the unclaimed luggage of the dead.

"Oh, well done, mate. Really well done. That's a hard track. Did some of that myself during Desert Storm back in '91." Eli was much more serious as he thumped his shoulder again. "So what's going on here? Who are these fine folks?"

"Everyone, this is Eli Jackson, the CEO of our airline. Sir—"

"Eli."

"Eli, these six people are the NTSB investigation team." He turned to make the personal introductions, but Miranda interrupted him before he could start.

"To answer your first question first, what's going on here is that we've found possible evidence of sabotage. Our next step will be a detailed reconstruction of the sequence of events."

Eli's face lost some of its color. He rested his hand lightly on Miranda's arm. "Sabotage, you say?"

Miranda didn't answer, instead staring fixedly at Eli's hand.

Holly slapped his hand aside. "You can't touch her lightly. You do and Miranda can't think of anything else."

"Really? Sorry." Eli glanced at Quint, but he could only

shrug. He had no idea what was up with that. Must be some part of her autism. Within moments, Miranda shook her head as if waking up, then spoke as if nothing had happened. Was she even conscious that she was rubbing her arm over and over where Eli had touched her?

"Possibly. We're trying to determine if it was sabotage right now."

"By who?" Eli stuffed his hands in his pockets.

"That comes later, Eli. What and how come before who." Miranda said it like he was a bit of a simpleton, not the president of the second largest airline in the southern hemisphere.

Then she simply turned her back on him.

"Holly, please lead us through your observations in detail."

Eli appeared taken aback, but he kept his silence and watched the others. It was damned decent of him to fly out so fast. Of course, he'd just lost a several-hundred-million-dollar plane and fifty-three passengers, so maybe it wasn't about decency.

Holly, on the other hand, looked like she really needed to take a sickie.

So slowly that it was painful to listen to, she recounted the events.

29

IT DIDN'T HELP THAT JEREMY SEEMED TO HAVE EIGHT questions about every single observation Holly made. He was clearly the resident whiz-kid, but Quint wondered if he ever slowed down.

The less Holly spoke, the more questions Jeremy fired off, until—

"Jeremy, hush," Mike just cut him off.

Mike had already interviewed him about the crash. And he was so damned smooth that Quint hadn't figured out what was going on until they were mostly done. They'd each grabbed a roast beef sandwich and a warm soda from the shattered galley, then gone and sat on the edge of the runway with their feet in the sand.

For an hour, while the others were investigating things he couldn't begin to understand despite a lifetime of flying planes, they'd just talked. Right through every single aspect of the flight from the moment he'd left his layover hotel, met Dani in the foyer, and headed for the airport.

By the end of the hour, he knew that Mike was the human factors investigator for Miranda's team.

And the way he figured it, Mike knew more about him than his ex-wife had after two years together. And they'd been pretty good years.

Now he stepped to the fore again.

The first thing Mike did was lead them all to a group of seats that the dozer had shoved aside with the rest of the wreckage. While the dozer operator struggled with the big central section and the still-attached right wing and engine, they tipped the seats upright in the sand.

The late afternoon sunlight was easing its hammer blow and the breeze felt pleasantly cool.

And with no obvious transition, Mike was interviewing Holly from the moment she'd boarded the plane. Rather than asking her questions, he...guided her explanation. No detail was too small.

"Take me on a journey down the aisle, Holly. Anything about the crew?"

"Shit, Mike. I didn't even notice I was sitting behind the air marshal until he threatened to shoot me. How's that for situational non-awareness?" Holly had pulled out the Glock as if holding a deadly weapon gave her hands something to do. She explained the series of events.

"Really? You can break it down one-handed? I've never seen that."

And nothing would do until she'd showed him how to do it. The weapon seemed to simply be an extension of her hand, which was a little creepy.

"Cool!" Mike gave an encouraging nod as she slotted it back together and rammed the magazine home with a hard slap. "So you missed noting the air marshal and dropped into your seat. Which one?"

And just that smoothly, he led Holly through each detail.

Leg cramps keeping her awake.

The initial vibration.

The increased shaking.

The visible shaking of the engine once she'd opened the window shade.

The clean breakaway, followed by the iron fist of the fan failure shredding the engine and punching the wing.

The amount of detail she unearthed under Mike's guidance was astonishing. She'd observed far more than she'd told them in the cockpit. Of course, they'd been on the verge of losing a wing at thirty-nine thousand feet at the time.

"Pure luck the uncontained fan failure didn't puncture the hull." Quint had never been through a depressurization event at thirty-nine thousand feet, and he never wanted to try.

"No," Miranda was shaking her head. "Pure luck does not apply in this case, Mr. Dermott."

"You call the CEO of my airline by his first name, but you've called me Mr. Dermott throughout the day."

"Yes." She didn't say anything else.

"Why?"

"You didn't ask me to call you Quint, Mr. Dermott. Eli did."

"Oh."

She waited.

"It's okay to call—"

"Shut your yap, Quint," Holly rolled her eyes at him.

"Miranda likes to focus on one question at a time. Miranda, you were saying why it wasn't chance that saved the hull?"

"This failure constitutes a terribly unlikely chain of events," she continued as if returning to the primary topic was physically painful.

She was a strange little woman, but there was a weird logic to her that he rather liked.

"The most likely source for vibrations severe enough to cause a breakaway would be an engine containment failure —though the shear pins in the engine mount can typically withstand that type of shaking. However, the events occurred in the reverse order. To cause the kind of vibration you're implying, someone must have mounted a hydraulic pressure booster pump in the system somewhere."

"Yes. I get it!" Jeremy was nodding excitedly. "The most likely place to mount a pump like that would be directly above the leading edge of the high-pressure fan. When the engine mount ultimately let go—*BANG!*—that would have severely weakened the engine containment housing at the top. The engine breaks away..." he punched a fist forward, "...then it inverts to clear the wing—per design..." he swung his arm up until he was looking straight up at his fist, "...and at the moment of fan failure, the punch would have been directed entirely at the wing below." Then he actually smacked the back of his fist against his own forehead.

"But...why?" Quint couldn't imagine someone doing that.

"That's still as irrelevant as 'By who?' was seven minutes ago." Miranda seemed to be studying his left ear.

Quint checked his watch but since he had no idea what time Holly had started speaking, he had no idea how long it had been. He did notice that Miranda hadn't looked at her own watch. He rubbed at his left ear. Miranda's focus shifted to his right shoulder.

"I do wish we could recover the Number One engine to verify that conjecture."

Jeremy was back to studying his tablet computer. "There's an over-pressure surge on the Blue Loop hydraulic loop at about the time Holly is referring to."

"How big a surge?"

"Well, it doesn't really make sense. Ten thousand psi? Four-point-four times normal operating pressure. A remarkably high frequency for an aircraft hydraulic system. Three-point-seven pulses per second."

Holly started slowly, "The vibration was induced by the high-pressure pulsation of the hydraulic system. It would be enough to damage the engine. Once the vibrations hit that harmonic of three-point-seven pulses per second, they would tend to amplify rather than dampen. *Until something broke.*"

Holly's voice radiated more anger than a ticked-off water buffalo ready to shred your truck.

Quint considered clearing a detonation zone around her in case she went off.

"Yes," Miranda said perfectly matter-of-factly. "Though without recovering the engine itself, we'll never know quite what gave way, which I find rather..." She pulled out a notebook and consulted it briefly. "...annoying." Then she tucked the notebook away as if her feelings were somehow stored in there.

"There was no alarm in the cockpit," Quint would remember that. "Wouldn't what happened be enough to trigger an alarm?"

There was a grim silence that answered that question.

Holly looked at him. "You had no alarm because during your supposed 'engine service', your saboteur simply disconnected the alarm sensor. They must have missed that when they were initially jury-rigging the system to fail."

"Which means..." Eli looked grim, "...that it really *was* sabotage."

"Possibly," Miranda spoke up. "These are all elements of the conjecture meta-sphere so far."

She didn't explain what that meant, but no one else was commenting on it, so Quint kept his mouth shut.

"There is also the nonconjectural evidence from a phone call Mike mentioned."

Mike tapped a phone. Unlike the others who carried a myriad array of tools, it was about the only thing in his NTSB vest. "I spoke with your Seattle maintenance facility. They have no record of a call for engine service during your three-hour turnaround and crew changeover in Seattle. Someone unauthorized worked on your engines. And then again to unplug the Blue Loop hydraulic alarm. The fault that *was* noted in the plane's log was not corroborated by the Seattle office."

"Which also fits the known facts," she conceded.

"Of one of *my* planes?"

"As you are the CEO of the airline, and I assume that you are referring to responsibility rather than direct ownership, then yes, this is the remains of one of *your* planes." She waved a hand toward the wreckage.

Quint fought to hide his smile. He'd had all afternoon to get used to Miranda's curious way of stating the obvious in a very particular fashion.

"And, while I wouldn't state it with the same certainty Holly just displayed, I would say that sabotage was a remarkably high probability at this time. There is another factor missing, something isn't quite correct with the math. I wouldn't be comfortable reaching any conclusion until that discrepancy is resolved."

"It *isn't?*" Jeremy jolted as if he was suddenly told he was on a plane about to crash. He plunged back into his modeling software.

"But," Miranda continued, "I hope to discover that either on the flight recorders or the section of wing we preserved for investigation."

There was a stunned silence. Despite the tropical heat, Quint felt a cold shiver up his spine. They really had been that close to death.

"Whoever sabotaged the plane will be disappointed." Miranda said it as if her simple words carried the entire emotional weight a sabotaged airliner called for.

"Aye," Holly nodded. "Disappointed enough to send an SOG team to break up any remaining evidence."

"What the hell are you talking about?" Eli roared.

Quint figured Eli was feeling just as overwhelmed as he himself was. He did his best to explain. Three women, with one gun between them, taking down a six-man CIA death squad had been pretty amazing to watch—even if he'd been doing his best to cower out of sight at the time.

"Why was the CIA trying to kill my plane?"

Holly's look went from sickly to almost barfing.

"Again you're asking *why*, Eli. Such conclusions aren't possible until I have completed my analysis," Miranda said.

Holly just looked down without saying a word.

30

"Are you sure, Holly?"

She wasn't sure of anything.

"Look, Mike..." She didn't even know what to say anymore.

Too weary to stand, she sat and leaned back against one of the three-foot-tall tires of the US Coast Guard C-130J's nose gear. The sun was now low enough to beat on her even here under the plane. Even though it was a desert island, it was the only place they could find some privacy.

The cleanup crew was nearly done. In minutes, Johnston Atoll would once again be left to the gulls.

Eli had offered her and Quint a lift to Australia in his Gulfstream, rather than them backtracking to Hawaii on the C-130J with the rest of the team and then catching a flight to double back.

"Seriously, I don't mind going with you if you need some company. Or just want a friend along for the ride."

It actually sounded good. Leave it to Mike to always say

the right thing. And he did it so well that she couldn't even get annoyed at him for it.

"If it was anywhere..." except where she had to go. She just shook her head.

"Christ, Holly. Now you're scaring me a bit. Maybe more than," he offered one of those consoling smiles of his.

"It's nothing dangerous, Mike. It's just something I have to do—alone." And if she survived, it would be more of a miracle than surviving a sabotaged plane crash.

"Any chance of you at least telling me what it is?" He rested his hand lightly on her arm.

It was all she could focus on. Offering comfort and consolation. Reminding her of a connection that she didn't want at the moment. And overloading her sensations as Mike so often did. Their bodies positively hummed together in bed.

Well, it gave her a little more insight into what it must be like for Miranda when someone touched her lightly. Yeah, right. Probably times a thousand for her.

Holly eased out from under his touch and stared out across the shimmering runway.

Home.

The place she'd left at sixteen.

The very last place in the world she'd ever expected to set foot again.

31

AT LEAST HER LEGS WERE ENJOYING THE RIDE IN ELI'S Gulfstream G650, even if the rest of her wasn't.

Even stressed out, her leather chair in the executive-class cabin *was* genuinely nice. The facing-four let her stretch her legs out and rest them on the opposite seat. Her body began to unkink, one vertebra at a time.

The morgue flight had left Johnston as soon as they were loaded.

After the dozer and sweeper were finished—other than the pile of debris along one side of the runway and some staining of the tar where the excavator had burned—the runway was clear again, and the island was much as they'd found it.

The second Coast Guard C-130J had headed aloft and turned for Hawaii at the same time Eli's plane turned for Australia. Holly could feel the connection with Miranda, Mike, and the others stretching thinner by another mile every four seconds.

How long until it snapped entirely?

Such a cheerful thought. She slouched lower in the seat.

After making sure they were settled in the front seats, Eli Jackson had become the pure businessman. He'd gone to the conference table, already set up in the second group of seats where his work was all spread out. In minutes, he'd been on the phone, deep in his computer, and worrying about whatever airline CEOs worried about after a crash. Still, he'd personally flown all the way to Johnston to see the crash for himself, which was saying a lot about his personal investment in the company.

When Quint handed her a cold Tooheys New and a foot-long Continental Roll of crusty bread, Italian meats, and roasted red peppers, she started feeling a little better about the flight. A Continental might be a Sydney treat, but it was still more the taste of home than even a New York submarine sandwich.

"I could kiss you for this."

"More than welcome to," he rumbled out cheerily as he dropped into the kitty-corner chair and rested his feet on the seat beside her.

Holly was tempted, but decided that Mike wouldn't like it.

Mike wouldn't...

Christ! Being in a relationship, even just a strictly physical one, was more trouble than it was worth. She and Mike had been shacking up for... Shit! Eight or nine months? Way too long!

And he kept acting like there was more there. Was that why he'd offered to come to Australia—as if she'd want him to see the hole she'd come from? Or maybe he was just trying to stay between her and Quint. Yeah, far more likely, even if there was nothing there.

"What's changed in Tennant Creek?" she asked Quint to make conversation.

He barked out a laugh and almost choked on his sandwich. "You're joking, right? TC hasn't changed since they put in the McDonald's."

That had her jolting in surprise. "When the hell did that go in?"

"Never," Quint grinned at his own joke. "That's how much TC hasn't changed. Though there's a surprisingly good Chinese place now."

"Well, that's something." She'd always liked Tennant Creek, except for the fact that her parents lived there. Three thousand people, half of them indigenous, all in a space of two miles from the airport in the north, to Kelly's Ranch in the south.

They sat in silence for about half a sandwich.

Holly was just as glad that she couldn't see the engines mounted to either side of the tail. Something falling off? She was too damn tired to care. The ocean continued to lie far below her, and would for the next five hours of the seven-hour flight to Tennant Creek.

Eli had insisted on delivering them direct. Quint was on a mandatory two-week leave—the airline's standard time to detox after an incident of any significance. He'd chosen to head for home.

Hanging out with Quint for a couple of weeks...she could do worse.

"You headed back for your parents?" Quint broached the subject softly.

"No real secrets in TC."

"Hardly."

"Yeah. They left no will or anything. The courts tracked

me down. They wanted me to come down personally. For myself? I'd vote against it, but..." She shrugged. Some tiny thread of obligation had her flying back. Though she'd made sure they were buried before she got there. "I don't even know how they died."

"Your dad died about a year ago on a run down the thousand klicks from Darwin. He spread his road train all over the Stuart, closing it for most of a day until they could get it shoved aside."

A road train was a long-haul truck typically with five full trailers all strung together. They traveled fast on the flat line of the Stuart Highway and didn't stop for anything. Dumping one of those would make a major mess. Especially as a run down from Darwin meant he'd been fully loaded. Not much shipped out of Tennant Creek to anywhere.

"A nighttime run," Quint said it flat.

"Jesus, nobody's that thick." Except she could see Dad doing that. Nobody ran the Stuart after dark except for the crazy-ass night buses. That's when the roos came out to feed on the thicker grasses that grew to either side of the sealed highway. Tiny bits of morning dew collected on the pavement, flowed to the sides, and created the richest feeding ground for hundreds of kilometers around. Hitting a two-hundred-pound big red kangaroo at speed destroyed a vehicle—even the ones with bull bars.

"And Mum?" Holly didn't want to know, but couldn't help herself.

Quint looked uncomfortable, then mumbled out, "Died pretty much like she lived."

Drank herself to death.

The stories had all been there, part of the family legacy.

Sixteen and had me a skinful when your brother was

conceived. Right smashed when I had you the next year. We was... Mum used to spin endless tales of how drunk she was on this or that occasion. The way she told it, she remembered them all—in painful detail—and seemed to love recounting each bout at length. Holly knew all the detailed variations of a drunken-high and a hangover-low long before she could read.

Broad Strine had a hundred words for being a drunk, and Mum had a story to go with every single one. *I 'member we were havin' a shoey blast and your dad filled one of his Wellies with beer. I finished off a pair.* A party to drink out of shoes. And Dad's Wellington boots stank plenty under any conditions. But Holly hadn't doubted the story then and, sadly, she didn't doubt it now.

"They wouldn't even let her in The Memo by the end," Quint grunted out like it hurt him.

"That had to be a blow." Took a lot to get banned from The Memorial Club's bar.

Never violent or nasty—except once—but never exactly functioning either. Holly could clean house by the age of four and could cook by six. Between that and the waitressing jobs she'd had before the army, she'd never cooked again if she could help it.

Mike wanted help in the kitchen? She always waited until someone else volunteered—even Jeremy, the can-barely-run-a-microwave kid. Taz being an avid cook made her an exceptional addition to the team for that reason alone.

Growing up, it had been her and her brother against the world...until she'd killed him.

She glared down at the glistening darkness of the Pacific Ocean's depths. This Gulfstream was flying ten thousand feet higher than the Airbus had been but it looked no different.

It seemed that almost everyone who'd known her was dead.

There was an idea that had been tickling at her all day, even before the SOG team had showed up. It had begun when Miranda, who never repeated herself, who *hated* repeating herself, had said multiple times how unusual an incident this was.

But now the evidence was piling up against her desire to pretend it was in any way a normal crash.

Sabotage.

Coordinated attack by the CIA's black squad—*without* the CIA Director's knowledge. Which, much to her surprise, Holly actually believed when Clarissa had denied knowing about the SOG team.

The idea that was itching at her didn't make any sense; there had been two hundred and forty *other* people on that flight from Seattle to Sydney.

But, despite how unlikely it seemed, she couldn't quite shed the thought.

A plane crashed.

Fifty-three dead.

Chance? Or had *she* been the target?

32

JEREMY WAS THE FIRST OUT OF HIS SEAT WHEN THE C-130J reached cruising altitude. He hurried forward to the section of the Airbus plane's wing that the Coast Guard had flipped over, then chained in place at the front of the cargo bay.

"Look at those shear bolts," he already had his camera out, had squatted down, and was blocking Miranda's ability to see them. "I've never seen ones that actually sheared in flight before."

Holly would have just nudged him aside with a knee to the ribs so that she and Miranda could see as well.

After he still didn't move, Miranda tried nudging his ribs lightly with her own knee. He moved aside without even appearing to notice. He didn't tumble aside as he would have when Holly did it; she must not have done it right. Holly had so many useful skills; she really needed to learn more of them. Top of her list: nudging force and appropriate application of same.

"They look like...shear bolts." Andi stood on the other side of the wing, with Mike and Taz beside her.

Miranda waited half a beat. She'd learned to always hesitate after any overtly obvious remark as Holly was sure to spin out one of her Strine sayings. When she didn't hear anything, she looked around to see if Holly had spoken more softly than the roar of the C-130J's four big six-bladed scimitar propellers.

That's when she recalled *again* that Holly wasn't there. It was an odd sensation; she was so used to Holly's constant presence at her side.

Miranda leaned in to look more closely herself.

The fuse pins and bolts were sheared cleanly.

"This one's color isn't correct," she pulled a graduated punch tool out of its vest pocket and dialed in a setting. Placing its point against the metal, she leaned her weight into it.

"This one is also different," Jeremy said from where he was aiming a flashlight into the other end of the engine mount pylon.

With a loud snap, the spring released the point of the punch in a sharp jolt at the selected force.

They all leaned in to look at the small divot. Then Miranda turned the punch for them to see.

"A *hundred?*" Jeremy's exclamation was loud enough to hurt her ears, even over the engine's roar. "It dented the metal at only a hundred ksi? That can't be right."

"Why?" Andi was a rotorcraft specialist and wouldn't know much about airplane shear bolts.

"Inconel 718 is used a lot in high-stress, high-temperature situations in aerospace." Miranda was always glad to explain the details; there was something comforting about the process. Curiously, she knew that Andi—unlike Jon, who was always a bit haphazard—

would now remember that and integrate it into any future situations.

Haphazard? Was that another metaphor? She turned to ask Holly…who again wasn't there. This was hard.

"Inconel is a nickel-chromium superalloy used in places like engine shear pins and fuse links," but Jeremy was right there with her.

"Exactly. It should have a yield strength of a hundred and sixty ksi—"

"That's kilopounds—thousands of pounds—per square inch," Jeremy interjected but she didn't let it sidetrack her.

"—and this is testing below a hundred. That shouldn't happen unless—"

"It's superheated to over thirteen hundred degrees at the time of the test."

"Latent degradation from overheating?" Yes, Andi was already asking the relevant question.

Miranda placed the punch against another pin—two of the four were distinctly shinier. Again she pressed on the punch until it snapped loudly, unleashing the spring to drive the point in. The sheared-off remains of the second pin wasn't so much as scuffed.

"Not overheating. Two key pins were replaced with an under-spec material. The real question is why it took them so long to fail."

"Are these pins manufactured in multiple grades?" Mike sat down on the wing flap, which groaned and creaked but held.

Miranda shook her head.

"Then it's definitely sabotage, just like Holly said." He reached out and wiggled an element of the engine mounting bracket. "This all got pretty twisted, didn't it?"

Miranda focused on the bracket. It *was* badly bent. Even though Mike was decidedly nontechnical, it was an astute observation. Far more so than Jon's "Hell of a mess." Maybe she needed to be open to changing things more often, even if she didn't like change. She made a note in her personal notebook for later consideration.

The engine's mounting brackets had been bent and twisted, though not—

"Which direction was the wing dragged?"

"Holly said—" Mike twisted as if turning to Holly, then looked confused for a moment.

It was comforting that she wasn't the only one having problems with Holly's absence.

"She said," he looked down and wiggled the bracket again, "that the wing didn't drag. Not the root of it. The tip did, then it ripped off when the landing gear failed. It probably skidded some, but it was still perpendicular to the runway. It never dragged sideways."

Miranda touched the kitty-corner end of the mount bracketing. She could almost feel its pain. But more importantly, it had been bent in the opposite direction to the one Mike still held onto.

"This wasn't caused by the sliding of the wing, in any direction."

Andi gasped, then held out her arm with her forearm over the wing where the engine would be. Then she simply twisted her hand one way and her elbow the other.

"Yes, the engine was torqued strongly counterclockwise, away from the main fuselage at the time of failure."

"So, these two pins," Jeremy pointed at the dulled ones, "with their softer material, failed as the engine swung *outward*. Wouldn't you expected them to fail on the inward swing?" He raised his arm and twisted it in the opposite direction to the way Andi had done.

"Yes. In fact, when you run the match, you'll find that it's really chance that the airplane survived. No more of a window than a few hundredths of a second out of every twenty-seven-hundredths per vibrational cycle."

"If it had failed in any other part of the vibrational swing..." Miranda saw the scenario and found herself unable to finish the sentence.

"What?" Mike looked at her. "What?" he asked the others.

Jeremy looked grim. Andi had gone sheet white.

It was finally Taz who answered him. "Picture it. The engine mount fully fails on an inward swing of a hard side-to-side vibration. What sits immediately to the right of the left engine?"

"The fuselage? The engine would have flown into the fuselage."

Taz nodded. "Straight through business class and into hell."

"The plane—" Mike didn't finish.

Then he spoke so softly that Miranda could barely hear him over the C-130J's engines.

"Holy shit!"

Mike didn't ever swear.

33

THE THWACK OF THE ELECTRONIC BOLTS IN HER CELL DOOR jolted Elayne out of sleep.

Two in the morning by the clock.

That had never happened before.

She didn't waste time getting dressed, she didn't need to.

Since finding out about Holly Harper's survival, she'd slept fully clothed—ready at a moment's notice for the slightest chance.

Maybe this was it.

She dropped her feet to floor, ready to rush whoever came in the door.

Her sneakers splashed ankle deep in cool water.

An incredibly good sign. When things went wrong, opportunities arose.

By the time she reached the door, it was swinging open and the water had increased from ten to twenty centimeters.

The common room was in darkness. The only light was that red-lit "Exit" sign above the vault door—plenty for her night-adapted eyes.

One inward-swinging cell door was blown outward off its frame, and water continued to spill out of it. A body washed by. Whoever had been locked up in there had drowned in bed.

Others were emerging from their rooms. Some half dressed, some in their PJs.

No time for them.

She sprinted for the stairs.

High-kneed steps, like a prancing horse's, sped her passage through the knee-deep water. A splash of water on her lips. Salt. This prison block was below sea level—and the tide was definitely coming in. How far below was the big question.

Alarms must be sounding somewhere if an automatic system had unlocked all of their doors. Guards would be coming in to secure the area.

Nonstandard operations, like an emergency, definitely meant opportunity.

Up the stairs, she reached the door, then slammed back against the wall beside it to be ready.

Nineteen seconds.

Nineteen long seconds she counted as others began slogging through the now-thigh-deep water. Some idiots doubled back into their rooms—probably to put on their favorite fucking tutu. What kind of fools were locked in here with her?

In the lead, a slender Arabic woman, had just reached the bottom of the stairs when the vault door opened.

"Shit, Harv! The pit is flooding!"

Then he stepped through the door. A knife-hand blow collapsed his larynx, making those his final words ever— and, she'd hit him hard enough, his last breath too.

As he collapsed, she ignored his rifle. Instead she simply reached out to grab his knife and sidearm before he slid out from under them.

"Harv" caught a round from his buddy's Glock in each eye. The loud gunfire reverberated in the small room past the vault door.

No one behind them.

She recognized him as she stripped Harv's weapons.

"Aw, my little phone tech. Did you lose your connection somewhere?"

M4 rifle with the Aimpoint CompM4 scope and two extra thirty-round mags. Oh sweet, a KAC flash suppressor and silencer—she took an extra couple seconds to mount it on the end of the barrel. Two more mags for the Glock. A pocketful of flashbangs, and a knife—in a sheath this time.

The Arab woman was stripping the first guard with a fast professionalism.

Elayne tossed her the first guard's knife. She caught it in midair, tapped the tip to her forehead in quick salute, then took the guard's sheath and strapped it to her own thigh.

While Elayne had been arming herself, she'd also assessed the room.

A little waiting area. Dim with a single work light. Coffee machine, couches, a desk, and another set of stairs leading upward.

More feet sounded at the head of the upper stairs as well as the other prisoners climbing the stairs beyond the vault door.

Again, she moved fast to the wall beside the second flight.

She again waited for the guard to step into view.

Except he fired first. Firing down at the concrete floor to skip bullets ahead of his being visible.

The Arab woman screamed as she went down.

He continued firing. By the changing angle, Elayne gauged his progress as he raced down the flight.

At the right moment, just as the gun barrel passed her, Elayne stepped around the door edge. She rammed her blade under his chin—upward with a hard thrust to scramble his brain—a sharp twist to snip his spinal column.

He switched off like a toy.

"Girl still has it!" She gave the air a little hip check and ducked back out of sight.

For fifteen seconds, no one else came down the steps.

One of the other prisoners, a tiny Chinese man in his twenties, picked up the dead Arab woman's rifle and rushed the upper stairs. He held the weapon wrong. Didn't even know to flick off the safety.

Just the kind of idiot she needed.

Elayne raced upward tight on his heels—but not too tight.

He made it five feet past the upper door.

Night, humid, tropical, ocean. Her senses registered each fact automatically.

When the Chinese guy went down, his body pitched right and back. Bullseye on the heart.

Shooter out there with night vision—low and left.

Another round hit the corpse, but she wasn't sure from which direction.

Elayne heaved one of the flashbangs out the door, then closed her eyes and covered them with her forearm.

When the bang fired off, she rolled out the door.

Two cries of pain sounded as the pyrotechnic glare forty

times brighter than the sun overloaded the shooters' night-vision optics.

To the left—a soldier standing clear in the dying light—she popped off three quick rounds.

The other shout of pained-surprise was dead ahead.

He ate another three rounds before the flashbang's light completely faded.

She dove behind a thick tree. She was in a dense coconut grove.

A coconut lay against her hip.

She tossed it high to land in the clearing by the door.

No one shot it.

Just silence.

And air. Fresh air.

Two deep breaths was all she allowed herself as she listened.

Sound of the sea to both sides. Island or a coral atoll.

The only human noises were from the open door.

Ten cells. One drowned, the dead Arab woman and Chinese guy, there should be six more.

There were four.

No loss.

She didn't need them, but they might be useful cannon fodder.

"Let's go!"

Zaslon operative Elayne Kasprak didn't wait to see if they followed. She was out of her cell. From here on, the rest of it had to be easier. In fact, the next piece of her trap should be springing soon.

That would be something to see.

To watch them writhe *in person*?

Oh! Maybe it *was* good that Harper had survived.

Now Elayne could take care of that bitch herself.

Maybe she'd find that Mike Munroe and fuck him right in front of Harper first.

Fuck him to death.

So sweet!

She licked the salt taste from her lips, almost the taste of blood.

She dodged into the thick trees.

After a year locked in a virgin's cell, she couldn't wait!

34

They'd been wheels-down in Tennant Creek at seven p.m. It had been full dark as the sun had set half an hour before. Holly wasn't even functional as Quint had thanked Eli, got her down the steps, and walked her over to his truck.

The jet, after taking on just enough fuel to get back to Sydney, was aloft before he'd driven out of the parking lot.

Their conversation had been short.

"You have somewhere to stay?"

"My parents' place is empty." She hadn't turned to look at him.

He'd made an executive decision, driven to the duplex he'd bought for himself and his parents, then dumped her in his bed. Turning for the living room, he thanked God he'd bought a comfortable couch for watching the games on the telly when he was home.

In the morning, the sun blasted him awake because he'd forgotten to close the curtains on the living room window. He made it to the bathroom before he missed her.

The bed was shipshape, military neat, and squared away.

"You did *not* skip out on me, Holly Harper."

No. Her gear bag was still propped up by the side of his dresser.

He dressed, hurried out to the car, and went looking.

She wasn't hard to find.

The Harper place lay on a chunk of dirt track out at the far end of Standley Street. Out past the power and water station at the southwest corner of town.

The house was the last of four at the end of the track. It faced the achingly dry sand and scrub of the Red Centre—so barren it made the Barkly Tablelands to the east appear as lush as the American prairie. The next civilization larger than a wandering indigenous family was Perth out on the west coast—over two thousand kilometers across the Gibson and Great Victoria deserts.

The wide roof overhangs to shield the house from the Outback sun sagged like unhappy frowns off each porch post. Two sections of wall had been painted a bright blue too many decades before, the rest were an orange so sun-bleached that they were more gray than faded yellow.

Her dad's tractor truck may have died on the highway when he did, but the yard was strewn with old fenders, giant worn tires, and a ratted-out ancient Datsun Bluebird coupe. Cars didn't rust in the Outback, but this one would be in better condition if it had. With the nearest big towns five hundred kilometers in one direction and a thousand in the other, the years had been hard on the old rattletrap.

As a kid, he'd never understood what the Harper place was really like the few times he'd seen it. Not that Holly or Stevie ever invited anyone over, but he'd shown up now and then to hang with Holly, and she hadn't chased him off.

Since she'd died (or rather left), he'd done his best to never even drive by the turn onto the dirt track.

The door was open, which didn't mean much out here. There were still indigenous who removed all the doors the day they moved in because they didn't like the trapped feeling of being indoors.

He parked on the red sand and climbed out of his truck. The only sound was the steady grind of the gas-fired generators at the nearby power station, and the only movement was a pair of buzzards high on the wind.

Without warning, a noisy crowd of red-tailed black cockatoos swarmed the dead white gum tree at the center of the yard. For a brief instant, the tree was alive with a hundred or more black, foot-tall "leaves" all chattering at one another. Then, with a brief flash of the crimson stripes on their tails, the whole flock of parrots swarmed aloft and the dusty yard was once again plunged back into silence.

"Holl?" he called out as he stepped onto the porch and into the shady interior. The morning sunlight was still low enough to shine inside, but it only showed how bad the place was. If there'd been more belongings, it would have been a mess. Instead it was more barren than cluttered. Even the dust motes caught in the light seemed lifeless. As if no one really lived here, or ever had.

He found her sitting on the back stoop and staring at the yard. There was an old fence that rimmed about half of it; the other half lay in the dirt.

"See the beans and tomatoes. Peas climbing up the poles there. Green peppers, eggplant..." Her voice sounded drifty.

All he saw was the parched, sandy soil and a few stray sticks of wood.

"My brother and I planted this together. Fed the whole family from this garden on most days."

"Looks like you did what you could."

"I guess."

He sat in silence with her, flapping a hand to keep the flies off his face. She was barely even doing that.

The times they'd gone into the bush together swam back over him.

A double handful of the indigenous kids—it was still okay to call them "aborigines" or "abos" back then—Holly, Stevie, and himself would go out into the deep Barkly Tablelands on most weekends. Often for a week or more during vacations. Sometimes they'd be figuring out bush tucker, or hunting up the odd snake or lizard for cooking, but other times they'd just all sit quiet with their own thoughts until someone had something to say.

"I miss those times."

"Which ones?" Holly didn't look over at him.

"The quiet ones. I get all wrapped up in the pilot world. Always busy. Always a schedule. Layover in one city or another. Checking out the bars. You know."

"And the women."

Quint shrugged. It wasn't worth denying. "But then I come back here and I remember."

"I wish I didn't."

He didn't have a convenient answer to that.

"I went by the churchyard cemetery, but I couldn't find them."

"They're out at the old cemetery, south of town. I'll drive you, if you're done here."

She didn't even look around. "I'm *so* done here."

"Want anything from inside?"

She held up a square-headed Ford truck key.

"Stevie's?"

She nodded.

Christ! The truck that had been washed away by the same flood that took her brother's life. He should grab it and throw it out into the dust where she'd never find it.

"Anything else?"

"Not on your life!" She actually shuddered before pushing to her feet, then circled wide through the yard as if even getting near the house hurt her.

35

THE OLD TENNANT CREEK CEMETERY LAY TWO KILOMETERS south of town along the Stuart. Or it had when Holly left. Now the town had expanded most of the way here on the Tennant Creek side of the track. The gully beyond the cemetery would occasionally have some flow during the Wet season, but it was the Dry now.

The graveyard's red sand surface was broken up with thin clumps of gray-brown Mitchell grass and wide-scattered Mulga acacia trees. Their leaves were red-dusted to such a pale green that it was a wonder they could use the sun at all. It would still be another three months before there was a chance of a December rain rinsing them clean.

Holly let Quint lead her out among the gravestones. She felt as if she was merely floating along, disconnected from anything that could possibly be real.

The Holly Harper who had left here at the age of sixteen —exactly half a lifetime ago—had been a wild, angry, and impetuous girl. After years of pushing her younger self away, at the house Holly had been able to see her so clearly.

Laughing with her brother. Tending her garden. Watching Mum drink and Dad sit in silence, watching the telly between runs, never knowing it was anger that was eating her alive.

Quint led her past the grand crosses and imported black gravestones.

Past the simple white headstones.

In the back corner, the grave markers were foot-high chunks of concrete with a brass plaque glued to the surface. Out here, that could last a thousand years. Far more permanence than any Harper deserved.

Mum and Dad shared a marker, nothing but their birth and death years. Not even "Husband and Wife." It was fresh and shiny, barely dusted at all.

With an odd hesitation, Quint pointed at the next marker. There was a small pot of wilted flowers close beside it.

She read the plaque.

Holly had to read it out loud to make sense of it.

"Stevie and Holly Harper. Brother and sister. Died 2004."

No birth dates.

No—

"What the fuck?"

"This," Quint spoke softly, "is why I thought you were dead."

"My parents *buried* me?"

Quint nodded.

"Your flowers?"

"Your birthday last week."

It had been.

She'd never mentioned it to anyone, not even Mike. Her sixteenth birthday had been a big day. Stevie had taken her in personally to get her learner's permit. It also marked three months until she killed her brother by drowning him in his pickup truck during the wet season.

Not a date she was much interested in remembering.

The pressure started building all over again.

The horror of finding Stevie's body.

The fight—that final long, horrid, drunken (on her mom's part) brawl.

First the screaming match.

Then the words that could never be taken back on either side.

Finally, they had battled up and down the length of the house. Throwing accusations—and whatever else came to hand.

It was the only time Mum had ever done more than give Holly a slap of admonition.

Holly had never seen the fist coming.

The massive nosebleed stain had marked the biggest change ever in her life. How appropriate that blood marked the day she lost all illusions. The same rug still lay there this morning—as soiled as ever.

The stain should have been there.

Instead? Gone, as if it had never happened.

As if she'd never existed.

The only thing in the entire place that showed she'd ever been there were the remains of the dead veggie patch.

After the fist to the face, she'd bought herself a moment to recover by kicking Mum in the crotch so hard that it blasted through even her drunken haze.

It had taken under a minute to staunch the flow of blood from her nose.

Another minute to pack.

Then she'd been gone while Mum was still curled up in fetal position.

Dad had done absolutely nothing. He just sat in his chair and watched them with a long neck of XXXX Gold brew in his hand as if they were just a show on the telly.

And now Mum was dead.

Holly needed to either laugh or cry as she stood over her own grave.

But she couldn't find it in her to do either one. Not even when Quint slid an arm around her waist and pulled her into a hard hug.

36

Clarissa stared at her phone.

She needed to make the call, but she didn't dare. It didn't matter that she was the Director of the CIA and her husband was the Vice President. Holly wasn't the sort of person to care about position when seeking revenge.

But an entire night of hounding her hacker twins hadn't erased the truth. Neither had an entire day of cyber-searching by the on-site teams revealed the first link in the chain, even though she knew where it must be. There was no way through the firewall of the Diego Garcia Black Site.

And yet, there was no other answer.

Someone had found a way.

And of the ten "guests" incarcerated there, only one had any connection to Holly Harper.

The origin of the attack had to be Guest Seven, the Zaslon operative Holly had caught and the CIA had incarcerated at the Diego Garcia Black Site.

Zaslon were Russia's version of her own Special Operations Group. They used them to poison defectors and opposition leaders. Assassination of counteragents, theft of secrets, and anything else that required the stalk-kill-vanish trifecta. If it was a mission for which a president needed plausible deniability: Zaslon, the SOG, Israel's Kidon, France's Action Service, the UK's E Squadron...

There was an entire clandestine global war that was mentioned only when a mission went wrong. A war carried out by tiny elite cadres—numbering no more than a hundred or so in any country—in contravention of every legal accord.

And Holly had actually captured a Zaslon operative, without ever revealing how.

Though now that she had the reports from Kurt Grice, she could guess.

The SOG team sent to Johnston Atoll had been less than forthcoming. In fact, the leader had made it clear to Kurt that his life now had only one mission...the eradication of Holly Harper.

While Clarissa could think of worse things to happen, she couldn't have someone going rogue.

She'd authorized Kurt to proceed with the leader of the SOG squad as he saw fit. It really was a pity that the SOG team leader of the Johnston Atoll cleanup mission had become so upset during his debriefing that he'd died of a heart attack. One induced by what method, Clarissa would never know. She appreciated the plausible deniability that Kurt had afforded her.

If the rest of the team had any suspicions, none of them had seemed terribly upset by it. He'd been very efficient but he hadn't exactly won himself a lot of friends inside the SOG operations teams.

No, the useful report of the events on Johnston Atoll had

come from the Air Force crew of the C-17 Globemaster III. Miranda's three warriors had taken down six of her agents in mere seconds, using such a simple tool: distraction.

Holly must have done something similar to capture the female Zaslon operative originally. Or maybe not. Clarissa had seen what a battered mess Holly's team was afterward that capture. One Special Operations Forces warrior was even hospitalized for over a month. It didn't matter how, she'd done it.

The deal had been simple. Clarissa could do anything she wanted with the intelligence asset that a Zaslon operative could be, but she must never be allowed to touch the outside world again in any way.

Clarissa had even been careful not to learn the Russian woman's name. She was simply Guest Seven.

Yet they'd gotten to know each other in the long phone calls. They were remarkably similar. She had a ruthless edge that Clarissa recognized in herself. In a different world they could have been friends, coworkers, collaborators. They could have helped each other.

But this wasn't that world.

The Russian Zaslon operative and the Director of the Central Intelligence Agency.

The distance was too great.

But her one guarantee to Holly of Guest Seven's permanent isolation had failed.

She'd somehow orchestrated the downing of the Airbus plane—and put the blame for the cover-up orders directly on Clarissa's desk.

Yet it was impossible for her to have issued the order to mobilize the SOG clean-up operation. That had still come from one of her directors.

Holly was going to be beyond pissed. For that, she just might follow through on her threat to hunt down Clarissa and make her pay.

She should have erased Guest Seven when she had the chance.

But that chance was gone. And she'd lost half of her assets on Diego Garcia just during the escape.

Before she could talk herself out of it, Clarissa dialed the phone.

It rang for a long time.

37

"WHAT THE FUCK DO YOU WANT?" HOLLY ANSWERED AFTER breaking from Quint's embrace when she saw who was calling.

"I have a problem."

"Good!" Holly hung up the phone just because it felt good. Something had to on a suck-ass day like this.

It rang almost immediately.

"What? You having a bad hair day, Clarissa?"

"I need your goddamn help," the snarl behind the words said she'd struck home. Clarissa was very particular about her long blonde ponytail.

"I'd rather have a sharp poke in the eye." Of course, staring down at her own grave was doing a depressingly superb job of that.

"It's important."

"Not to me. Not right now." What she wanted to do most was go get bloody lost in the bush until she woke up as somebody else or the world ended—whichever came *second*. Just her and a sharp knife, and she'd be fine. Surviving out there only took experience and a certain bloody-mindedness; today she had the latter in boatloads.

"What the hell, Harper? You know that it's a major problem if I'm calling you."

She did. "Still don't care."

"Jesus. Who rammed a stick up your butt? Your parents?"

"They're dead." Holly felt even less like talking after that came out.

"Good thing or bad thing?"

"Fuck you, Clarissa." And there was the problem. It *was* a good thing, and Holly *hated* that she felt that way as she stood staring down at their graves.

"I had one and one," Clarissa's tone was suddenly soft. "The day Mom died was the single worst day of my life. The night I executed my father was the best."

Holly kept her mouth shut. For Clarissa to admit that casually seemed unlikely.

But when she didn't speak either, Holly was left to wonder. Clarissa continued after a long pause.

"That was over twenty years ago. First time I've said that aloud—ever. Shit! Do me *one* goddamn favor in your lifetime, Harper, and don't ask."

"Okay." Holly had never thought about why Clarissa Reese was always as mean as cat's piss, but now maybe she didn't need to.

"Thank you." Another long pause.

Holly supposed it was her turn. "Mom's been dead under a week. Drank herself to death. First time I've been home since I was sixteen."

"Sixteen was when I bought my freedom." When Clarissa had killed her father.

"Goodonya." Her own father might as well have been

dead after twenty years living with Mum. Holly supposed it was much the same for her. She'd killed her *connection* to her family. Once her brother was gone, there was no reason in the world not to.

"Thanks." There was a tapping in the background, like Clarissa was fidgeting with a pen or something. Clarissa never showed her nerves.

"What's going on?"

"You remember the guest you gave into my care?"

And in that instant, Holly knew.

It hadn't been mere paranoia bothering her.

The destruction of the Airbus A330-900neo and the death of fifty-three people had been aimed at a single target.

Her.

The crash. The deaths. They were all her fault.

Russian Zaslon operative Elayne Kasprak had returned from the grave.

38

"Next person who makes a noise is going to die very painfully."

Elayne stood over the three bodies of the Air Force roadblock.

Once out, it had only taken her minutes to figure out where in the world she'd been incarcerated. The bright moon had revealed the narrow strip of land and the extensive line of it around a great central lagoon. Bright lights on the far side of the lagoon revealed what must be a military base. She'd managed to confirm that only minutes later when a large four-engine propellor plane had departed. Definitely military in profile. A C-130 Hercules.

She was on the eastern arm of Diego Garcia base, halfway between Africa and India in the middle of the fucking ocean. There was no other base like it in the world.

The Brits and Yanks had purchased it outright—in a manner that both the International Court of Justice and the UN said was utter crap—and then kicked out all the natives in 1971. Dubbed the "unsinkable aircraft carrier", fifty years of military operations had relied on the runway, submarine service docks, and a three-sixty-degree protected lagoon big enough to moor an entire carrier group of ships.

The atoll itself was a lumpy oval stretching eleven by twenty-one kilometers.

And she was on the wrong goddamn side.

It was all connected by a single dirt road that ran all sixty kilometers along the top of the narrow atoll.

So, of course, they were going to set up a roadblock.

A roadblock that had spanned one of the atoll's narrowest locations—and been put on full alert by the curse of one of her four tagalongs.

She'd wanted a nice quiet takedown, no one the wiser.

Instead, it had become a goddamn firefight—a short one, because the Latino was almost as good a shooter as she was —but still.

In answer to her order for silence, she received nods and the flash of a smile, moonlit on the Latino's face.

She'd never had a Latin lover. But after a year-long enforced dry spell, she'd want to take her time...and no witnesses.

For now?

The distant airbase remained quiet—no airborne helos rushing at them across the lagoon, no flash of headlights racing south along the atoll road.

At least they got a vehicle upgrade, from SUV to salt-eaten Humvee.

"Saddle up!" She'd watched far too many movies while locked up—all American, of course. Only John Wayne was worth watching.

They climbed aboard: the piece of Eurotrash who couldn't keep his goddamn mouth shut—he'd be the first she'd throw in harm's way—a slender Indian woman, and a husky Chinese woman who moved like a soldier. The Latino took the back center and stuck his head and shoulders up into the roof-top gun turret.

"No shooting unless the shit really hits the fan, *comprendes?*"

"*Si*, lovely *señora*," he racked a round into the chamber, flicked off the safety, then offered her another of those smiles.

Definite possibilities.

39

"Did she get out?" Holly's voice was dead cold. Completely unreadable. Whatever unexpected window they'd briefly ripped open into each other's pasts had just slammed shut.

Clarissa paved over it quickly. "One hour ago. A pump failure caused the, ah, site where she was being held to flood. The automatic safety systems released her...and others. Maybe as many as seven. Information on the ground is still sketchy."

"I don't give a flying fuck about them. Your site should have locked down hard and let it flood."

"You think I don't know that? I didn't design the damn system!" Clarissa knew she was shouting at the wrong person. She tried a deep breath; it didn't help.

Holly waited her out.

"I lost an entire team. And..." A message appeared on her screen. "Oh shit! Three minutes ago the Air Force discovered that one of their roadblocks had been terminated—with prejudice."

"And?"

Clarissa sighed and forced herself to set down her fountain pen before she flipped it onto her skirt and stained everything blue.

"*And?*" Holly was no more patient than she herself would be. Clarissa *hated* having anything in common with Holly.

"We don't know how she was getting messages out. But she must have been the source of the attack on your plane. She was in an isolated accommodation."

"A what?"

"A fucking Black Site, okay, Harper? Solitary confinement. No other contacts."

"For a year? She was already crackers back then. Must be full-on mental now."

"We allow television in and she has a phone—a landline. It automatically dials me directly when it's picked up. Fully encrypted."

"But she's getting out messages."

Clarissa hated to admit it. "Worse. They look as if they're routed from *my* desk, through a long-lost Finnish back door onto a Russian server farm, then a lash through Syria."

"Couldn't happen to a more deserving drongo."

"Drongo?" Clarissa didn't know that one.

"Raw recruit. It's another word for an idiot who—"

"Bitch."

Holly didn't argue with the accusation. Well, at least they were back on their old terms. It had been an extremely uncomfortable feeling that she could actually like Holly Harper. Something that would never, ever, under *any* circumstances happen.

"We can trace the message origin to the island, but we can't trace them any farther."

"The island?"

Clarissa got up and paced across her office. Leaning her forehead against the glass, she stared down at the small executive parking lot on the north side of the New Headquarters Building. Looked down and saw Clark's motorcade parked below. By the movement of the agents, she could tell that he'd just entered her building.

She checked her watch, four p.m. He'd been on the ground for barely the length of the drive from Andrews Air Force Base.

Leave it to Clark to come to the CIA first after returning from Alaska. He couldn't just go to his office in the White House or home to the Vice President's mansion at One Observatory Circle.

No, he was a sentimental slob who would make coming to see her his first stop. And then, of course, he'd want sex in her office, just as they'd started out when the office had still been his.

She spoke quickly. "Where are you? I'll get a fast transport to pick you up and deliver you to her location. I've locked down all departing flights with full security on each plane. The Air Force is beyond livid, but there's no other way out. They're sending out hunt-kill squads but we both know she has the skills to just walk right around them—or rack up the body count if she's in the mood."

"A year in solitary? She's definitely in the mood."

"Yeah," Clarissa would be too. "I'll give you full authorization to do whatever you deem necessary."

"I'd rather be licking a dingo's balls."

"You can enjoy yourself later, Harper. Where are you?"

Holly didn't answer.

"Look, Harper. We need to capture this bitch. I'd like to

just put her down, but we need to know what else she's done, and who her inside contact was because there was no way for her to order the SOG team—that came from one of my directors. I hate to admit it, but you're the only one who managed to capture a Russian Zaslon operative—ever. You're the best qualified to catch her, and get the truth out of her."

"Fuck me."

"Not my department. Where?" There was a knock on her locked office door. Security really should have taken away Clark's key to the executive elevator when he became VP. She didn't have time for him right now.

"Tennant Creek, Australia," Holly groaned out like she was in pain.

Clarissa did a quick search on her tablet, then made an arrangement to borrow a Falcon 7X passenger jet from the Royal Australian Air Force against—damn, she hated to do this—an open IOU. "They'll be there in two hours and take you direct to Diego Garcia. Clearance will be there by the time you arrive."

Again the silence stretched long before she answered.

"Yeah, that'd be right." Holly's tone was so resigned that Clarissa actually felt bad about sending her. Not that there was a better choice.

"Do you want me to mobilize an SOG team to assist you? I have one in Italy."

Holly's laugh was bitter and short enough to feel like a slap.

Then she hung up.

Clarissa sent the clearance for one Holly Harper to land at Diego Garcia and have access to any assets.

This whole disaster had to stay completely isolated inside the CIA—and Clark was Executive Branch since becoming Vice President. Well, she knew one sure-fire distraction.

After slipping off her underwear and making sure her skirt and blouse were in order, she hit the remote unlock on the door.

She met Clark halfway across the carpet.

He might be twenty years her senior, but he was still in excellent condition.

"Hi, honey."

"Missed you," he dragged her into a kiss, one hand tight around her, the other freeing her long hair from its perennial ponytail. Only Clark ever got to see her with her hair loose, and they both liked it that way.

His eagerness was already apparent as he pressed against her.

His fingers traced the curves of her ass muscles through the skirt's material.

His smile shifted from happy to greedy.

"Ah, the old days," he whispered as he leaned down to kiss her and dug his fingers into her butt more tightly.

She'd made a policy of never wearing underwear to the office after they'd become lovers. Their sex life had started as stolen moments against his cherrywood desk. Now that they were married and he was no longer her boss, it had taken some of the edge out of it.

On the plus side, Clark's skills had continued to improve.

Rather than just diving in for the home run as he used to, he took his time about it. When he was finally done with her, all she wore was her Christian Louboutin pumps. Her body burned from a most pleasant ravaging.

And while she kept the CIA's secrets from him, he didn't see any need to withhold Executive Branch information from her. She lay against him while he played with her hair and recovered—and told her about everything that was new in Alaska and over at the White House.

When the news had run out—turnabout being fair play, and it was the end of the day after all—she turned the tables on him.

By the time they would be finished—both naked, prostrate, nursing rug burns in awkward places, and gasping desperately for air on the Director of the CIA's carpet—Holly Harper would be airborne.

40

HOLLY STUFFED THE PHONE INTO HER POCKET.

"Bitch," she whispered at her mother's grave because she was well and truly trapped.

"That didn't sound good, Holl."

She'd forgotten Quint was there.

"I have to be at the airport in two hours."

He squinted at her. "There are only two flights a day out of Tennant Creek. First one just heads down the Alice and it isn't for another four hours. If you're wanting Darwin, that's not until midafternoon."

"Special flight. The RAAF is sending a Falcon for me." She kicked a boot at the dirt. Not really intending to, she sprayed a layer of red dust over her mother's new grave marker. She did it again, hoping she could obliterate it. The additional dirt merely slid off the angled plaque.

"Shit, woman. I thought it was me that Eli was being nice to last night, flying us so far out of his way. You in all tight with the Queen or something?"

"Oh yeah, me and the Royals, we go way back. Only too bloody right, mate." She studied the dirt.

"But you just got here. Didn't you have things you wanted to..."

He must have seen the look on her face.

"Okay. You don't *want* to be here at all. Got it. You've got two more hours in Tennant Creek. What do you *have* to do?"

"Sell the bloody mansion. I tried giving it to Harry and Meghan as a wedding present, but they didn't want to show up the Queen with such a posh cubby."

"That place wouldn't pass for decent dunny when you've got the shits." Then he turned a little red and mumbled a soft, "Sorry."

"Not half as sorry as me, Quint. And only too true."

"Don't know as there are any estate agents up and about at six in the morning. But we can try."

Holly closed her eyes. She didn't want to see the graves anymore. Didn't want to witness how Quint was seeing her as a woman to pity. Didn't want to see Tennant Creek.

"How about you sell it for me? If you get anything, put it in your pocket. Or donate it all to the Julalikari Council Aboriginal Corporation. Hell, just *give* the house to them. I'll sign a paper for you to hand off. They still doing job training, food service, and all that?"

"They are. Some of the old crowd are there as well. Do you want to—"

Holly just shook her head. It had been her only freedom from the psychotic Harper household. Getting out into the deep bush. Toward the end, she'd gone far more often on her own than with the the usual crowd. Barely cared about water, not at all about food, only about...away. It was a miracle she hadn't killed herself through being teen-stupid.

"I used to dream of going walkabout."

"Shit, Holl. You evaporated half a lifetime ago. That wasn't enough of a walk for you?"

"Out there," she nodded toward the Barkly Tablelands. A person could live out there for a hundred years and maybe never see another soul.

"Seriously?"

She could only nod.

Quint turned to stare out at the bush with her.

The land was rough, not tall with mountains like southeast, but a vast trackless terrain filled with unexpected gullies, harsh precipices, and little fodder. Even at their densest, the low gum and Mulga trees were fifty or a hundred meters apart. The brush and grass between could only maintain a few cattle per acre—sometimes less. Cattle stations, ranches, were typically measured in hundreds of thousands of acres. Whole generations of cattle might never see a person.

"In God's name why?"

"There's water enough. And bush tucker." She'd learned how to find them as a kid. Gotten even better at it during SASR survival training.

"Still."

Holly kept staring, feeling the pull. "I was a wild pain in everyone's behind back then."

"You were incredible."

She looked at him.

"Oh come on, Harper. Everyone—even Stevie— worshipped you, and not just because you were his kid sister. Most people in TC move through life at a good, steady pace. You were like a lightning bolt. Always on the move, always doing something exciting. The weekend trips out into the

Tablelands?" He nodded toward the desert. "They pretty much died along with you. You know, back when we all thought that was you." He had the decency to grimace as he waved toward the gravestone behind them. "They said you were the one who started them in the first place."

"No. I..." But she had been. Pushing her friends to find out what the elders knew about survival. She'd spent more time at the Julalikari Council Community Center than a lot of the indigenous, asking endless streams of questions. Always looking for ways to turn the wilderness of the bush into school projects.

"It's a cliché, Harper, but you were a force of nature in this sleepy small town. No wonder you left."

"I loved it here." The words hurt her throat. She nodded toward town. "Maybe not there so much, but..."

"*Out there?*" Quint's disbelief was clear.

"It was like those endless stretches of the bush *drew* the wild out of me. It was the only place I could ever be myself. Might still be the closest I've ever come to that." And she'd lost that—somewhere along the way.

"The road hasn't been that hard, has it?"

She nodded at first, but could feel the wrongness of it and shook her head instead. No, it hadn't.

Holly remembered laughing it up with her SASR demolition squad after a hard day's dance with the ISIS or al-Qaeda sharpshooters in Kandahar, Lashkargah, or wherever the muck-up of the month had been.

There was the NTSB team. Sitting back on the office couch debating the failures in aircraft structures. Sharing a meal around the big table up on Miranda's private island.

Mike. No, she wasn't going to think about Mike.

And she'd never met anyone like Miranda Chase. Never

had a friend like her. There was a real purity to Miranda. Not that she wasn't a total mess as well, but there was a clarity and purpose to Miranda that just shone out of her. Holly had lost that too.

A lightning bolt? She was more like fulgurite—lightning sand. The lumpy, hollow tubes of fused silica glass sometimes formed when lightning struck and superheated the sand. Yet she remembered the stick-figure girl who loved to run beneath the burning sun. She could almost see her racing ahead of the pack to be the first out into the bush.

When she'd been away, the main thing she'd remembered about Tennant Creek was her disaster of a homelife.

Now that she stood on the familiar soil, Mum, Dad, and the house seemed more mirage than real. The bush. *That* had been what was real. The kids, even Quint—so eager to please, so happy to be there—they had been the real family.

"Maybe it's not the road behind that's bothering me so much." Though her family's two grave markers still called horseshit on her for that.

"The phone call that bad?"

Holly could only nod.

"Okay. I'll get rid of the place for you."

She nodded her thanks.

Then she fished Stevie's truck key out of her pocket and studied it carefully. It had been her ticket out, her ticket away. Freedom...chopped off by stupidity as Stevie had shouted not to drive into the running wash and her wild younger self had taken it as a dare.

She'd thought to carry this one memory out into the world with her.

But maybe it was better if it was left as a memory.

She knelt down and buried the key in the dusty soil against the raw concrete gravestone bearing her and Stevie's names. Kissing her brother's name seemed too little, too late, but it was all she had to offer.

"I'll get them to change the grave marker. Take your name off."

"No, Quint," she brushed a hand over her own name. "I think maybe it's time I left the sixteen-year-old they buried here in...peace."

She pushed back to her feet.

"And thanks for my birthday flowers."

Quint spoke after a long silence filled only with the soft wind rattling the acacia leaves.

"Pretty dead now."

"But they were alive." Just as she'd been back then. What would it feel like to be that way again?

"You've got an hour and fifty-five to flight. What do you *want* to do?"

41

Holly lay in Quint's bed and wasn't sure who she hated more, herself or...herself.

Quint was in the shower being pretty damn pleased with life.

Her body was all sappy happy as well.

Yet somehow—without once committing to anything more than sleeping with Mike when they were both in the mood, which she had to admit had been far more often than not lately—she'd just cheated on him.

No words of exclusivity, monogamy, or any of that crap had ever passed between them.

But still...

She'd just cheated on him.

Telling herself to shut up didn't help.

Telling her body to stop being so damned liquid and content didn't seem to bother it for a moment.

For one lousy hour Quint had helped her forget everything. But now she was—

"That's not a real happy look for such a fine-looking

woman to be wearing." Quint was still naked, except now he was naked and wet. A right nice look on him. All big and solid. Nothing like Mike's lean and smooth...

"Someone should just feed me to a saltie and put me out of my misery. Why do I feel like such a shit?"

Quint finished drying off and wrapped a towel around his waist. "Never told you about my ex, Darlene."

And she really didn't want to hear it now. She'd meant the question for herself, not for Quint.

He sat on the foot of the bed and waited.

"Shit! Okay. What about her?"

"For two years after she left me, every time I had me a little naughty, I felt like you look right now. You *are* in a relationship."

"No!" She never had been and never wanted to be. Not one long enough to ever be counted as a relationship anyway.

"Sorry, Holl. I saw, but I maybe didn't let myself see. Not saying I didn't enjoy it, just saying maybe I should have said no when I said yes."

"I'm *not*—"

Quint held up his hand to stop her, resting his fingers on her lips. "The more you protest, the more it hurts. Just the voice of experience here trying to save you some pain."

"I'm *not* anyway. Definitely not with Mike," she mumbled around his fingers. And there was Quint's shot of pain. Damn him for being right. She yanked the sheet up over her head.

"Aw, crap. I'd have seen how deep it was if I hadn't been so busy thinking these kind of thoughts. It sucks for me that he's a nice guy. So I don't get to begrudge you even that. I liked him."

"Everyone likes him!" Holly bolted to sitting upright and knew she was shouting, but couldn't seem to stop. "Even me! And you know what that's going to get him? It's going to get him fucking killed because I didn't have the balls to off a Russian assassin bitch when I had the chance. I should have dumped her into the goddamn Siberian Taiga from thirty thousand feet when I had the chance."

Quint waited out her rant.

"Okay, tell me you didn't just hear that. Because it was one hundred percent classified."

"Not a word, Holl. Not a word. Once you sat up and that sheet fell into your lap, I wasn't thinking about anything so dumb as words. I'm just sitting here congratulating myself on being smart enough to have a crush on you when I was twelve. You shaped up damn fine."

Holly looked down at her breasts. "They're just—"

"The finest pair of bazoomas this boy has ever handled."

"Christ! You *are* still twelve." She so didn't feel like laughing.

"No, I'm Australian."

"Next you'll want to tit-fuck me."

"You offering?" He said it with a twelve-year-old's excitement as he clasped his hands together like a kid at Christmas. "Please say yes."

She sighed...and pulled up the sheet.

"I guess that's a no," and he plastered on an overdramatic sad face.

"That's a no." She knew that he was just trying to cheer her up, but it wasn't working.

"What is it, Holl? We crashed out of the sky on the only piece of land for a thousand klicks in any direction and most of us survived. In the middle of that, you were on your toes and kicking sass the whole way. Never mind that we'd have all been dead without you."

Holly realized she was crumpling the sheet into a thousand tiny folds of worry in her hands.

She tossed it aside, climbed to her feet naked, and headed to shower before her flight. At the door jamb, she hung on with both hands to keep from just collapsing to the cool tile as her head spun with vertigo.

"Quint?" She called out without turning.

"Yeah?"

"Once I'm gone, never mention my name. Not to anyone."

"Jesus, Holl. You kidding?"

"No one, Quint!" She spun around to face him.

His look said she was as crackers as a Melbournian riding a roo—which wasn't even close to how screwed up she was.

"I mean it. Everyone I've ever cared about, I've killed. If this bitch knew I liked you, she'd kill you just for the fun of it. And she's not the worst I've faced over the years. Well, maybe, but well within a cooee of some others."

"But—"

"Everyone, Quint! My brother, my SASR team, and now I have to figure out how to save Miranda's team before someone gets them, too. They're in danger because of *me*. For the sake of *your* life, you've never seen me. They interview you about the crash, I was just some blonde bimbo you got to fuck afterward—can't remember her name. The air marshal is bound to back up the bimbo part of that story."

"Well, shit, Holl. That's a whole swagman's bundle of unload."

"Yeah, sorry. But it doesn't make it any less true."

"I just don't believe it."

"Well, for your own sake, you'd better, Quint."

"I mean after all these years; you actually like me?"

He finally earned her laugh. It didn't even last until she reached the shower, but she did like him. Maybe not as much as Mike, but she could definitely do with a few more Quints in her life.

42

"It's weird not having Holly here," Mike wouldn't stop fussing with the television remote, and it was giving Miranda a headache. The remote for the big screen television was usually in Holly's control. During an investigation, it was filled with data. During these rare slow times between investigations, she'd put on a movie. When it was some exciting thriller, Miranda was more comfortable turning her back but didn't mind listening in.

Unless it had planes. Very few of those passed any grade of reliable accuracy. However, Holly had gotten her hooked on science-based futures. *Star Trek, Star Wars,* though her favorite was *WALL-E*.

Mike was flicking from CNN to a movie, then over to a sitcom. He stopped to watch a car tire commercial, then—

Andi finally yanked it from his hand and turned the television off.

Miranda felt as if she could breathe again.

Her team's secure office was in the back of her airplane

hangar at Tacoma Narrows Airport. Jeremy was busy at his workbench, running a chemical analysis on the false shear pins they'd extracted from the crashed Airbus 300 engine pylons.

Taz was reading out instructions to the new spectrum analyzer for him.

Miranda sat on the sofa with her laptop and was trying extremely hard to concentrate on the data collected during the long flight. There should be some clue to what kind of alteration had been made to the lost engine to cause the breakaway.

The Flight Data Recorder was useless. It was designed to track accident information and to survive the crash. It only stored the last two hours of the flight. Any stress data from the Seattle takeoff and climb to altitude had been overwritten three times prior to the crash, which had finally cut off the recording.

The QAR had a longer buffer and more detailed data, but she still wasn't finding any useful indicators regarding the type of sabotage to the engine or what had caused the fatal hydraulic overpressure pulse.

Perhaps a study of other flight equipment on the Blue Loop of the hydraulic system would—

"I mean why is she in Australia anyway?"

Miranda had learned that listening to Mike was immensely helpful in most circumstances, so she'd trained herself to listen when he spoke. But—

"Mike."

He turned to look at her.

"That is the twenty-third time you've asked that question today. You already know that all she ever said to any of us was that it was personal business. What else are you anticipating learning by repeating your question?"

"I..." he shrugged, "...nothing. She wouldn't let me go with her. She barely let me interview her after the crash. I spoke more with that big Australian pilot she was so buddy-buddy with than I did with her. He was fine being interviewed about the crash. So was the captain when we caught up with her in Hawaii. They were glad to tell me everything. But Holly? She's the one I'm sleeping with, and I couldn't get her to say two words to me. Worse than a clam."

"You know how to talk to a clam?" Miranda had never considered that as even being a possibility.

"Sure, with a steamer, a butter-garlic sauce, and a small, sharp fork."

"I don't think that would be a very useful interview technique to—"

"Bloody hell, Miranda. I was making a joke." He thumped his head against the back of his leather armchair. "Sorry, Miranda. Now I'm *sounding* like Holly. I'm totally losing my shit."

"The bathroom is over there," Miranda pointed.

"Thanks." Rather than heading there, Mike kept thumping his head against the chair. At least the padding was thick so she didn't have to worry about him hurting himself.

"It's okay, Miranda." Andi sat down next to her. "He's just worried."

"I would think that he'd be more worried when she was crashing rather than merely visiting Australia."

"Sometimes we worry about people we care about no matter where they are. Especially the ones we love."

Mike jerked upright in his armchair as if he'd been electrocuted. "I never said I loved her."

Andi rolled her eyes at him; which Miranda had learned meant something to others but never meant anything to her. Whatever it did mean had Mike slouching. Mike never slouched.

43

Miranda tried thinking about how she felt about people she herself cared about who weren't here. Like...Jon. It had been twenty-five hours since she'd last seen Jon on Johnston Atoll. Because of how they'd parted, should she have expected to hear from him?

It was the sort of question she typically asked Holly. She'd learned to ask Holly about her relationship questions. Her advice had proven to be more helpful and measurably more comprehensible than Mike's on the subject.

But now she wasn't here.

Mike jumped to his feet and stalked away to the kitchenette to fuss with his espresso machine.

"Andi? Should I be hearing from Jon? We did not part amicably."

Andi almost laughed. "That is putting it mildly. It wouldn't surprise me if Holly threatened to castrate him if he ever contacted you again."

"Oh. So that *is* a disincentive for him."

"Absolutely. Are you okay with that?"

Miranda studied the bright red tips of Andi's hair. "Feelings are difficult for me to assess. My own as much as in others."

Andi nodded, setting up an interesting swirl pattern in the tips that dampened as the hairs' colors transitioned to gold, yellow, and finally flame blue before fading into the true black of her natural colors. Miranda didn't think that the pattern was related to the weight or stiffness variations of the coloring products, but it was an interesting phenomenon nevertheless.

Mike served her a mug of hot chocolate and Andi an espresso—exactly like the ones he'd given them each less than an hour before. She dutifully took a sip, the proper thing to do when someone offered you a hot beverage, but she didn't want more than that.

"It just nerves," Andi whispered as soon as Mike was out of earshot. "About your feelings for Jon..." Andi looked puzzled for a moment. Then she turned to Jeremy and called out his name.

"Uh-huh," he didn't even look up from his equipment.

"Do you have that card deck of yours handy?"

He barely turned to toss it over before he and Taz were making some new calibration.

Andi spread out the deck. "Wow! Jeremy's really been working on this. These look great!" she called out the last to him.

"Uh-huh," Jeremy didn't sound as if he even understood.

She and Andi inspected the cards shoulder-to-shoulder. Jeremy had added several categories of cards in varied sizes. She had no idea how they all fit together, and she was worried about how much she was supposed to already understand.

"Okay, let's ignore the game dynamics for a moment," Andi split them into the different decks. "He'll have to tell us later how they work together."

That was a relief. Miranda always felt like she was so far behind in new games.

"Twenty-four map cards of time zones around the world." She began laying them out from the International Date Line.

"Why didn't he lay them out from GMT 0 in London?"

"Well, this way, the entire world is functioning on the same day."

"Oh," Miranda herself had always preferred to think of time zones from 0 to +24—she'd never been comfortable with the implications of negative time such as when her present Pacific Time Zone was designated GMT -8 when it was really GMT +16 but not because it was the same day for nineteen hours out of every twenty-four. Of course, what really needed to happen was that 0 needed to be jumped to the International Date Line. But, on consideration, she doubted that would ever happen and dismissed the entire framework.

It was a good thing that she had bought such a large coffee table when she'd furnished the office—twenty-four cards across took up a lot of room.

Andi called out again. "Jeremy, for the map, you need to make twelve cards with two time zones each. This is crazy."

"Oh," he looked up, "that's good! Thanks." He looked back down.

"So," Andi shuffled through the aircraft cards. "Here, you're the Sabrejet, right?"

"Right." Mike sat down to Miranda's other side.

Andi set the F-86 Sabrejet card down on the GMT -8 map card, which was their own time zone here in Tacoma.

She recognized the other cards that Andi plucked from the deck as the ones Mike had used to describe each of them once over dinner. Holly was the Russian Havoc helicopter, a metaphor she still didn't understand except that they were both warriors. Andi was the experimental S-97 Raider helicopter that she used to fly—easy to remember. Taz was the F-35 stealth fighter always thinking like an attack plane, and Jeremy the reliable Chinook helicopter.

When Andi pulled the Mooney M20V for Mike, Taz spoke up from where she was now leaning on the back of the couch.

"No. Mike's the A-10C Thunderbolt close air support attack jet."

"But—" Miranda understood the association of Mike with the Mooney he so often flew, "—he's not a combat jet pilot."

"Trust me," Taz insisted. "He may fly way below the radar, but he's dangerous as hell in the role of close support for the team, just like the Warthog."

Mike sighed, "This is when Holly is supposed to say, 'But he's so pretty' in my defense."

"She would," Andi laughed as she found and laid down the A-10C Thunderbolt. Then she spread out the rest of the cards. "So that's all of us. Which one of these others seems like Jon?"

"He's—"

Andi reached across to slap Mike's leg to stop him. "I'm asking Miranda."

"But she's terrible at metaphors."

"Yes," Miranda agreed looking at the bewildering array of possibilities. "He's right."

"Well, for the moment, we're going to pretend he's wrong. Choose one."

Miranda studied the options.

Jon often flew a sleek C-21A Learjet transport, but if Mike wasn't the Mooney, then the C-21A must also be too obvious for Jon.

They'd met during a crash investigation of a massive Russian AN-124 Condor cargo jet—not that he'd really ever fully understood what had happened to it.

He wasn't a rotorcraft as that implied an agility of thought that Jon had never demonstrated. And he wasn't very observant on crash investigations, which removed the remote-sensing and command specialists like the E-3 Sentry with its big radar dome or the several presidential command planes: Air Force One and Two, and the E-4B Nightwatch.

As she pushed each card aside, Andi gathered it up, simplifying the choices.

Jon had none of the attack-jet capabilities that Mike had assigned to Taz. Though he *was* good at investigation organization, which discarded a number of poor aircraft designs.

He was old-fashioned like a B-52 Stratofortress, which was the only remaining combat aircraft, but it was so old-fashioned that she handed that to Andi as well.

That left only a few of the cargo planes. She eliminated them one by one until only one remained.

"I know that he isn't these other planes. So why is he the KC-135 Stratotanker?"

"Not flashy," Andi offered.

"Reliable," Mike said carefully.

"Useful?" Jeremy made it more of a question than a statement. The sixty-year-old design was finally being phased out in favor of the ten-year-old KC-46 Pegasus tanker. Though it was much better and fifty years newer, that plane also had issues of its own.

"Outdated and needs to be replaced—big time." Taz had been the one to shoot Jon with her Taser.

She looked at the map. All of the team's cards were in GMT -8 except for Holly's Havoc in GMT +9. Or maybe +10 or +8. They didn't even know where she was in Australia.

It felt like a piece of herself was broken off.

Not knowing where to place Jon's card didn't bother her at all. Which probably meant something.

She handed the Stratotanker flight card back to Andi.

44

"I CHANGED IT FROM A COMPETITIVE GAME TO A COOPERATIVE one." Jeremy was in the middle of excited explanations of his new mission cards—that actually followed a clear logic if not a quite realistic methodology. "We get to solve missions together instead of..." He stopped and glanced sideways at Taz.

There was enough of a hesitation in his look that Miranda pulled out her emoticon reference page...but nothing matched his look.

"Cautious," Andi whispered.

"Oh, thank you." She put her notebook away.

"He got tired of the women kicking the men's asses, especially his," Taz gave Jeremy a friendly hip check that almost flattened him to the floor despite his being nine inches taller.

"I didn't like the feeling of—"

"—always being the first to lose," Taz finished for him.

"—of us working against each other instead of together."

She blinked at him. "Are you trying to turn me into a goddamn mush, Jeremy?"

"I dunno. Is it working?"

"Not a bit." Then, rather incongruously to Miranda's way of thinking, Taz leaned her shoulder against Jeremy.

"So," Jeremy returned to his explanation, "the mission cards spread aircraft crashes around the globe and we have to roll dice and move to solve them before—"

Miranda's phone rang.

It was the startup whine of a C-5 Galaxy's General Electric CF-6 engines, which only meant one thing.

"Hello, Jill. This is Miranda Chase. This is actually her, not a recording of her."

Jill's burst of laughter every time Miranda answered the phone was always unexplained. She assumed that Jill simply enjoyed laughing.

Miranda waited for it, but the Launch Coordinator at the NTSB didn't laugh this time.

"We have a bad one, Miranda. An Air Force C-40B just went down with a Senate fact-finding mission aboard. There are three senators, two generals, and an entourage of forty others—all dead. The President wants answers fast. He needs to know if it was an attack, just a crash, or maybe a hijacking or hostage situation gone wrong. Depending on the answer, we could have a major diplomatic crisis. How fast can you get your team to Whidbey Naval Air Station near Seattle for transport?"

"I have my Citation M2, I can fly to the crash site myself."

"Not this time, Miranda. They went down in the Middle East."

"Oh," she'd never been there before. "We'll be at Whidbey NAS in twenty minutes."

It was only after she hung up that she recalled that Holly wouldn't be there. The jolt of worry made her finally understand Mike's agitation.

45

Whidbey Island Naval Air Station lay two-thirds of the way from their office at Tacoma Narrows Airport to her house on Spieden Island. It was the primary Navy air base in the Pacific Northwest. Its permanently stationed squadrons specialized in electronic surveillance and search-and-rescue. Also, whenever an aircraft carrier was brought into the naval port in Everett, all of the deck aircraft were flown here as well.

They also had a separate field set up for practicing carrier launches complete with catapults and arresting wires that Miranda had always wanted to try. When she'd inquired, they said that she had to be a naval aviator. But now that she was doing so much military work, the training might prove useful.

As soon as she landed, an armed escort arrived complete with bomb sniffer dogs. The team scoured them, their site investigation gear, and her plane.

The instant they were cleared, the Navy whisked them

aboard the C-40A Clipper. The Clipper was a modified Boeing Next Gen 737-700 that could be easily switched between all seats, all cargo, or half-and-half.

As they boarded, she saw that all of the standard seats had been removed.

The entire front was stacks of litters and body bags.

A conference module had been installed in the midsection. The carpet was deep pile Navy blue and there was a big oak, Scandi-design worktable and business-class flight seats along either side. It looked strangely out of place. Yet the module had no walls or ceiling. This slice of corporate office sat exposed on a durable steel cargo deck under an undulating arc of thick white sound insulation that lined the fuselage.

To the rear past the conference section, a bunks-and-shower module said this was going to be their home for a while.

"Sweet!" Taz nodded at the accommodations. "The Navy always has the right amount of class. The Air Force is a little too convinced that looks are everything, and the Army that they don't need any luxuries because they're rough-tough soldiers. This middle ground definitely works for me."

"Christ, I thought I was done with body bags for a while." Andi hurried past the forward stockpiles.

"Just another reminder that we're still alive," Taz answered.

"That's a good perspective, Taz." Miranda made a note of it in her notebook.

She tucked it away and noted that Taz was watching her. "What?"

"Nothing, Miranda. Just think that might be the first

thing of mine you've ever written down. Does that mean I belong?"

"No, I have several entries. The first was how you felt being five inches shorter than I am had affected your perceptions of the world around you. And why would you ever doubt that you belong?"

Taz's shrug wasn't any answer that she could interpret.

Before Miranda could ask for an explanation, she called out, "Come on, Jeremy. Let's check out the rest of our new home. Maybe they have a king-size bed for us to try out." An odd statement as the eight single bunks were clearly visible.

Miranda was about to point out that it wasn't a home but then recalled Holly calling the Airbus crash survivors on Johnston Island "natives." If that was possible, perhaps this was a home. For the seventeenth time since departing the atoll, she turned to ask Holly—only to find that she wasn't with them.

Jeremy had ignored Taz's invitation, instead connecting his computers to the Clipper's onboard systems, which included a large computer monitor at one end of the conference table.

Mike was the next to sit at the table.

"Miranda," he called out and picked up an envelope with a large red *Classified* stamp on it with her name beneath.

She sat beside him and nodded for him to open it, which he did. She'd just given a nonverbal agreement and designation of responsibility to act—an interesting achievement. Had there been something of that in Taz's shrug? Perhaps it had meant—

"What the hell were they doing in Syria? That's a war zone," Mike had pulled a report out of the folder.

"Syria? Shit, man! That's ugliness personified." Taz returned to the table, apparently having determined that no king-size bunks would be available for the flight.

"It says that several witnesses saw it go down. No one saw a missile strike. It blew up during final descent into al-Tanf airfield in southern Syria."

Taz snorted out a laugh. "The runway there is a chunk of desert they barely flattened enough to land on. Miranda, your island runway is a better strip."

Mike tossed a thumb drive to Jeremy as Andi hesitated beside the empty chair to Miranda's right.

Her gesture, nonverbal, asked if it was okay to sit there.

Miranda considered how to ask her own question in silence, but couldn't think of anything short of American Sign Language—which she didn't speak. Speak or gesture? What did they call that? Oh, sign. You *spoke* words. You *signed* ASL. You *gestured*...gestures. At a loss, she asked aloud why Andi would ask about sitting there.

"Holly always sits beside you."

"She," Miranda managed not to look over her shoulder, "isn't here. Always?"

Andi nodded, but finally sat.

Jeremy loaded the files onto his computer, calling them out as he did. "Passenger and crew manifest. Plane flight log and maintenance history. Schematics. Oh, photos. Just three." He put them up on the big screen.

There was a grim silence during which the C-40A Clipper started its engines and closed the door.

They were photos of the debris field. It took experience to see that there was enough volume to show that there was no crash, *just* a debris field.

The plane hadn't crashed.

It had shattered in the sky and rained down onto the desert.

Any hurry that the President was feeling wouldn't be able to accelerate the analysis of such a wreck.

46

HE PAGED THROUGH THE THREE PHOTOGRAPHS SLOWLY IN THE privacy of his secure Washington, DC, office.

The largest remaining objects were the mangled remains of the two engines. There wasn't a single thing left that looked like the plane he'd watched take off from Andrews Air Force Base last night.

Zooming in for details revealed a wide field of bodies.

He glanced at the report again.

No survivors.

Good.

It had been so easy, coaxing the three liberal-leaning senators from conservative states aboard. They *needed* to have a little junket to "properly understand" the Middle East situation. Now, the more conservative governors could choose who filled their seats until the next election. Ones who understood the threat of Russia's presence in Syria, the Saudi's kill squads, Iran's Quds Force—and had the balls to do something about it.

How convenient that the Russian presence there was about to be brought forcefully front and center.

By the time he was ready to step forward, the Senate's support would be in place—and he would be the one with the *right* answers.

He and the trapped Zaslon agent had proved particularly useful to each other. It was too bad that she now had to die.

No back doors. No leaks.

He sent an order to his man embedded at the Diego Garcia Black Site.

47

"THIS COULD BE USEFUL," MIRANDA GLANCED AT THE ON-screen images again, then looked around their plane. There were two military pilots and the five of them in a plane that could normally carry a hundred and twenty.

"What? Oh!" Jeremy nodded as he looked around.

Taz leaned over to buckle Jeremy in, which made Miranda feel much better about his safety as they were already taxiing. Jeremy continued without appearing to even notice.

"This is a C-40A and they said the crash was a C-40B. There are some key differences in radio and loading configurations but you're right. This could be particularly useful if we need an aircraft for comparisons to existing conditions. That was very nice of them."

"Trust me, Jeremy," Taz patted his knee, "nobody in the Pentagon thinks hard enough to get that right, especially between the Air Force and the Navy. This one is pure coincidence."

"Oh, I didn't know that. You see, the—"

Her phone rang sharply. It seemed very intent on interrupting Jeremy every time he spoke.

"Oh, it's Holly." She forwarded the call to the secure phone on the conference table and set it to speaker as the plane began its takeoff roll.

"Hello, Holly. This is Miranda Chase. This is actually her, not a recording of her."

"Hey, Her. I need you to— What's that background noise?"

"It's a pair of CFM56 engines on a C-40A Clipper. It is currently in an unusual combi configuration which may explain the unexpected quality of the noise signature." The jet rotated and became airborne. Three loud clunks announced the raising of the landing gear.

Then she listened to the sounds over the phone.

"Are you on a Falcon 7X? It's hard to tell with the sound from our own airplane."

"You're very good, Miranda."

"Thank you. The triple Pratt & Whitney 307 makes quite a distinctive sound, which made that relatively easy to guess."

"To you maybe. Where is the team going?"

"The Middle East."

Holly remained silent for a long moment. "What went down there?"

"A C-40B with three US senators, two generals, and their entourages went down in Syria."

"What the hell were those idiots doing in Syrian airspace? Never mind. Forget I asked. You can't go."

Miranda looked around the table. She didn't even need to pull out her notebook to check: the other four team members' expressions could be easily matched with the surprise emoticon.

"There's a crash. We have a launch call. We're already en route." Miranda didn't usually have to point out such simple facts to Holly.

"Miranda, trust me. You can't go to Syria."

"Why? Will it be more dangerous than anyplace else?"

Again a lengthy pause before Holly continued softly. "I don't know, Miranda. I just don't know. Just...I guess...be careful."

"I'm always careful."

"Miranda," Holly sounded like she was either choking or laughing. "You're *never* careful about anything except a plane crash."

"Isn't that all that matters?"

"Taz and Andi, you watch her goddamn back. I'll join you as soon as I can." Holly didn't answer her question but Miranda didn't feel comfortable asking it again.

"We're on it," Taz assured her after trading nods with Andi. "Where are you?"

"Mike there?" She ignored their question as well.

"Right here, Holly."

"Mike, explain it to the others: Elayne Kasprak is loose."

"Please tell me you've got a sick sense of humor, Holly." But Mike's look would definitely match the "grim" emoticon in her notebook.

With reason.

Miranda had only met her briefly, and never suspected at the time that she was other than she'd said—a representative of Ukraine's Antonov aircraft manufacturer. But she'd seen what it had taken to stop her.

"I wish, mate." Holly sounded no happier than Mike looked.

"You be careful, Holly," Miranda felt she had to speak up. "Remember, that woman is an airplane killer."

"And a killer-type killer. I'm on it, Miranda. They've got her trapped on a tropical island."

"Tough life," Mike muttered.

"Yeah, we cobbers should be so lucky. Though the last one wasn't incredibly fun either."

Miranda agreed, a sabotaged plane was *never* fun. She hadn't enjoyed her time on Johnston Atoll very much either. She'd never understood the allure of tropical vacations.

"How hard will it be to hunt her down this time?" Last time, Holly and Jon had— Jon! He wasn't available anymore, was he? How essential was he to the task of capturing Elayne Kasprak?

Holly was answering, "The island is twelve square miles, which is a lot bigger than it sounds when it's all stretched out. It has four thousand people and a joint military base presently on full lockdown."

"Diego Garcia." It was the only base that Miranda knew of anywhere in the world that fit that description.

"Yes. You'll certainly be safer in Syria than Diego Garcia."

"That's good," Jeremy spoke up. "Does that include factoring in that we're flying into a mostly Russian-occupied Middle Eastern war zone? I mean that—"

Holly cut him off. "*Anywhere* away from Elayne Kasprak is safer."

There was a long pause before Holly spoke again.

"Mike?"

"Right here."

"I... It's just..." Holly huffed out a hard breath, then she spoke quickly. "I just wanted to say I'm sorry, Mike. I really am."

Before Mike could speak again, Holly rushed on.

"Taz? Andi? Full alert mode every second, or I'll come back from the grave to haunt your asses." And then the phone clicked off.

"What was that about?" Taz was the first to break the silence that followed.

"From the *grave?*" Andi asked softly.

Mike just nodded.

Miranda knew. It was because Elayne Kasprak really was that dangerous.

"Where we're headed," she pointed at the images still on the big screen, "the plane has already crashed. That should be safe. It's just like this one, which is flying without a problem."

She turned to Andi, "Did I say it right this time?"

After swallowing hard, she nodded. "Close enough, Miranda. Close enough."

48

HOLLY GLARED AT THE EMPTY INTERIOR OF THE FALCON. IT had room for a dozen VIPs. The back two couches dropped down into a bed.

And she'd never felt so trapped in her life.

Seven hours to Diego Garcia was eighteen too many. Yes, it was a damn sight closer to Syria than Australia, but it was still in the middle of the fucking ocean. She needed to be in Syria with Miranda to keep her safe.

Could she possibly be any farther from where she needed to be?

Maybe if she parked her ass back on Johnston Atoll, but that was about it.

With the way her luck was running, maybe the Falcon trijet would just fall out of the sky. Though she'd already done that once in the last thirty-six hours, and all it had done was make things worse.

One of the pilots wandered out of the cockpit.

"Can I get you anything, Miss?"

"Can you make this jet go supersonic? Maybe Mach twenty or ninety?"

"Not unless you want to be ripping off the wings and walking outta the Great Sandy," he nodded toward the windows.

A glance down showed they were still somewhere over Western Australia. Go down in that desert and it could take months for someone to stumble on them. Even her skills would be tested to the limit to survive there.

"Sorry, I don't have time for that. Any other suggestions?"

"Pop a longneck, kick back, and enjoy the flight? Got some brew in the galley if you want. Passengers only, of course." He offered a friendly wink.

She slouched lower in her seat. "No. I'm good. Thanks."

He offered a friendly shrug, grabbed two sodas and a couple bags of chips before ducking back into the cockpit.

Bloody hell!

She'd just survived a major plane crash. Returning to Tennant Creek had only been depressing rather than the horror she'd expected. Quint had done an unexpectedly effective job of alleviating most of that with his kindness—and by screwing her so royally that even the Queen should be applauding his skills.

Curling up with Quint for a week or ten was a nice little fantasy. He'd be a lot easier than Mike. He was Australian and wouldn't expect more than she was willing to give. Aussies still embraced their personal independence like the God-given right it was.

Mike was...

She didn't even know how to answer that.

Kind, funny, thoughtful, such a good lover, a good cook, incredibly kind—

She'd already done that one.

Kindness wasn't something she had much experience with, or need for. Every time she got near him out at Johnston Atoll he turned all thoughtful and solicitous. It wasn't what she'd needed so she'd kept brushing him off.

Freaked-out passengers. Lines of bodies like she'd never had to deal with. Clarissa's bloody Special Operations Group.

It had been a situation of pure edge, and he was distracting her with...that!

And now...

How was she supposed to deal with Elayne Kasprak?

That was the real issue.

Clarissa had given her a carefully worded *carte blanche: I'll give you full authorization to do whatever you deem necessary.*

If anger had made the Zaslon operative dangerous before, what had imprisoning her for life without trial done?

Blind fury opened many unexpected doors.

49

THE SECOND VEHICLE UPGRADE HAD GONE DOWN MUCH MORE quietly and neatly than the first. Close by the munitions bunkers, they'd gotten an unbloodied guard's uniform and a truck.

The clothes were too small for the Chinese woman, Mr. Eurotrash, or the "Latin Wonder" as he'd introduced himself. That left Elayne and the slender Indian. She'd hardly said a word and, unlike the dead Arab woman who might have actually been an asset, she had no idea how to hold a weapon. Besides, her English sucked. Elayne took the uniform and the driver's seat.

One more roadblock, but she'd barely had to wave her ID and crack a John Wayne joke about "Gettin' these hosses back to the stable" before they flagged her through.

As soon as she'd cleared it, the Latin Wonder stuck his head in through the small window that connected the truck box to the cab.

"You know, we're totting a very nice load of eight two-hundred-pound bombs."

"Any timers?"

"Not that I can find."

"Well, I can always get creative if I have to. Hotwiring a detonator isn't exactly magic." She kept driving.

"Ah, Señora, you make my heart go pit-a-pat."

"Stay out of sight."

He didn't argue, just pulled back and closed the window to a crack.

Elayne eased along like she was in no hurry.

Two armored personnel carriers raced by them, headed south. Gone to see why they weren't hearing from their first roadblock. Or maybe why the underground prison had gone offline.

Time was running short.

Holly had survived the crash on Johnston Atoll.

She was probably all back and cozy with her little team. Or maybe she was in Australia—that's where her plane had been going when Elayne had knocked it out of the sky from inside her prison cell.

Except now she was *outside* her prison cell.

Oh yeah! Can't keep a good woman down! Uh-huh! Uh-huh! She did a little rock-and-roll beat on the truck's steering wheel as she rolled along. Butt-dance in her seat. Feeling the rhythm.

Finding Holly again wouldn't be hard though; she'd be coming to her.

Because Elayne was going to have her hands around the throat of that lying little Miss Miranda Chase bitch.

Oh, I have no idea what actually caused this AN-124 Ruslan Condor to crash.

She'd goddamn *known* Elayne had sabotaged it! And

Elayne had *bought in* to that crappy little lie—which was even worse!

To fall for the spacy-naive-crash-investigator act *demanded* payback.

Yes, Miranda as bait for Holly.

And once she was done destroying Holly, she'd take Miranda apart with her own two hands.

She'd already beaten Holly once, downing her plane.

Twice, by now, wiping the Syrian desert with those US senators.

It had to be something that high profile to draw their precious Miranda Chase out into the open where even conventional forces could grab her. How convenient that it had also served her unknown benefactor's agenda.

Now? She could do the final step herself. So much more exciting.

Yes, Miranda would suffer and Holly would know.

Even better, she'd do Miranda first.

Maybe right in front of Holly.

Oh...yes!

Slow and painful. Draw it on. And on. And...

So good!

So—

The release slammed into her with such an intense viciousness that she almost lost control of the truck.

Yes, it would feel just that good knowing Holly would live to watch her precious Miranda die in agony. And shame. Agony and shame. Oh, yes!

When Elayne finally rode the searing arc back down and her head cleared, the truck wasn't moving.

"Why did we stop, Señora?" The Latin Wonder called from the back.

Straight ahead lay the American airbase.

No fences. No base security. The island was all British and American forces; no civilians to keep away. They didn't need anything else because the next nearest land was over a thousand kilometers away.

"Have a look."

The Latin Wonder stuck his head through the small window at the back of the cab and then sighed lustily.

"Oh, that is *soo* sexy!"

Lined up in along a big, paved runway were a half dozen US military jets.

Big ones!

50

ANOTHER BLOODY ISLAND ATOLL, GLARING IN THE SUNLIGHT.

Holly stared down at Diego Garcia from above.

Quint had kissed her goodbye at the foot of the Falcon 7X's stairs.

"Welcome on my doorstep anytime, Holl."

She'd kissed him again for that, then climbed the stairs.

"Tropical island. Fruity rum drinks with muddled fruit. You in a bikini," he called after her.

"In your dreams, Quint." Then she'd gone without looking back.

He belonged in Tennant Creek. She had too...long ago. Not anymore.

Approaching Diego Garcia from the south, the view was a laugh. The narrow, sixty-kilometer-long slice of white coral and coconut palms drew the white outline of a bikini babe against the blue ocean. Complete with curvy hips, a wasp waist, and a massive bustline to the east.

"Oh, if you could only see me now, Quint."

On the ground, there was a car waiting for her.

"Are we headed back to Australia?" one of the pilots asked. The other one was stretching his legs and chatting with the driver of a refueling truck that had pulled up—a big Latino guy with an easy smile.

"Don't know, mate. I've got a problem here I have to deal with, then we'll see. Get on a full load of fuel."

"Aye, aye, ma'am."

"I'm not a ma'am, I'm a Holly."

"Ray." They shook on it.

They raced her out of the equatorial heat and over to a small office building along the east side of the runway.

Ernie Maxwell turned out to be six feet tall, athletic build, with melting-pot coloring that was part Arab, part African American, and part just plain striking—not particularly handsome, but the kind of face you couldn't forget.

The meeting room had all the friendliness of a street thug interrogation room. Four sides of concrete broken only by a steel door. White table. Four chairs. One camera —unplugged.

"What do we know so far?"

"The woman is pure business. Excellent," he unrolled a map of the island across the table and put a long finger on a spot across the lagoon.

She looked at the scale, thirty kilometers by road. And there were places where the atoll was so narrow that road was about all there was.

"Twelve hours ago at two a.m. local, something went wrong at our detention site, and it flooded out of control. I have two dead and two unaccounted for. The site was below sea level, and I haven't been able to get any divers over there yet. We had ten guests—"

"Inmates."

"As you wish," he nodded without pausing. "Two bodies accounted for, both apparently shot during the initial escape."

"Okay, now give me the bad news."

"Within two hours of breakout," he touched a spot near the very southern tip, "a three-man Air Force roadblock was gunned down here. And here," he tapped near some unlabeled buildings, "a munitions truck loaded with eight, two-hundred-pound bombs went missing. An Air Force sergeant had been knifed in the back. And a senior airman's body was found, naked. No blood, her neck broken, and no uniform. We found the truck two miles north of the airfield, parked in ten feet of water. One bomb is missing."

He stopped.

Holly looked at him.

He didn't say anything.

"And?"

Ernie Maxwell shook his head. "We haven't found any sign of them in the last ten hours."

Holly rubbed her forehead and felt a headache building. "Boats, planes—"

"Full lockdown. The Air Force had a full squad locked aboard each aircraft and they're required to check in every hour."

"Jump it to every ten minutes."

He nodded.

"The only boat in the lagoon right now that can go deep sea is one of the Brit's submarines."

"Let me guess, they're now off the dock and submerged in the lagoon."

"The woman is smart," Ernie nodded.

"As are the Brits. And from me you want to know...what?"

"Quite simple, Ms. Harper. What are they going to do next?"

"And how the hell am I supposed to know that? Got some tea leaves or maybe a divining rod? Tried making one of those in the Outback as a kid, the indigenous just about laughed their asses off."

"No, not handy," Ernie barely cracked a smile.

Holly tipped back her chair until she found the balance point on the back two legs and rocked there.

Balancing act.

It was all a goddamn balancing act.

Elayne had escaped a flooding CIA Black Site, taken out armed guards, busted one roadblock, stolen a munitions truck, and rolled through another roadblock. Yet the moment she'd reached the airfield, she'd evaporated.

"Gone to ground until dark?"

Ernie stared at the wall for a moment, then shook his head.

"No," Holly agreed. "She's casing everything out. Looking for any way off this place."

"That bomb she kept?" Ernie offered.

Now it was Holly's turn to shake her head. "Not unless she's desperate for a distraction. She's Zaslon. Stealth is her preferred method. Busting up that first roadblock wasn't her style. Stealing a truck and an identity to cruise through the second block, then evaporating? That's absolutely her."

"She was in there for a year. Maybe she..." but Ernie tapered off, finally shrugging.

"Elayne Kasprak spent a year waiting for opportunity.

That flood was it and she grabbed it. Doesn't matter who else made it out, she's the one in charge."

"Is she really that dangerous? We had Guo Cheng—she was China's top assassin. We caught her just feet away from Taiwan's President. And Najila Dawoud. She masterminded two embassy bombings. Paolo Ortiz has personally toppled at least three Latin and South American govern—"

"Doesn't matter. Elayne is in charge. If anyone argues with her? You'll eventually find their corpse. No, what she's doing is watching for any break in security. Any pattern variation that might—"

The front legs of Holly's chair thudded back down on the hard concrete.

"Oh, fuck!"

"What?"

"Ortiz. Big guy? Handsome? Leads with a smile?"

Ernie's eyes went wide, confirming her worst fear.

"Shit! Shit! Shit!"

Holly raced from the room with Ernie Maxwell close on her heels.

51

EVEN THOUGH IT WAS PAST MIDNIGHT PACIFIC TIME, NO ONE had yet gotten any sleep on the flight from NAS Whidbey. Other than Andi, who had stayed in her bunk since they'd taken off eight hours ago. She hadn't even moved through the refueling and crew change stop at RAF Mildenhall, northwest of London.

Miranda had asked, but there'd been little added information overnight about the Syrian crash of the Boeing 737 C-40B. Most of the official news had been about attempts to identify various remains, as if that was what was important. She did hope that they were recording the position and description of each body as at least *that* might contain some information relevant to the crash.

So, the team had gathered around the conference table to wait. All except Andi. Perhaps she'd been exhausted by her PTSD episode on Johnston Atoll.

Miranda's exhaustion was very deep—oh, *that's* what "tired to your very bones" meant, she understood it now. But she could only envy Andi her ability to sleep.

With Jon gone, Holly flying over the Indian Ocean, and Elayne Kasprak on the loose again, Miranda's mind simply wouldn't settle.

For once, she couldn't lose herself in Jeremy's reports on the spectral analysis of the faked engine pylon shear pins. Nor the pilot interviews of the 757 freighter that had slid off the icy runway in Juneau, Alaska. Not even...

She sighed, closed all of the files on her computer, and turned to watch the others.

They were playing Jeremy's newest version of his card game.

Per Andi's earlier advice, he'd thrown out every other map card and scrawled two time zones onto each one. The map's longitudinal pattern was strangely broken by missing every other card. Seattle abutted Chicago, the UK and Ukraine had become neighbors, and Japan was missing entirely. She knew he would fix that later, but it still looked strange.

Just as fractured as the team. Mike sat beside an empty seat.

Miranda considered going to sit in it. From there she could be Holly, tossing out Strine witticisms...exactly the kind of thing she could never think of. She considered trying out an Australian accent anyway, but still didn't know what to say. Besides, that was Holly's role.

The empty seat to her own left... Had Jon ever had a true role on the team? He gave them occasional access to military transport. He'd been her sporadic lover when a military crash had brought them together. There had even been a few holidays together. But she couldn't think of what else he'd done that was useful for a crash investigation. He'd flown a

Russian Condor, but any multi-lingual C-5 Galaxy pilot could have done the same.

Was her relationship with Jon like Jeremy's game?

From the outside, it was a confusion of dice, three distinct types of cards, two of them in the same deck—which didn't seem in the least bit logical.

From inside the game, well, she wouldn't know as she hadn't played it yet, but she could see that the others were following what was happening easily enough.

Sitting here with her team that was bigger than her former team, it was still as incomplete as Jeremy's world map.

Unable to sit still, she rose to her feet to walk the length of the fuselage. Except to the rear were bunks, and she didn't want to disturb Andi. Forward were piles of litters and body bags. She hadn't even met the Navy pilots who'd taken over the flight in London.

The ping to fasten seatbelts was a relief. Now she had something to do.

She returned to her seat and buckled in.

Then she checked her watch. It was nowhere near time to land.

But—

The plane jounced.

She sighed. Midair turbulence.

Hours to go.

52

THE FALCON 7X RACED DOWN THE RUNWAY AND TWISTED aloft.

And Holly could only glare at it in frustration.

If she had a rifle, maybe she could do something. The air marshal's Glock didn't stand a chance.

The goddamn Aussie pilots. What was it with guys and blondes? Elayne had clearly bamboozled them but good—at least enough to get on board. Were they still flying or—

Then the Falcon made a hard bank and a too-abrupt recovery. That too was bobbled before the plane stabilized, turned for the northeast toward India, and raced away. No Royal Australian Air Force pilot would make such a mistake. But a woman who knew how to fly but didn't know the handling of that particular jet might.

Good bet there were two more bodies either on the tarmac or getting a funeral ride in the back of their own plane. Two Royal Australian Air Force pilots down.

"We need to chase that plane and shoot it down."

"We don't have any fighter jets here at the moment.

There's a big exercise going on with India off Kerala. That's hours away."

"You have a military airbase with no protection?"

He pointed toward an AC-130J Ghostrider gunship.

Maybe half the speed of the Falcon, if she was willing to get on board—Mike and Jeremy hadn't had much luck the last time they had.

She yanked out her phone and called Clarissa.

53

"Go west?" Elayne kept her voice calm and friendly. She sat in the pilot seat of the Falcon 7X. The other four had dealt with the pilots lounging in the back while she got the plane moving and in the air.

"Yes," the heavy Chinese woman was apparently their mouthpiece. "In Africa, we can disappear."

"I'm not going to Africa. I'm going to Syria. I will drop you at the Kuwait-Saudi Arabia border."

"No. Khartoum, Sudan. We can get out from there. I have contacts."

"And who is going to fly you if I say no?"

The woman pointed at her own chest.

Elayne glanced over her shoulder.

The Chinese woman stood close enough to hold on to Elayne's seatback in a very proprietary way. The Latin Wonder, Mr. Eurotrash, and the quiet Indian woman crowded close enough to listen.

"Any of the rest of you pilots?"

All three shook their heads.

Elayne made a show of sighing.

"Africa? You'd get off there?"

The woman nodded.

"O-kay." Elayne banked the plane to turn from her original northeasterly heading—to at least temporarily deceive anyone who gave immediate chase—toward the west. As she reached her desired northwest heading, she abruptly leveled the plane.

The woman spread her feet to brace and grabbed on to the copilot's seat with her free hand to keep her balance—which occupied both her hands.

As she did, Elayne kept her left hand on the wheel. With her right, she slid her knife out of its thigh sheath and rammed it between the woman's legs.

The woman shrieked in agony as Elayne drove the big blade upward. With a twist, she scraped the blade along the back of the abdominal cavity. The geyser of hot blood over her hand told her that she'd managed to cut both of the femoral arteries.

"So," she looked up at the woman's face, "are you *getting off* on this? Real good for one last time?"

Elayne twisted the blade to make her point, eliciting a fresh shriek of pain with each movement. Making her dance on knife point.

Then Elayne tipped the point, still buried inside, and probed for the spinal column. She found it—and gave a vicious sideways yank. When Elayne felt it sever, she jerked out her blood-drenched blade. Red ran down over her entire forearm and dripped from her elbow.

With her spine cut above the legs, the Chinese woman collapsed to the deck.

Elayne looked at the others, "Everyone else okay with the Kuwait border?"

The Indian woman nodded.

Mr. Eurotrash wasn't visible, but she could hear someone puking—hard.

The Latin Wonder merely smiled. He placed a hand over his heart and mouthed, "Ah, Señora."

Elayne wiped the blade on her pantleg and pushed it back into the sheath.

"Good. I'd appreciate it if you could get *that* out of my cockpit."

At the rate the Chinese woman's whimpers were fading, she'd bleed out before she reached the back of the cabin where the pilots were stacked.

Then she looked at her arm before calling out.

"Could someone bring me a wet towel?"

A warm wet towel was always nice after sex.

Even knife sex.

She doubted if the dead woman in the back would appreciate the joke.

She was still laughing herself when the Latin Wonder brought her the towel.

54

"Do you know what time it is? This had better be important, Harper."

Clark grunted beside her. He was a ridiculously deep sleeper.

Clarissa slipped out into the hall and sat on the carpet of the staircase's top step. The old Queen Anne Victorian of the Vice President's home was dead silent. She couldn't hear the Secret Service patrol that was bound to be outside, even at this hour.

"Elayne's gone," Holly told her.

"Who?" But she felt a chill and wished she'd grabbed a robe instead of just wearing her nightgown.

"Elayne Kasprak, your fucking Guest whatever-the-hell number it was. She's gone. You've got at least four dead CIA guards. Another five US Air Force people aren't going to be breathing again anytime soon, and I'd wager that you'll have to explain two dead pilots to the Royal Australian Air Force."

Clarissa hadn't risen to being the CIA Director by being slow, but it was three thirty in the morning, and her brain simply couldn't keep up with Holly's single-breath list of disasters.

"Waiting here!" Holly sniped at her.

"Do you have her?"

"Two dead Aussie pilots, remember? Come on, Clarissa. Get it in gear. She just stole the Falcon 7X. Last seen headed north. You need to shoot that bitch down."

"I'll—" Do what?

"Wasting time here, Clarissa," Holly rasped into her ear. "Bitch!"

"Let's worry about the bitch in the sky, okay? Get her ass down and into the ocean. Though I'd rather have her alive. I need to know what she's got planned for Miranda."

"What she *what*? Never mind. Hold please." Clarissa muted the call and resisted the urge to throw the phone and Holly down the stairs to shatter on the marble of the entry hall.

Once she could trust her voice, she dialed the number for her head of station at Diego Garcia.

"I'm standing right next to him," Holly shouted over Maxwell's greeting.

Shit! She'd been hoping for a moment of sanity.

"Situation?"

He put his phone on speaker. "Other than what Ms. Harper said? We have an unknown number of guests—"

"Hyper-violent sociopaths!" Holly shouted over him. "You lock them in a box for not even Her Royal Highness the Queen knows how long, and you think they're *guests?*"

"—unaccounted for," Maxwell was always steady under fire. "Possibly as many as seven others—we have two bodies so far. The site is flooded. Now that Guest Seven is no longer posing a threat here on Diego Garcia, we can lift the lockdown. We should be able to dispatch a dive team to make a more accurate assessment within the hour. The Chinese hacker and the Arab bomber Najila Dawoud, Three and Nine respectively, are accounted for."

"Get the divers moving in the next five minutes. I need to know which ones to put back on the Most Wanted list."

There was a brief sound of scuffling, like someone grabbing the phone, though it remained on speaker.

"Clarissa! That's goddamn ninetieth on the list. Start at the head of the track."

"Holly, you don't understand. These are the very worst. If these people get out—"

"Grab a clue off the apple tree, Clarissa. They're out. And there's not a plane here fast enough to catch them."

"So tap the Air Force." She knew the CIA kept very few assets on Diego Garcia other than the Black Site.

"No," Ernie spoke up, "They don't have one. The only jets on the ground right now are cargo and fuelers. Not even an aircraft carrier within a week of the lagoon. No fighter jets to borrow."

"It's a goddamn Air Force base with no fighter jets?" Clarissa slapped a hand over her mouth. Clark might be a deep sleeper, but shouting just outside the bedroom door wasn't going to help.

She headed down the stairs.

"Not at the moment."

"Hell of a stupid way to run an Air Force." But Clarissa sure wouldn't be calling the Chief of Staff of the Air Force to complain. He hated her guts almost as much as he hated the CIA. He was so old school that he believed that diplomacy or military action were the only two necessary tools to maintain world order. He wanted the third option of clandestine operation eradicated—as if every President all the way back to Eisenhower didn't love having their own squad of assassins.

"What do you want me to do?" There was a reason she liked Ernie Maxwell. After they'd graduated from the Academy and entered the field together, he'd stayed out there. Assistant to the CIA Chief of Station in Moscow until his cover was blown, then reassigned to Tel Aviv followed by Riyadh. He'd recently crossed Gavin Chalmers on the Middle East desk and been sidelined to the Diego Garcia posting.

Maybe it was time to bring him to DC.

Actually, there were several reasons she liked Ernie Maxwell all of the way back to their last assignment in the field together, setting up one of the first Black Sites in Afghanistan.

"Get assets along the routes to the northeast on the lookout for the damned Falcon. And get Holly on the fastest plane you can find." And out of Clarissa's hair. "Anywhere she wants to go."

"Anything else?"

"No. Yes. Get me that diver report. I want photographic proof of each one. Then you can flush the whole damn mess for all I care."

"Done." And Maxwell was gone.

Clarissa hadn't quite meant it that way. Though she'd learned the hard way in Afghanistan that once a Black Site was exposed at all, it was best to shut it down, erase all the evidence, and set up somewhere else. There was a reason that the Diego Garcia site was all below ground. It had intentionally been placed so that they could turn off the pumps that kept it dry, and the sea would reclaim the site very quickly.

A simple set of explosives to collapse the upper stairwell, and all evidence would be gone. Flushed.

Well, if Ernie did that, she wouldn't be shedding any tears over the inmates. Nor would anyone else in the world. She'd have to smooth it over a bit—two of the guests had been escorted in by the Brits' E Squadron and one by the Israeli Kidon.

That's when she noticed that Holly was still on the other line.

"What?"

There was a long pause before Holly whispered softly, then hung up.

She couldn't have just said, "Thanks"...could she?

Clarissa stood in the middle of the foyer; her bare feel cold on the chill marble.

Seven guests—psychopaths—on the loose? Eight with Elayne. Eight of them unleashed, under *her* watch. It could be the worst bungle by the CIA since the mid-seventies.

That disaster had come about with the 1974 leak of the internal "Family Jewels" document, chronicling every illegal activity since the 1950s. The four failed assassination attempts against Castro, including the disastrous Bay of Pigs fiasco, right up to Watergate—all exposed on the front page of the New York Times. It had launched the crusade by the Pike and Church Congressional Committees. In the end, they'd stripped the entire action division from the CIA. It had taken decades and, ultimately, Osama bin Laden to rebuild it.

These eight could wreak havoc across international boundaries.

The blame for their release was going to follow right back along those illegal orders to the Special Operations Group. Even if that knowledge never reached past the Gang of Eight congressional leaders or the President, she'd be quietly dismissed—driven from the CIA and politics.

Years. *Years* of planning, intelligence gathering, political maneuvering, including her goddamn marriage to Clark and the manipulations to make him Vice President—for nothing?

She tried to dial the hacker twins.

Clarissa stopped with her finger hovering over her phone.

It was shaking.

Her hand never shook. Not when she'd put down her father like the rabid dog he was. Not when she'd negotiated the deal that had placed her in the director's chair. Not even when Harper was finding some new way to crawl under her skin.

Focusing on it didn't stop the motion.

The phone began to shake as well.

Then the light went away when the screen timed out.

Now she could acknowledge that it was just being woken in the middle of the night. Or low blood sugar.

Yes, she'd get something from the kitchen and be fine.

Yet her feet remained rooted to the cold marble floor.

55

HIS CONTACT AT THE DIEGO GARCIA BLACK SITE WAS ON THE deceased list.

While disappointing, it wasn't particularly relevant now that Guest Seven was on the loose.

Could he trust the woman to stay out of the way for long enough? He didn't need complications...not that she had any idea who he was.

He looked at the report again.

Four CIA agents down, five Air Force people too, and an unconfirmed number of escapees.

But it didn't conclusively tie back to where it was needed to. He needed one more piece to do that. One tiny link. Regrettably, the telephone that only connected to the Director/CIA was now under two stories of water on a remote island atoll.

Maybe if he came at this another way.

The Middle East was anything but peaceful.

Perhaps he should have crashed the Senators' plane

where Guest Seven had told him to. Get the Russians right in the Americans' faces. Too late to change that.

But still...

Perhaps he could give the Syrian situation a nudge in precisely the wrong direction. A nudge that could only have originated from one person's desk.

He headed into the office even though it was only five in the morning.

By noon, it would be done.

56

Elayne had taken careful note of what planes were visible at Diego Garcia. They hadn't finished scouting the hangars when the Falcon 7X showed up.

When she'd seen Holly Harper climb down from the sweet jet, Elayne *knew* she had to take it. It was being offered to her and Holly would be shown up for a complete fool.

The others had said it was a reckless act in broad daylight.

Not reckless—calculated.

Calculated to cause Holly Harper the maximum amount of misery.

Like most Zaslon operators, Elayne had been trained in basic airplane and rotorcraft flight, precisely for situations like this one. But a twenty-four-meter-long trijet was a new experience. It would have been nice to get the Aussies' cooperation, but there would be no way to trust them. She'd put a round in each one's face, then left it up to the others to make sure they were dead.

Of course, Holly Harper had been flown around the

world in a luxury jet while she'd been rotting in prison. It was definitely *not* enough to just off Miranda Chase as she'd originally arranged. No, it had to be much worse—not all of the Siberian gulag labor camps were gone.

She liked that idea. Then Elayne could keep sending little pictures to Holly at random times of Miranda in the mines of some closed city. Perhaps as a test subject for one of the poison labs in the closed city of Shikhany-2 where Novichok was manufactured.

No, she had to be alive so that Holly would come looking for her.

But first, Elayne herself had to survive. When no fighter escort appeared off her wing in the first fifteen minutes, she took it as a good sign.

Staying extremely low, under any radar, she crossed the Arabian Sea. The tensions between Saudi Arabia and Egypt made the Red Sea on the other side of the Arabian Peninsula a no-go. Especially with Israel and their American radar systems sitting at the northern end.

Following the Iran-Iraq border north was a possibility. But last year's accidental downing of an airliner by an overanxious Iranian missile officer said that might be too big a gamble.

In the end, she slalomed up the Persian Gulf, then slithered over the northern border into Saudi Arabia. Ten kilometers inland, she touched down in the desert. She braked hard enough to force everyone to stay in their seats.

As she jerked to a final halt, she spun out of her seat and pulled her sidearm.

She aimed it down the cabin.

The other three looked at her in some surprise.

"This is the middle of the desert," Mr. Eurotrash whined.

She didn't shoot him, because she didn't want to risk damaging this plane before she was done with it.

"Not the middle. Wafrah, Kuwait, is ten kilometers due north. You even get to walk with the sun at your backs. A two-hour stroll, you'll be there before dark. Now, leave your weapons on your seats and get off my plane." She didn't want anyone shooting up her plane.

He stumbled out the door and into the heat.

The Indian woman took several water bottles from the small galley. She bowed her head briefly in thanks.

The Latin Wonder stopped in the middle of the aisle. "Sure you don't want some company, lovely Señora? You and me, we could do some wonderful things."

Elayne considered it, but he would just be a burden where she was going. Too many things to explain as she dragged Miranda Chase across the Syrian desert into Russian territory, then back into Mother Russia.

Pity. She liked a confident lover, and there was no doubting his fighting skills. She'd wager he still had more than the knife he'd strapped to his thigh, but he didn't worry her.

"Maybe some other time."

He nodded with a half smile of regret, but his dark eyes still shone. "Paolo Ortiz."

"Holly Harper." Elayne wasn't about to give him her real name. But maybe he'd cause Holly trouble someday.

He pocketed a couple bottles of water himself, gave her an easy salute, then descended the steps.

She tracked him with her sidearm until he'd swung the door back into place and locked it.

Once more aloft, she climbed to just civilian high as she flew directly above the border between the Iraqis (who were too busy destroying themselves to notice anything) and the American-friendly Saudis (what a joke—there were few they hated worse than the US, except for Iran and all Shia Muslims).

Only one controller pinged her radio during the entire flight.

"This is unscheduled corporate flight for Saudi Aramco," she shifted her flight to the Saudi Arabian side of the border. "I'm flying a Falcon 7X. My executive passenger wishes to remain anonymous."

"Roger, flight."

Nobody in the region would think to argue with a pleasure cruise flown by the eighth largest company in the world. The only surprise would be that it wasn't a luxury Boeing 777 or Airbus A350. Top executives of Saudi Aramco didn't travel in piddly little Falcons.

But they let her through.

When she jogged north along the Jordan-Iraq border, no one said a word.

Six minutes later, she was over Syria.

57

THE TEAM DEPLANED AT THE AL-TANF GARRISON, SYRIA.

The heat slammed into Miranda.

One of the waiting military escort must have seen her reaction. "You're lucky it's October; just ninety-five degrees today. July cracks a hundred with room to spare most days."

Al-Tanf was a small cluster of buildings set in a featureless expanse of brown-beige desert. The dry expanse and lifeless rounded hills were broken only by the gray sliver of the M2 Baghdad-Damascus Highway. The garrison was a small outpost surrounded by absolutely nothing.

There was nothing here. To the southeast, the Iraqi border twelve miles away. A Jordanian refugee camp, just twenty miles south by air, was almost unreachable by road. The nearest town lay over seventy miles in the opposite direction. Which, according to Jeremy, was no bigger than al-Tanf.

The outpost itself was surrounded by a continuous line of HESCO barriers. The cloth-and-wire mesh barriers stood seven feet tall. Each five-foot-square section was filled to the top with dirt.

She wanted to study the weight-to-load issues but—she could feel Holly quietly reminding her—there was a crash.

"Do you want to freshen up first or—" The officer who'd come over glanced out toward the desert.

"I wish to proceed to the crash."

"Let's go. It's only a couple miles north."

They moved in a caravan of vehicles. Her team was loaded in the back of two M-ATVs.

"Aren't these sweet?" the driver called out. "We just got them in. Still way tougher than the old Humvees, but way smaller and way more agile than those monstrous first-generation MRAPs—that's Mine Resistant Ambush Protected."

"Are we safe out here?" Mike asked her across Andi, sitting in the middle.

The driver answered before Miranda could speak.

"This close to the garrison? You're fine. We control the Deconfliction Zone out to fifty kilometers. Ruskies wouldn't dare come this far. And any Syrial killers try?" He made his fingers into a handgun and pretended to shoot through the windshield. "Syrial? S-Y, not S-E. Get it?"

Miranda didn't. "C-E would also be a homonym. Though why you would want to kill a bowl of cereal, I can't imagine. Besides, that wouldn't work."

"Why not, ma'am?"

"Your windshield is rated bullet resistant to Level 8. That's five rounds from a 7.62 mm. Your rifle is only 5.56 mm. If you shot from inside, you'd be far more likely to be injured or even killed by a ricochet."

The driver laughed. "I'll be sure to be careful about that,

ma'am. Thanks for the warning. No shooting Syrial killers through bulletproof glass."

"You're welcome."

"But I'm still okay shooting at bowls of cereal?"

"No, I—"

Mike rested a hand on her arm and shook his head.

"But he's not making any sense," Miranda whispered.

"That's kind of the point, Miranda."

She was never going to understand people.

The commander in the righthand seat ignored them.

Miranda looked out the window and began to wonder what they'd gotten into. Their two transports were being escorted by four other vehicles, each of which had a gunner standing at the ready with only their head and shoulders showing in a roof-mounted gun turret.

She looked up. Over Andi's seat, there was a hatch in the roof. If she were to stand on her seat and open the hatch, she would be in position to operate the M240 machine gun.

Miranda didn't often leave US soil. Sometimes, when a US-made aircraft went down overseas, the investigating agency would ask for the NTSB's assistance. But it was her first military overseas crash.

She had extraordinarily little to judge by.

"Andi?" Miranda leaned close.

"What?" Andi's shout definitely sounded like surprise. Then she continued closer to a whisper, "Oh, sorry. What is it?"

"Mike's question. Are we safe?" It seemed like it was okay to repeat Mike's question; especially as Andi's yelp had him leaning in to listen for the answer. Besides, Andi would know far better than either of them would.

"What!"

Miranda had seen this look on Andi before. Her hands were clasped and pinched between her knees. Her breathing was too fast, and she was staring straight ahead but didn't look as if she was seeing anything.

That's when she remembered and looked out the window herself.

"Oh!"

"Oh what?" Mike's voice sounded panicked, and Andi didn't respond.

"This is al-Tanf Garrison, at the center of the American Deconfliction Zone. Andi's copilot was killed here." And her research into Andi's condition had indicated that revisiting a location was a key factor in triggering a PTSD attack. Was Andi even now picturing her copilot curling up around a grenade to save her life as they flew from Syrian airspace into the DCZ? They'd been shoulder-to-shoulder—pilot and copilot—when he'd died aboard their tiny MH-6M Little Bird helicopter.

"Shit! I totally forgot. Sorry, Andi." Mike wrapped an arm around Andi's shoulders.

Offer comfort when a person is upset. The rule was in the personal interactions section of her notebook but she hadn't recalled it soon enough. Or was delayed comfort still comfort? She tested the theory by placing her hand over Andi's clenched ones.

Andi freed a thumb and used it to pin Miranda's hand over hers.

Apparently, yes. Delayed comfort was still appropriate. How long a delay could occur with undiminished effectivity would have to wait for a separate set of tests.

"It was thirty-seven kilometers straight ahead. You

know...before...when..." Andi's voice was rough and her eyes were still wide. "Here we're in the center of the DCZ."

"I've paid very little attention to geopolitical conflicts." She glanced over at Mike.

He shook his head. "I always figured that was Holly's or Taz's gig."

"Well, you're in the middle of one of the worst ones here," Andi's color came back slowly as she was forced to explain. "We took over al-Tanf and formed the Deconfliction Zone when ISIS chased out the Syrians. We, in turn, drove ISIS out again. Then we kept it to support the Syrian rebels, not that we'll ever admit that's why we're here."

"And another crash here? Are you okay with that?" Mike pointed straight down at the floorboards though Miranda presumed that he meant the rough ground currently jouncing their vehicle. It was inherently inaccurate as Andi had said her crash was thirty-seven kilometers away.

Andi shook her head. "I don't have a lot of choice, do I."

"You could have stayed on the plane."

Andi shook her head. "Holly said that Taz and I had to protect you guys. I don't think pissing off Holly would be a good choice right now." She eased the pressure of her thumb over Miranda's hand, finally slipping her hands free to scrub at her face. "Besides, I already spent long enough lying awake in that bunk trying to pretend I wasn't coming back here."

"Will you be okay?" Miranda withdrew her own hand now that it was no longer providing comfort, belated or otherwise.

Andi shrugged. "When I met you three months ago, I can promise I wouldn't have been. Now? How the hell should I know?"

"Well, I would think that through self-assessment—"

"It was a rhetorical question, Miranda. I don't have an answer and I wasn't looking to get questioned on it. Do you think I have *any* idea of how I'm feeling other than screwed up? I'm afraid of my own feelings." Andi's voice seemed to be getting louder and more strident.

"Oh," Miranda forced herself to not continue her interrupted sentence as it didn't appear to be welcome. Besides, "I didn't know anyone else felt that way. I almost never know what I'm feeling."

Andi went still and just looked at her.

So intently that Miranda actually looked back without having to dodge her gaze aside.

"What do you do?" her whisper was almost softer than the racing M-ATV.

Even leaning in from Andi's other side, Mike didn't seem able to hear them.

Andi's soft voice prompted her again, "When you're feeling that you don't know what you're feeling?"

"Well," Miranda knew the answer to that one. "I remember to breathe. It's what I do when the world is becoming too much."

Andi laughed roughly. "Yeah. That's actually good advice."

The rest of the way to the crash, they sat side-by-side in silence—breathing.

58

ELAYNE WAS FLYING OVER THE DESERT TWO MILES NORTH OF the American base at al-Tanf. The American air controllers had picked her up the second she crossed the border from Iraq. Once ascertaining who she was, or rather who she said she was, they advised her with a tone of polite threat to avoid al-Tanf by a minimum of two miles and to remain above ten thousand feet—if she didn't wish to be "accidentally" shot out of the sky.

She complied.

The planned crash zone for the US Senators' plane was fifty kilometers to the north anyway. There, the Syrian and especially the Russian forces patrolled the edge of the American's precious DCZ line in the desert sand.

She'd planned that point of impact most carefully. It would allow the Americans to feel safe investigating the crash inside the DCZ. And the Russians could easily cross the short distance undercover to grab Miranda Chase.

Now she could reconnect with Spetsnaz Special Operations Forces herself. Then together, they could wreak some bloody retribution on Holly and her whole team of precious crash investigators.

Down on the desert floor, she spotted a line of six dust plumes. A phalanx of six vehicles were heading across the DCZ.

"Where are you headed in such a hurry?"

And then she saw it.

An airliner lay shattered across the desert sand another kilometer past the racing vehicles.

"No. No. No! You're not supposed to be in their backyard. You're supposed to be crashed at the edge of Syrian space." When she found out who'd screwed up her explicit instructions, she was going to murder them—personally! In ways that would...

Think. She had to think.

The crashed American plane was supposed to be at the *edge* of the DCZ so that the Russian forces could grab Miranda Chase and whisk her into Syrian-controlled terrain before anyone could stop them.

Here. There was no chance of them striking this deep into the DCZ.

She made a bet with herself that her contact hadn't even contacted the Russians, even after she gave them the emergency direct phone code and password.

Oh, what she would do to him would paint the very skies red. She'd—

Think.

Right. He was for later. Now was Miranda. Then Holly. Then the bastard on the phone who—

Why was it always up to her to do things right?

She circled once more high over the wreck.

At least ten vehicles were already at the site. It was busy, cluttered with personnel poking through the wreckage. There was no way to snatch one person from that confusion.

Confusion.

That gave her an idea...if she could just find the right solution.

59

SERGEANT CHARLIE WIGGINS RACED HIS M-ATV ACROSS THE
Syrian desert. Two soldiers cruising all day along the DCZ
border was not the kind of sexy deployment he'd been
imagining when he'd signed up for the Minnesota Army
National Guard.

Every day at 1600 hours, drive the fifty klicks with his
border partner out to the edge of the DCZ. Then spend eight
hours running back and forth along his hundred-kilometer
section of the zone's perimeter. He'd run it so many times
that he knew every damn pothole and dust mound
intimately—an M-ATV was made to be tough, not
comfortable.

The Russians—dressed as Syrians, of course—had run a
parallel course so many times that there was another worn
track a hundred meters to the north. He had no interest in
crossing the line and the Russians didn't dare because he
could have a line of attack helos tromping their asses faster
than your hand froze to your car door handle during a
Minnesota winter.

No friendly camaraderie across the line. No trading whiskey for vodka, or even peanut butter for their syrniki. These guys looked like bad asses with heavy weapons and no sense of humor.

After only her first week, Corporal Betty Glaser looked as bored shitless as he was. She was okay. New enough to still believe, but the shine was already coming off. Another couple months and she'd shake out as either in for the long haul or a sour bitch. He'd seen it often enough to know. Gender didn't matter. Bitchy guys weren't any less of a drag. The women, if anything, adapted better. They—

"Holy fuck!" His rearview was blotted out by the nose of a jet. *Objects may be closer than they appear!* Fuckin' A! It was right up his ass!

He swerved aside, barely not rolling the M-ATV as a plane screamed by not twenty feet to the side. Not an airliner, but not some crazy fighter jet-jock either. Bizjet.

"They're landing," Betty shouted out. "Without gear."

Even as she spoke, the plane bellied onto the sand a hundred meters ahead of them.

It bounced aloft, then slammed down once more. He twisted back onto the track it had flattened across the landscape and raced after it.

Just before it slowed to a stop, it caught a wingtip and slewed around.

Charlie stopped nose-to-nose with the plane.

Now that he'd chased it down, he wondered if he should back up in a hurry. He knew shit-all about planes and had no idea if they hadn't exploded when they hit, were they about to?

Then a pilot raised her head and looked at him through

the windshield with shocked-to-be-alive wide blue eyes and wheat-white hair.

Both he and Betty jumped out of the M-ATV.

He grabbed his rifle. Glaser hadn't. She'd learn that you never got separated from your weapon. But she had her sidearm, which should be fine. They wouldn't need it. A crashed civilian aircraft in the middle of the desert didn't seem likely to be much of a threat.

At the door, there was a clear sign: *Pull handle for emergency release.* He figured this counted and yanked it.

The door flopped down onto the sand.

He stepped in.

The main cabin was seriously classy. The airplane seats looked more like armchairs. In a space that would fit twenty economy seats, there were six.

"Fancy," he commented to Glaser as he turned for the cockpit.

Then Sergeant Charlie Wiggins froze in his tracks.

The blonde was dressed in a blood-stained Army uniform. All down one side. Then he saw the carpet.

"Holy shit!" He'd never *seen* so much blood. It squished beneath his boots.

He looked back up at the pilot.

"Are you okay?"

She held a pair of handguns with silencers. One aimed at Glaser's face; one aimed at his own.

"Weapons in the front seat. Then walk backward away from them."

He just stood there, trying to figure out what was happening. She didn't look ready to faint.

Ready to *faint?*

"All this blood, you should be dead."

That's when he finally connected the two guns and all the blood. It wasn't hers. Which meant it was someone else's blood that covered her. It must be—

"Now!"

Her shout was loud enough to jolt him into swinging his rifle partway up from his side.

The next moment his shoulder erupted with pain. He looked down at the blood pouring from the wound just one inch to the side of where his left shoulder emerged from his Kevlar vest. His rifle clattered to the deck.

There was a scream of pain. It might have been his.

He clapped a hand over the bullet hole, but the blood kept spilling out.

"Don't!" Her eyes were now steely blue as they shifted to Glaser.

His Ma would always joke about when Charlie would get really mad, his eyes would go "kitten-blue." Not this woman. She could do welding, like heavy machine shop welding, with those eyes.

She seemed to be wavering on her feet.

But she wasn't.

It was him.

"Slow," the welding lady said to Glaser.

Glaser took her hand off her holstered sidearm, then carefully plucked it out of the holster with her thumb and forefinger before setting it on the seat. She dropped a knife and a backup piece beside it.

"Unload him. No tricks or the round will go through both your heads. And don't get any blood on your uniform."

Glaser mouthed a "sorry" as she took his sidearm and knife. She didn't bend down for the rifle, instead nudging it forward with her foot.

"Sit!" She waved one of her pistols at him.

His knees were weak enough that he collapsed back onto one of the plush seats. His shoulder roared with agony again as he instinctively tried to use his arm on the armrest. Instead, he tumbled into the seat—which hurt even worse!

Glaser had missed his backup piece, but it was on his injured left side, no way to reach it with the right.

"Strip."

Charlie didn't know if he could manage. But then he realized that she was talking to Glaser, not him.

He faded in and out as she did so.

Vest, weapons belt, boots, clothes. The blonde insisted on the t-shirt too until Glaser was standing there in just bra and panties. She had a far better body than he'd thought. Betty Glaser was soldier hot. About time *somebody* at al-Tanf was.

She stood half a row in front of him.

A tattoo at the base of her spine was of a red-and-gold dragon. That tattoo changed a lot of his guesses about her. He'd bet that she'd learn to fit the job just fine.

Had to be tough to wear a dragon like that. Make a good soldier—

The shot to Glaser's heart was almost silent, just a click of the slide ejecting the round and loading the next.

Blood fountained out her back, partly hiding the dragon behind a spray of red rain that spattered over him too, though he could do no more than blink it away.

She seemed to collapse in slow motion to lie flat on her back in the aisle. It was funny that she lay down there when there were all these ultra-classy seats on the plane. Or maybe it was better. The bloody red hole in her chest was making a mess.

The blonde stripped off her own blood-soaked uniform.

If Betty was—had been—soldier-hot, the blonde was in a whole other league.

Model-hot? Nope.

Magazine-hot? That wasn't it either.

Oh! Centerfold-hot.

That was it.

Though maybe not with the crazy welding eyes.

The right side of her bra was blood-soaked, too. As were her ribs and hip.

Some jingle about rinse the stain out slipped by, but he couldn't quite latch on to it.

She followed the direction of his gaze and looked down at the stains.

They both looked at Glaser's bra, but even not counting the bullet hole, it was in far worse condition than her own. Too bad. It looked as if Glaser's had been nice breasts. He supposed he should feel something looking at Betty Glaser lying there all dead like a piece of roadkill, but he couldn't think of what at the moment.

Cold! When did it get so cold in the desert? He couldn't even shake with the chill.

The blonde said something that sounded very foul and... Russian. Shit! He'd been trapped but good. The Ruskies had crossed *way* inside the DCZ border, and he hadn't called in anyone.

She looked at him and muttered something about, "Waste of another bullet."

Between one slow blink and the next, she was fully kitted in Betty's clothes and gear, including vest, helmet, and sunglasses.

The next blink she was outside the window, setting

something under the wing with a metallic clunk. Twice more, fore and aft.

Next: his M-ATV was leaving without him. He'd bet that it wasn't heading to the US patrol line.

He again thought about calling it in.

That's when he noticed that his radio was missing, not that he had the energy to care.

He watched Glaser's dead form.

Not squished like roadkill after all.

Just lying like she was asleep in the aisle...just waiting for him. By the blood still welling under his hand, he supposed that would be true soon enough.

Twenty minutes later, though his heart was still beating slowly, Sergeant Charlie Wiggins didn't notice when the timer set by Zaslon operative Elayne Kasprak ran out.

She'd placed three breaching charges along the Falcon 7X's three lower fuselage fuel tanks: fore, center, and aft.

The airplane had been fully refueled at Diego Garcia in preparation for the long return flight to Australia. The flight to Syria had used just half of the forty-seven hundred gallons.

The JP-5 jet fuel went up in a fireball that would scatter everyone's remains far too wide to ever be gathered together again.

60

"Thanks for not shoving me out midflight, Captain."

"Our pleasure, ma'am." The Air Force pilot was a patient man, but Holly knew she'd pushed his limits during the flight.

At a loss for where Elayne might have gone, she'd headed to rejoin Miranda on the fastest plane remaining at Diego Garcia—an ancient US Air Force KC-135 Stratotanker.

It had been developed from the same prototype—and at the same time—as the original Boeing 707. The newest one was fifty-five years old, this one was closer to sixty-five.

But it was still a jet, just thirteen miles an hour slower than the Falcon 7X would have gotten her there.

To the Air Force's credit, it had only taken them twenty minutes to get the plane aloft from the end of Clarissa's phone call, not that she'd ever admit her appreciation for that efficiency to Clarissa.

From the inside, a Stratotanker looked like your average cargo plane: steel decking below, exposed sound insulation along the entire curve of the hull above, and incredibly uncomfortable fold-down seats along either side. This jet wasn't about moving people, it was about moving airplane fuel—thirty thousand gallons at a time. They refueled everything from jet fighters to Air Force One.

At the rear, under the deck, was a large window and three lay-down tables, like you were waiting for a massage. A boom operator could lie there on their stomach and, using tiny winglets, literally fly the refueling boom to mate with thirsty aircraft in-flight.

And in the six hours and twelve minutes of flight, she'd walked an untold number of miles from the cockpit to the refueling boom and back.

As she'd paced end-to-end of the KC-135's eighty-eight-foot cargo bay, all she could think to do was to get to Miranda and protect her. Elayne could have done anything, planned anything, while stewing in her luxury cell.

And now that she was out?

How was she supposed to guard against someone like Elayne twenty-four-seven?

It just wasn't possible.

Holly knew that the best preparation for a mission was sleep, but that wasn't going to happen. Only her training forced her to eat, and only her iron will kept her from puking it back up.

The pilots had let her strap down in the jump seat for the final approach and landing on the dirt at al-Tanf.

"Do me a favor, mates, don't be ripping off any wings on landing or otherwise."

They laughed, "Well, okay. Just because you asked so nice."

She was glad that *they* thought it was a joke. Jump seat,

short final, in a large jet. After yesterday's crash on Johnston Atoll, it was no longer on her list of fun places to be.

They were less than a thousand feet up when a flash of light had her looking to the east.

"Is that where the crash is?"

"No. That's due north. There." The copilot pointed at a cluster of vehicles around a plane's worth of wreckage.

The flash of light turned into a fireball, then a pillar of black smoke raced up into the sky. It lay ten miles away.

This time Holly didn't ignore the itchy feeling.

A crashed plane and a second explosion deep inside the DCZ didn't feel like a coincidence.

Elayne had departed to the northeast. Toward India.

Was it chance that she'd been set free or part of some plan?

Had the crash in Syria been Elayne's next move?

Oh shit!

Holly willed the plane onto the ground.

Please don't let her be too late.

61

THE PERIMETER GUARD FLAGGED HER DOWN AND DOUBLE-checked Betty Glaser's ID. She and Elayne didn't look at all alike. Thankfully, full combat gear left very little exposed.

"Thought you were on perimeter patrol today," the guard offered a smile, then handed back her ID.

"Hey, I just go where they tell me."

"Ain't that the truth. None of us getting out of the sun today," he glanced upward.

"Whoa, take 'er easy there, Pilgrim. Don't peak too soon."

He laughed and waved her toward the wreck.

She wondered if John Wayne quotes always work on Americans.

Elayne sat in her M-ATV at the edge of the Senators' plane crash and waited. Her timing was good; she'd had to sit less than a minute before the fireball of the Falcon distracted people around the site.

Climbing out into the blazing heat, she headed toward the NTSB team. Their methodical progress stood out like sore thumbs from the military personnel hustling through the wreckage. Four of them wore bright yellow ball caps as well.

She recognized and avoided Mike Munroe. He'd get his later but she couldn't afford to be recognized as herself at the moment.

She'd also seen the Vietnamese kid at the crashes last year, but hadn't had anything to do with him. He could live—for now.

The other two women were new.

Just as she arrived at the group, they were all turning to face the growing smoke column.

All except Miranda Chase. Just like on the crash of the Condor a year ago, she didn't even look up. She was wholly focused on the ground as she tracked the perimeter of the debris field. Little Miss Anal.

Elayne stepped up to her, careful to keep her back to Mike, even if he was looking the other way and stood over ten meters away.

"Ms. Chase?"

"Yes."

"I've been asked to escort you to another crash that has just occurred," Elayne gave it her best cross of military hustle but patience with civilians.

"But I haven't even started this one."

"My orders state that this new crash has a higher priority." She should have had a "who" ready. Oh, she did. "It's a special request from CIA Director Clarissa Reese." Elayne had certainly talked to her often enough by phone over the last year. She was on Elayne's list not far below Holly Harper and Mike Munroe.

One at a time, she counseled herself. *One at a time.*

Right now, it was Miranda Chase.

"Okay. I'll just tell my team."

"I already took care of that for you, ma'am. I have a vehicle waiting." Elayne took her lightly by the elbow and turned her away.

And it was just that easy. Instead of watching where she was going, Miranda kept watching where Elayne's hand held her arm. Her grasp was too light, it couldn't be hurting her. It didn't matter, Miranda stumbled along fast enough to where Elayne was guiding her.

Out of sight of the other people working on the site, she gave Miranda a morphine slap shot from the M-ATV's medical kit to knock her out. Tape on her mouth and zip ties on her hands and feet, Elayne dropped her onto the back seat floor and tossed a blanket over her with no one the wiser.

She considered going back for Mike Munroe. Or just killing Miranda here, but then she saw the monstrous jet fly by low overhead as it came in to land.

It had a rear boom; one of those US Air Force tankers. The only aircraft at al-Tanf were a few helicopters. They'd have no need of an aerial refueler.

But there'd been a line of them at Diego Garcia.

Had Holly Harper somehow followed her from Diego Garcia? That should be impossible. She'd seen Holly get off the Falcon. It had totally jacked her up to be stealing Holly's plane from right under her nose.

But Harper hadn't followed her initial path toward India. So how—

Didn't matter.

It was too perfect.

Elayne hopped into the M-ATV and drove in the unexpected direction.

Holly would be certain she'd gone north, making the long drive to cross into Russian-controlled Syria.

Instead she turned south and drove toward al-Tanf.

62

AFTER GETTING OFF THE KC-135 TANKER, HOLLY GRABBED THE first vehicle she came upon, a technical. There was a line of two-seat Toyota Tundras, each with an M2A1 Browning machine gun mounted on a tripod in the truck bed. Each had a black-winged logo across the door and an infinity symbol across the entire cab's roof, presumably to mark them as friendlies from the air.

Even before she reached the gate, the KC-135 was already aloft and turning south. Couldn't get out of here fast enough.

At the gate, a guard flagged her down.

She didn't just run him over. That counted for major patience points.

"I'm headed to the crash site."

He eyed her carefully. She was still in the same clothes she'd put on after sleeping with Quint. But she wore a harness that Ernie Maxwell had given her. She'd hit him up for spare magazines for the air marshal's Glock, a battle knife in addition to the one she kept up her sleeve, and a rifle. He'd given her a Desert Tech MDR rifle that rested on the seat beside her, which was damned decent.

"Hang on, ma'am. I can't let you off the base like that."

She almost gunned the engine to just ram the barrier and see if she made it, when he held out a Kevlar vest and helmet.

Yanking on the helmet, she tossed the vest on the seat beside her.

"It doesn't do you any good there, ma'am. You should put it on before..." Then his voice finally petered out as he caught the look on her face.

He held up his hands for peace as he backed away, then raised the barrier.

She knew that the primary crash lay due north. Once she'd humped over the M2 highway, the tire tracks of numerous vehicles across the desert were easy to follow. She pushed the tough pickup for all it was worth over the rough ground. As she drove out, a lone soldier in an M-ATV passed her heading back to base.

Her arrival at the crash was so abrupt that a number of the guards spun to face her with weapons half-drawn. Not that they had a chance of targeting her because her sliding stop had raised a cloud of choking dust that forced her to waste twenty precious seconds holding her breath with her eyes closed.

When she opened them, several of the guards still had weapons aimed partly in her direction. When she waved, they finally eased off. Maybe the vest was good advice. She slowed just long enough to release her weapons' harness, don the vest, and strap back in. With the rifle over her shoulder, she went looking for the team.

They found her first.

"Holly, have you seen Miranda?"

It took everything she had to not drive a fist into Mike's worried face.

63

CLARISSA'S RECEPTIONIST CALLED OVER THE INTERCOM.

"You have a Kurt Grice here to see you, ma'am."

"Send him in," she pressed the lock release on her door.

Kurt walked up to stand directly across from the center of her desk. He didn't sit—never did.

He was of average height and build, almost completely forgettable. His slightly round face looked neither childlike nor overfed. His blond hair fell straight to his ears and might have a touch of gray. And he was also one of the most effective field agents in the entire Special Activities Division. Prior to taking command of the SOG, he'd been particularly adept at aiding or altering the course of South American coups.

He waited for the soft click of the door swinging back into place and locking once more.

"You asked me to confirm any future orders in person." About as many words as he ever spoke at once.

"I didn't issue one."

"The codes check." He pulled a piece of paper from an inside pocket, unfolded it, then slid it across her glass desk.

SOG Baghdad.

Acquire Iraqi Su-25 Grach jet.

Deliver minimum 2kkg—two thousand kilos!—*bombs to coordinates 33.567392, 38.613187.*

Eject and crash en route Tiyas.

"Steal a friendly military's Russian-built plane and drop four tons of explosives before pretending to run home to the Russians. What's there?"

He pulled out a photograph and repeated his earlier action.

It was an aerial image of an airplane wreck.

She hadn't really thought about the implications of a bunch of Senators being shot down in Syria.

"Someone really wants to implicate the Russians in a coverup of that crash."

Kurt nodded.

"Do we have any people there?"

Kurt shook his head.

"Who is?"

"Local Army forces from al-Tanf Garrison. And a civilian NTSB team just arrived."

Clarissa looked up at him very slowly.

"Miranda Chase?"

Kurt shrugged that he didn't know.

"Okay, make it look as if you're following the order. Borrow the plane. Get it aloft."

Kurt nodded and headed for the door.

"And Kurt?"

He paused without turning.

"Stay close today."

He nodded and continued out the door.

She dialed her phone.

64

ELAYNE HAD CONSIDERED JUMPING ON THE M2 HIGHWAY AND bolting toward Russian territory. But an M-ATV topped out at a hundred kilometers an hour.

She'd seen Holly clear as day racing toward the wreck. How many minutes until she was hot on Elayne's tail? And that truck could crack two hundred kilometers an hour. It was a two-hour drive to Tiyas Military Airbase, the closest Russian stronghold.

Holly might catch her.

While she was thinking, she reached the US al-Tanf garrison. Well, she could hide for a few minutes in plain sight. Not even Holly would think to look for her here.

Maybe even find a room to hide in with Miranda while Holly ran about like a chicken with her head cut off looking for them.

No. Too lame.

Elayne offered the guard a salute at the gate.

He waved her in with no further inspection. Not even checking Betty Glaser's ID.

The main compound was a small warren of mud-brick buildings. A row of technicals were lined up in the courtyard. If she had a driver, it would be fun to go hunting Holly with one of those. Riding in the truck bed, her hands latched onto the big M2A1 swivel machine gun.

Pop! Pop! Bang! Bang!

Then, as she cruised slowly across the inner compound, through a small gap in the HESCO wall, she saw an adjoining HESCO-ringed courtyard. There she spotted exactly what she needed. It was beyond perfect.

65

HOLLY DIDN'T WASTE TIME ON ACCUSATIONS. SHE SHOULD have thought there was some chance of Elayne coming here. Until this instant, she hadn't known why Elayne would do so, but now she did. "Lessons learned" were what post-mission debriefs were for.

They were still in the crisis.

Mike and Andi piled into the front seat of the technical —Mike holding Holly's rifle upright between his knees like it might explode. She really had to teach him to shoot someday.

Taz and Jeremy sat in the back with the M2A1 Browning machine gun.

The first thing she did was circle the debris field a couple hundred meters out from what had once been the Senators' C-40B transport jet. There was a multitude of tracks to the south in the direction of al-Tanf.

The farther she circled around the crash site, the more she didn't see any other tracks across the desert.

Nothing west, north...or east.

"Shit! I passed her. That had to be her."

"What had to be who?" Mike braced an arm against the dashboard as Holly pounded back over the track she'd just traversed from al-Tanf.

"Elayne Kasprak."

"No way."

Holly glanced over to see Mike's expression wasn't so much disbelief as fear. He knew just how dangerous Elayne was.

"Who?" Andi asked from where she sat between them.

"A Russian operative who just escaped the cage we put her in a year ago. Lethal as an Australian eastern brown snake, crazier than a wombat, and pissed as hell."

"Why would she target Miranda?"

Holly knew the answer to that one only too well.

Because Elayne knew just how much it would hurt Holly.

66

THEY WERE LESS THAN HALF A MILE FROM THE GARRISON'S front gate when a helicopter lifted over the HESCO barrier.

"Holy shit!" Andi's curse burst forth before she could stop it. She'd never faced this helicopter before, but she knew everything that the US Army knew about it. It had been a part of her training as a pilot for the 160th Night Stalkers, back when she'd still been qualified to fly.

The Mil Mi-28 Havoc was one of the nastiest looking helicopters in the sky.

Painted in the Russian mottled bands of dark green, light green, and gray, it was ten tons of lean, mean, gunship machine. It had a chin-mounted 30 mm cannon. And winglets to either side, which sported four rocket pods. Each side had an eight-pack of S-8 rockets capable of delivering three inches of hell up to two miles away, and the five-slot S-13 rockets were five inches across and punched three times the explosive charge—enough to really destroy a building's day.

It was built to instill terror—and to destroy anything in

its path.

It swooped so low that she cringed out of the way, sure it was going to fire at them. At the very last second it waggled from side to side in a friendly wave.

"Bitch!" was Holly's curse as she kept the M-ATV racing back to the garrison.

"Who—"

"Elayne Kasprak. And we can be sure she has Miranda."

Andi twisted around to see the helicopter racing away to the north.

"What is a Russian helicopter doing here?"

"Damn good question."

She blew through the barrier.

The guard had it only part way raised, so it smashed in the windshield, but still Holly didn't slow. Instead, she leaned her head out the driver's side window and raced through the compound. Soldiers scattered to either side.

Andi looked back. Some raised their weapons.

But it was clearly marked as one of their vehicles with no one standing at the rear machine gun, so they weren't sure if it was an attack or not.

Andi glanced out the back window.

Jeremy and Taz weren't cringing out of sight, they were waving. Definitely Taz's style to confuse.

"Someone really needs to teach these guys about security," Holly muttered as she charged through a narrow gap.

An AH-64D Apache attack helicopter was being prepped for flight.

Holly skidded to a stop that almost sent Andi flying through the barrier-shattered windshield.

"Can you fly one of those?"

"Sure. I mean I'm not certified on it, but Night Stalkers train to fly almost any—"

Holly grabbed her shoulder and dragged her out of the truck.

"Hey, Holly, they have real Apache pilots here." Andi tried digging in her heels to no avail; Holly kept dragging her forward.

"Not ones I can trust."

"Excuse me, ma'am," a pilot stepped in front of them.

"See?" Andi waved a hand but Holly didn't stop.

The pilot pushed against Holly's shoulder to stop her. "We're preparing for a flight here. You need to stay back. Someone has just stolen a military helicopter."

"A Russian Mi-28 Havoc. Why was it here?" Andi figured it was best to keep him talking.

"It was delivered by a defector. We were holding it here pending the visit by the Congressional team; the one that crashed in the desert early this morning." He had the decency to look both sad and angry for a moment.

"And who took—"

"Mike!" Holly interrupted her as she called out over her shoulder.

He lofted the Desert Tech MDR rifle to her.

She caught it by the grip one-handed and swung the barrel to press against the center of the pilot's chest.

"Our flight, mate. Give her your helmet and back the fuck off."

He did, then stumbled backward until he ran into the copilot and mechanic. They must have realized they were the only ones in the helicopter yard close enough to stop them. The three men gathered together, looking ready to draw weapons and charge.

There was a loud *clack-clack* from the back of the Toyota Tundra.

Taz had just racked the slide on the big .50 cal Browning machine gun mounted there. She aimed it at the ground in front of the flight team.

"You might want to think twice about getting in the way. This is a President-sanctioned codeword-classified operation."

The men cowered.

Holly half glanced at her, "You think I can trust any of them to fly right into a Russian airbase if necessary?"

Andi didn't hesitate any longer. She slid into the back seat of the Apache. The two positions were arranged for the weapons officer to sit low and forward, having the best view for weapon's deployment and navigation. The pilot's seat was behind and raised high enough for a clear view over the weapons officer's head.

Holly said something to Taz, then Andi didn't waste any more time looking.

She'd only flown a helo once in the nine months since Ken's death, and this was an unfamiliar cockpit.

But a helicopter was a helicopter, and she soon had the turbine whining on the starter and the four-blade main rotor whooping slowly around overhead.

By training, a Night Stalker pilot could start with a cold helo and be airborne in three minutes.

Andi cut some corners and was ready in two.

Holly climbed into the front seat and yanked on a helmet.

As soon as the intercom was live, Holly was shouting, "Go! Go! Go!"

Andi went.

67

It was a forty-five-minute flight to the Russian airbase at Tiyas and Elayne could only hope that she lived through it. Yes, Zaslon training included basic fixed-wing and rotorcraft flight practice—but *very* basic on rotorcraft.

Aircraft had always been one of her specialties. Because her father had been a submarine engineer for the Russian Navy, he'd taught her more about mechanics than any classroom could.

Zaslon had honed that for sabotage and attack of foreign military aircraft, but she rarely flew herself.

And definitely not in a highly responsive military aircraft like the Havoc.

It was so twitchy that a moment's inattention had her skewing across the sky, stall warning buzzers bleating at her.

She'd almost crashed when she'd overflown the Toyota pickup that must be Holly and Miranda's team. She tried desperately to fire a gun, a rocket, anything at them. Instead, she'd almost piled into the desert to make a fourth crash.

Such a pretty picture: an Airbus at Johnston Atoll, the Senators in the Syrian Desert, and the Falcon.

And that boy bleeding out in his full gear beside his dead girlfriend.

Though it would be better if she didn't make another hole in the desert herself.

Focus, Elayne.

You're Zaslon. You've got this, baby sister.

Thanks, John.

Together they'd ride their horses rough-shod over the West.

She laughed aloud. The West. The Wild West. Oh yeah, she and John Wayne had this wired.

They hadn't even had a guard in the helo yard. Granted it was an airless, sunbaked hole, trapped behind double-height HESCO barriers, but there should have been some sort of a decent shootout *Stagecoach* style.

They came out of the woodwork like angry bees once she was aloft, but a Havoc was armored against small round ammunition. It was also fast.

Once she had better control of the Havoc, going after Holly and the others was tempting, but that big machine gun mounted on the back of the pickup made her decide against it.

Besides, now she was making good progress across the desert—far faster than she could have driven.

She had Miranda Chase, still drugged out in the forward weapons position.

Maybe she'd do Miranda good—then send a video to Holly wrapped in birthday paper.

Elayne started to laugh.

Oh, yes!

That would be perfect!

So perfect!

Or maybe let her live and send a whole series. Then all she'd have to do was let slip where Miranda was stashed. Holly had proven that it wouldn't matter. Even if it was in a closed city in the heart of Russia, Holly would come for her.

Even better than perfect!

And Elayne would be waiting.

68

MIRANDA STRUGGLED UP AGAINST THE FAMILIAR FEEL OF drugs.

There were numerous periods when she was young and having an autistic episode that she'd been dosed with one sedative or another. Tante Daniels tapered her off those when she'd become Miranda's caretaker, but the feeling was familiar.

It wasn't some smooth emergence from a cocoon of safety that her parents seemed to think.

It was a scary, blurred journey rising through panic of a world gone mad.

Every perception blurred.

Every sound wrong.

Often, the metal taste of blood in her throat where she'd bitten her tongue or the inside of her cheek.

She'd eventually learned that the feeling passed, but she had to ride it out.

This time, she was in a seat.

The firm pressure of a five-point harness comforting.

The tape on her wrists was less so.

Sound.

The beat of rotors.

A helicopter.

Five blades. With an unfamiliar turbine. No matter how she listened, she couldn't make sense of the engine noise.

Somewhere, the unfamiliar sound of shrill laughter.

Her eyelids seemed to weigh a ton as she dragged them open.

Open enough to see the sky terrifyingly close in front of her. She was out at the very foremost point of the helicopter with a clear cockpit wrapped close around her.

The cockpit was...Russian.

Tandem fore-and-aft seating. The Russians only made three of them that way.

The rotors overhead weren't coaxial, so not a Kamov Ka-52 Alligator.

Two of them.

And a Mil-24 Hind was far larger with rounded cockpit glass.

One left.

How had she come to be in a Mil Mi-28 Havoc?

She managed to twist around enough to look at the pilot over her shoulder.

The helmet covered the upper part of her face, but Miranda tried never to look there—eyes were very confusing to look at.

But she recognized the chin even without the clue of the white-blonde curl of hair sticking out the edge of the helmet. The woman was smiling at her in a way that...that... reminded her of a dog about to bite.

Elayne Kasprak.

Miranda turned forward again. She'd been fairly sure that even if Holly hadn't killed her after the Condor mission that she'd arranged to have Clarissa Reese do it for her.

It had taken Miranda a long time to come to terms with that thought of Holly being a killer. She knew Holly had done that when she was a part of the Australian Army. But that was different from being a member of Miranda's NTSB investigation team.

Apparently that worrying had been a wasted effort as Elayne wasn't dead.

Though listening to Elayne Kasprak's cackles of delight, perhaps it might have been a good thing if Holly hadn't resisted.

Elayne also wasn't a particularly good pilot.

Miranda looked out at the barren desert of central Syria and began calculating her odds of survival.

The numbers were not encouraging.

69

"THERE!" HOLLY SHOUTED.

The blast nearly took out Andi's eardrums. "I can hear you just fine, Holly. It's called an intercom."

"Yeah, yeah, yeah. How do we get her down?"

"Without killing Miranda? No idea. All I have are guns and rockets." And she was totally helpless. She could drop the racing Havoc in a second, well, actually closer to three at this distance.

Until this moment, her main worry had been catching Elayne before she reached the Russian base. The Havoc had a sixteen-kilometer-per-hour speed advantage over her Apache. But Elayne was an inexperienced pilot and Andi had been trained on how to milk every meter per second out of a rotorcraft.

They now had just twenty kilometers to force her down —only a matter of minutes.

Actually, less than that. There were two low ridges close ahead. Past those, the Russian base's radar would have a clear view of them, as would their weapons.

"She'll start climbing any second, Holly. Do something fast."

Holly started viciously swearing to herself.

"Less swearing, more action."

"Big help. What if I shoot her engine?"

"No!" Andi shook her head, which was a strangely civilian habit. Gods! No pilot in combat would waste time looking at another pilot. It had been so long since she'd flown.

Was she losing her edge?

Hell, she'd *lost* it the day Ken had been blown out of the sky. What was she doing aloft anyway? She couldn't be trusted to fly. Should she? No. Not anymore. Not since—

"Why not?" Holly demanded.

Andi dragged in a desperate breath. "Because I'm betting..." another dragging breath, "...based on her weak handling skills, that Elayne...has no idea how to do an autorotate landing. She's all over the sky. Doesn't even know she should be climbing already."

"Bugger me with a tree branch."

"Ouch! I'd rather be shot. Though use a small caliber, please."

Holly froze in the lower cockpit. Then she slammed against the harness as she tried to turn enough to look back —another real mistake in an Apache. There was barely room to sit, never mind turn.

"You're brilliant, Andi. Get me alongside her. How do I open one of these windows?" She began poking around the edges of the right-side window in her cockpit.

Andi leaned forward to try and see what Holly was up to.

"No handle." Holly didn't hesitate. She pulled out her sidearm and placed it against the glass.

"No, don't! The glass is bulletproof. You'll shoot yourself with the ricochet. Miranda told us."

"Well, hell."

"Upper left corner of your panel. Canopy Jettison. Twist and punch in."

Andi had never been aboard when one had been fired. Couldn't even guess what was going to happen in flight at a hundred and fifty miles an hour.

"Helmet visor down firs—"

Her warning was too late.

Holly twisted and punched.

The two glass side panels blew violently outward.

The rotor roar blasted into the cockpit even louder than the wind.

Holly yelled something incomprehensible over the mayhem. Even the intercom couldn't punch through the noise.

Andi shouted back to show her the problem.

Holly sliced a hand toward the racing Havoc helicopter, then twisted her hand to show them pulling alongside.

Whatever she was up to, Andi hoped to hell that it worked because they were coming up on the ridge far too fast.

Holly swung up her Desert Tech MDR rifle.

"Too small!" Andi shouted as loud as she could.

"Does she know that?" Holly roared back.

The instant they were alongside, Elayne twisted to look at them.

And they almost all died at that moment.

70

Holly wasn't sure how Andi managed to not intermesh their rotors when Elayne twisted the helicopter along with her body.

But the Night Stalker training came through and Andi kept them right on station, with only a few meters between the tips of their main rotors.

Holly aimed at Elayne's face behind the canopy and fired.

The bullet skipped off the surface but sent Elayne slamming the other way.

Every move she made, Andi kept her close.

Holly kept firing, beating on the canopy. Never giving Elayne a moment's rest.

Elayne just wouldn't take the hint. She'd turned away from her direct flight to Tiyas military base, but she hadn't begun descending.

Holly's own training by the SASR was probably similar to Elayne's, far more about destroying an aircraft than flying.

She dropped the rifle across her lap and grabbed the

controls for the M230 chain gun mounted directly under her seat.

The Mi-28 Havoc might be fully armored, but not enough to stop a 30 mm round. Or the twelve hundred of them loaded in this bird.

Miranda turned just her head to look out at Holly from the forward cockpit.

"Thank God! She's alive."

Now to keep her that way.

Holly studied the targeting scope, lined up her absolute best guess...

And fired.

71

Elayne looked down in surprise.

The huge bang had reverberated through the hull.

A hole twice the size of her thumb had appeared in the left side of the canopy. On the right side, a massive round was buried in the glass.

Another round blasted through the canopy from side to side, so close in front of her face that she could practically taste it.

The wind whistled through the two holes.

The message was clear.

Holly was such a bitch that she was willing to sacrifice her precious Miranda Chase for revenge.

Well, wasn't that just so interesting?

Holly wanted to take her on personally. One-on-one and screw the consequences.

Ooh, they were more alike than she'd ever imagined.

Elayne locked the collective control for a moment to free up her left hand. Then signaled to Holly across the narrow gap between them.

You and me, she waved a single finger back and forth. Then pointed at the ground.

The last time they'd met, it had taken Holly and two Special Operations fighters to capture her. One-on-one, taking down Holly Harper was going to be easy.

Holly nodded her agreement.

This was going to be so awesome!

And way easier than landing this damned helicopter. The rugged foothills didn't offer a lot of options.

And each time she got close to the ground, a blinding cloud of dust blanketed everything, forcing her to climb aloft once more.

Finally, she picked a hockey rink-sized flat spot, managed to stabilize to a hover over it, and just eased down on the collective while she tried to stay in one place.

The world blanked behind dust.

Down. Down.

"How goddamn far away is the groun—"

The helo slammed onto the dirt and she bit her tongue hard enough to draw blood.

But she was down.

Holly's helo settled smoothly beside her, raising its own massive dust cloud.

When the dust cleared, Elayne could see Holly sitting in her cockpit without windows like the old witch Baba Yaga perched in her chicken-leg house.

Elayne popped the canopy and exited the Havoc on the side opposite where Holly had landed.

She'd show Holly exactly who was the best.

As she circled the nose of the Havoc, she was surprised to see Holly was still sitting in the cockpit. Her rifle was still propped between her legs, the barrel pointing skyward.

"Come out and play, Harper. Your call. Guns, knives, bare hands? I'll take you down any way you want. Twelve months. Twelve fucking months in that cage I've been wanting to do you."

Elayne tossed the boy's rifle aside—she'd never learned his name before leaving him to die on the Falcon.

"And the last three fucking weeks? All those little phone calls, but never once helping me get out of there. I did those guards good, by the way, just want you to know. Next after you, maybe that little phone caller, don't you think? I'll find out who it was. Him, I'll goddamn fuck to death. Not like we did to your precious Senators. *Poof!* Up close and personal for that bastard."

She heaved aside Betty's helmet.

"Senators scattered all over the desert. *Bang!*"

She discarded the weapons harness.

"We're gonna smear your Yankee asses right out of the Middle East. Then right out of Europe. But that boyo on the phone, ever so anonymous? Oh, I'm going to hurt him so good."

Then the vest, so hot in the desert despite the cool shadows.

"But the first ass I'm gonna fuck is yours! You're now! You know you want to do me yourself. Maybe like the old days?"

Elayne untied the knife from her thigh and tossed it aside.

"Skin to skin!"

She yanked off her t-shirt until all she wore was her bloody bra.

"Aww," she brushed a hand where the blood had dried brown over her breasts and was flaking away all down her side. "And I never learned the big Chinese bitch's name—"

then she grabbed her own crotch and yanked upward, "—
not even when I drove my knife so far up her that she just
couldn't stop squealing. Same kind of delight I'll give you,
Harper."

She waved toward the deep desert.

"Then *Pow!* I blew her up with your plane, Harper. Tiny
bits scattered everywhere. Come on down and play. You
know you want it—so *bad!*"

"I had something else in mind," Holly had still made no
move to climb down.

Her hand had been out of sight below the edge of the
canopy's missing window.

She raised it now.

It looked like a yellow plastic ray gun.

Then Holly shot her in the chest with it.

72

ANDI COULDN'T HELP HERSELF. SHE BURST OUT LAUGHING, even as Elayne Kasprak dropped to the ground convulsing.

"Oh, Taz will be so sorry she missed that."

Once more, Holly pushed the button on the Taser.

Elayne grunted inarticulately as the charge blasted into her again.

"Let's get this done," Holly showed no sign of humor.

They climbed down together.

While Holly was seeing to Elayne, Andi hurried over to Miranda. She pulled the tape off Miranda's mouth and untied her hands.

"Are you okay?" Andi massaged her wrists, then helped her get far enough out of the cockpit that she could cut the ties on Miranda's ankles.

"I shink sho. Dwugged."

Once she was out and standing wobbly on the ground, Andi hugged her because she was just so glad to see her.

Then she looked at the two helicopters.

"Uh, Holly. How are the three of us getting back in one

Apache helicopter? The Havoc has that small emergency compartment for crew rescue, but we can't just leave an American Apache here in Russian-occupied Syria." The AH-64D was a fighter aircraft with seats barely big enough for the two pilots.

Holly didn't answer. Instead she was dragging a well-bound Elayne toward the Havoc. An impressive pile of body armor and weapons lay on the sand where Elayne had been.

Even as they were loading her into the pilot seat of the Havoc, she began to regain control of her body.

Andi barely managed to avoid a vicious head butt.

"She's a real sweetheart," Holly didn't even look up from where she was strapping Elayne into the seat. The straps she was using were more appropriate for securing a car to a tow truck bed than a person to a seat. But the fury in Elayne's scream said that maybe the straps were a bit on the small side.

If Holly took any notice of Elayne's increasingly articulate imprecations and curses, she showed no outward sign. Not even when Elayne described in some detail how she was going to fuck Mike Munroe to death.

"She knows Mike?" Andi asked as casually as she could manage while having to shout over the continuing barrage. Actually, the screams of pure rage were almost a relief. Andi's own anger that Ken had died instead of her, widowed his wife and orphaned his child, almost seemed to be a quiet place compared with this woman's anger at the world.

"Likes to think so. Mike was too smart for her."

That unleashed a new barrage.

"Out-maneuvered me, too."

Andi couldn't have heard that right, but Holly was already walking away toward Miranda.

Without a word, Holly bent down and simply hugged Miranda hard. It was perhaps the sweetest thing she'd ever seen. Neither of them moved. They simply held onto each other like long-lost sisters.

Then she helped Miranda climb into the forward seat of the AH-64D Apache, slipping the helmet over her head and buckling the seat harness herself.

"I'm sorry about the windows," Holly waved a hand through the openings in the cockpit door where she'd blown away the glass to fire her rifle. "It's going to make the ride back pretty windy for you. But I can't take an American Apache helicopter where I have to go."

"Ish okay," Miranda assured her.

Holly handed the Taser to Andi as she came up to ask what the plan was.

"Give this to Taz. Tell her thanks. Now you get Miranda back. Keep her safe."

She was so serious that Andi could only nod. "Where are you taking her?"

Elayne's fuming was quieter but no calmer from behind the closed canopy on the Havoc.

"Do you hear how close she came to starting a war?" Holly just shook her head and pulled out her phone to begin typing a text.

Andi thought about the sabotage on the crashed Airbus at Johnston Atoll half a world away. Then she looked up at Elayne flailing ineffectively against the heavy straps securing her in her seat. Finally, she looked back across the desert toward the new crash that had made the fireball ten miles past the first wreck.

She turned back to Holly. "You already know what we're

going to find on the crash of the Senate committee members."

Holly nodded but stayed focused on her text.

Andi tried to picture it, but sabotage wasn't part of her Army past. She'd been a helicopter pilot. Her duty had been delivering people who *did* the black ops, not doing them herself.

"A... Oh my god! We're going to find that a Russian triggering device, even Russian explosives, are what downed a US military plane full of Senators."

"The first plane crash was to kill me. The second one was probably to entice Miranda into a kill zone. Or worse, a capture zone. The fact that Elayne would turn Syria into the next Vietnam by starting a major war would simply be an added bonus in her mind. The last place they had her wasn't secure enough. I'm going to take her where she can't...*do* anything. Ever again."

Holly turned toward the Havoc.

"Can you fly that thing?"

Holly's smile looked sad, despite the lilt in her voice.

"Just watch me, mate."

73

ELAYNE COULDN'T EVEN WIGGLE A FINGER. HOLLY HAD trapped her thoroughly.

"I'm not going back to that goddamn prison, Harper." Her throat felt like she'd swallowed steel spikes.

"Nope."

"Where are we going?" She was hoarse and hurting. But pain didn't matter to a Zaslon operative. "Somewhere I can screw you with a baseball bat? Where I can ram a—"

"Home."

"Fucking Australia? Oh no. I'm soo scared."

Holly's laugh sounded bitter as she closed the canopy and powered up the Havoc. "That's no more my home than it be yours. Not even close, mate."

"I'm not your mate, Harper. I ever mate with you, it's gonna be—"

"Too fuck me dead. I get it." She took them aloft.

Then she turned northwest and began to climb over the ridge.

"But that way lies Tiyas Airbase."

"Better than a slap in the face with a wet fish."

"What the hell are you talking about? I want to kill you myself, bitch. Not the goddamn Russian Air Force. C'mon, Harper, we have to do this. You. Me. You dying in agony, knowing I'm gonna screw your precious Miranda myself until it kills her. Harper! *Harper!*"

Holly didn't offer another word no matter what Elayne yelled at her.

74

ANDI HAD FLOWN SEVERAL MILES BEFORE SHE REALIZED THAT Holly wasn't behind her.

On the radar, there was a tiny blip that must be the Havoc. Even as Andi watched, the blip moved farther away —directly away!

That couldn't be right.

Andi turned the Apache around.

The radar wasn't nose- or belly-mounted like most helicopters; it was in a bubble dome that stuck up above the center of the main rotor. The sensitivity didn't increase with her turn as it did on most helicopters, but it still made no sense.

The blip of the Mi-28 Havoc was flying directly toward Tiyas Airbase.

"What are you doing, Holly?" She couldn't use the radio to ask. Even if they'd agreed on a frequency, the Russians would monitor it and scramble their defenses.

Andi raised herself as high as she could, barely enough to see Miranda's head slumped to one side. She'd fallen back asleep in the front seat. She hadn't even roused when Andi had checked her pulse before taking off.

Torn between rushing Miranda back to safety and seeing what Holly was doing, Andi finally raced after the Havoc.

Holly cleared the ridge in far better control than Elayne and disappeared from view. She would now be visible to the Russians.

Andi slipped her Apache up behind a sharp ridge edge, then eased slowly upward in a stable hover.

The reason an Apache's radar dome was mounted above the rotor blades was multi-fold. One advantage was a clear three-hundred-and-sixty-degree view for the radar sweep. But the main advantage was that it let her hover out of sight with only the dome visible. It let her look over the horizon—in this case, the mountain's ridgeline—without exposing her aircraft.

Holly had descended again, landing only a few kilometers from the Tiyas airfield. Already, a pair of Russian helos were lifting into the setting sun and turning in her direction.

The Havoc sat on the ground for another thirty seconds while Andi held her breath.

Then it fired an entire salvo of missiles.

Both of the approaching Russian helicopters managed to release chaff and get clear.

The missiles impacted the desert just this side of the nearest hangars, tearing up nothing but desert.

Then the Havoc took off and climbed straight toward the Tiyas Military Airbase.

The response was swift.

The two Russian helicopters that had been sent from Tiyas to investigate rushed in.

The Havoc was climbing through five hundred feet when it was struck by missiles from both gunships.

It didn't dissolve; it exploded so violently that it must have been scattered over a square kilometer or more.

Andi couldn't make a sound.

Her mouth was open, but no scream found its way out her throat.

Tears blinded her as she eased once more below the ridgeline and turned for al-Tanf.

Miranda slept all the way there.

And Andi couldn't stop crying.

75

"SORRY, I HAVE A TEAM ARRIVING AT THE SYRIA CRASH THAT I've been waiting to hear from." Clarissa excused herself from the conference table where she and Gavin Chalmers were discussing the Middle East situation.

She crossed to her desk. She'd left her phone there but had heard its sharp buzz as it rattled on the glass.

Clarissa opened the message.

A man made phone calls to Guest Seven's cell. Who at CIA wins with dead Senators and a war in Syria?

Somehow Holly Harper had done it again. She'd caught up with Guest Seven. What's more, she'd again taken her alive and found out about her channel of communication out of the CIA Black Site.

Clarissa's own phone was so rarely from her side that it was hard to imagine someone else ever accessing it.

Clark?

But that was ridiculous. She couldn't recall ever telling him about the Diego Garcia Black Site, never mind Guest Seven.

Maybe someone with more direct access to Guest Seven's phone? Ernie Maxwell out at Diego Garcia had the knowledge of Russia and the Middle east.

But no, he couldn't have issued orders to the SOG; it had to be one of her directors.

She looked about her office. But how?

Clarissa tapped a quick message before she replaced her phone carefully in its usual spot on her desk. The only other place she ever put it was in her purse. Someone had been close enough to grab it before it auto-locked.

Someone had been in her office, taking advantage of a moment she'd been away.

Someone who knew about Guest Seven.

And the landline connection to Guest Seven.

Or had found out about both.

Clarissa turned to look at Gavin, still seated at the conference table.

Gavin Chalmers, the Department Director of the Middle East Desk.

The most critical and powerful position in the CIA outside of her own and the Russia Desk.

She might step out of the room to get a file or something. If he waited and watched, he might have accessed her phone.

The SOG orders, supposedly sent from her desk. They would damn her, lose the directorship.

Holly's question, *Who at CIA wins with dead Senators and a war in Syria?*

That, *and* who would win at the CIA if she went down?

With a war in the Middle East, who would they call to replace her but...

The answer was sitting right in front of her.

Gavin watched her for a long moment.

Then he smiled slowly, before rising to his feet and approaching her.

"You're so slow on the uptake. I was worried about that but you were even slower than I thought. Now it's all coming home to roost on you, Clarissa. I don't have such pretty tits like yours, but I wonder if your precious Vice President will care so much about them when his wife is in jail for murdering two airliners. He'll have to resign in disgrace, you know."

Her intercom buzzed. She didn't turn to answer it.

She waited him out but it took everything she had to control her breathing.

"If you hadn't been fucking your way to the top, D/CIA would have been mine, not yours. *Mine, goddamn it!*" He screamed it right in her face.

"Yours?" She kept her voice soft to keep him close. His attention on her. In the background she heard the tiniest little metallic click. Unnoticeable if she hadn't been listening for it.

Gavin shook his head. "You'll see. There's proof. My back channel is dead, so you don't even get that."

He said it like a threat, but she knew he didn't have it in him—Gavin had been a political animal, never a field agent. His connection to Guest Seven had died some other way.

Oh!

Now it took everything she had *not* to laugh in his face.

Yes, Gavin had found a way to talk to Guest Seven, some operative at the Diego Garcia site who had tapped him straight into her cell's phone. He hadn't called from her phone, just using it long enough to find Guest Seven's calls, then set a trace of his own until he found it, doctored it. And Guest Seven had killed Gavin's accomplice during her escape, erasing the back channel.

"And as you sit in your ugly little cell," Gavin was gloating, "—because it won't be any pretty white-collar prison for you—I'll leave you to figure it out on your own. If you're an exceptionally good girl, maybe I'll come by and tell you a little fairy tale to pass the time. Someday. After you've rotted for a long, long while."

He backed her against the glass edge of her desk.

"Are you really that good in bed? I always respected Clark. Until you got your claws into him."

Clarissa saw a motion in the background, but was well enough trained to not turn and draw Gavin's attention there.

"Would you like to find out just how good I am?" She slid her fingers inside his pants.

His smile was slow and avaricious.

"No. Not that, you weasel," she leaned in and snarled right in his face. "You wouldn't last a single day as D/CIA."

"Oh and why is that?" He tried to back away, but she had a tight grip on his belt pinning him in place.

At least until the moment that Kurt Grice slipped an arm around Gavin's neck.

Gavin's eyes went wide with panic, but he was unable to make a sound.

The head of the Special Operations Group had answered her text even faster than she'd hoped—she'd told him to "stay close" and he'd taken that very literally. She'd texted him because she'd wanted to discuss the implications of Holly's message with him. Instead...

The intercom buzz had announced his arrival.

His sharp ears must have heard Gavin's shout despite the room's sound insulation. With his training, the locked door had probably only slowed him down for a few seconds.

Clarissa fisted her hand on Gavin's belt, and used her grip to pin him in place as she drove her knee into his crotch as hard as she could.

Kurt's tight air choke only allowed the smallest squeak to escape Gavin's throat.

She leaned in until they were nose-to-nose, almost lip-to-lip.

"You have no idea how good I am."

She took a half step back and looked at Kurt.

Kurt looked at her with no expression.

At her nod, he shifted from a cross-throat bar cutting off his air, to pin Gavin's jugular veins with his biceps and forearm in a blood choke.

Gavin was too busy not believing this could be happening to even struggle.

Twelve seconds later, he slumped against Kurt's arm, unconscious.

Releasing her hold on his belt, Clarissa placed her hand on the center of Gavin's chest.

She and Kurt continued to watch each other; neither of them moved a single muscle.

She wasn't worried about some "if I'm dead" letter of accusation; Gavin wouldn't think that way.

At sixty seconds, when his brain should just be starting to die, she felt it.

Respiratory arrest.

His heart was still beating—sluggishly—but with no blood flow, his brain had given up on his lungs.

She nodded and Kurt let him drop to the floor.

Drastic medical action in the next two minutes might save him. At four minutes, he'd be a vegetable.

They waited through three more long minutes.

Then Kurt pulled out a small radio, "Heart attack. Director's office. Call an ambulance."

After nodding to Kurt, she stepped into the private bath until his team was done.

Clarissa took her phone with her this time.

She sent a *Found him!* as thanks to Holly. There was no answer; she hadn't expected one.

Then she called the hacker twins. Knowing the missing link made it safe to purge the message paths so that nothing pointed to her.

If Gavin had his own connection to the Black Site...

"Any connections between Gavin Chalmers and CIA personnel at Diego Garcia?"

Heidi rattled some keys and then laughed. "A much-despised son-in-law."

"Died last night?"

Heidi sobered, "Um. Yes."

"Acknowledged," she hung up.

That meant Ernie Maxwell hadn't been a part of Gavin's bid for power.

She sent him a text.

Site down?

Crashed. They could be talking about the Internet.

A man of action. A genuinely pleasant change from Gavin Chalmers.

How do you feel about coming to DC?

?

Middle East Desk just opened up. He'd done time on the

ground in more of those countries than most Americans could even name, never mind locate.

On the next flight.

Yes, she'd always liked Ernie Maxwell.

76

For two long days, Andi didn't tell anyone what had happened to Holly.

Miranda—pronounced fit and healthy by the base's medic once her system had finished purging the morphine—had led the investigation. Stage by stage, they'd narrowed in on the cause.

Ironically, it was Mike who'd found it, the least technical person on the team.

When he had asked where Holly had gone this time, Andi had only been able to shake her head.

He'd looked ready to press her on it, but apparently saw something in her face that he wouldn't like the answer. Unlike previous times, he'd hadn't repeated the question even once.

Instead, he'd entered some strange mode of hypervigilance that Andi barely recognized as still being Mike. He drove them all as if solving this crash could somehow bring Holly back to life.

He'd been the one who found a small piece, deep in the debris field, with Cyrillic lettering.

Taz had known Holly's fate the moment that Andi returned the Taser. "Holly wanted you to have this. It...helped."

Taz had held it close.

Only Jeremy and Miranda remained safely unaware.

She accompanied Jeremy all through a long afternoon trying to find a way to tell him, but had never found it. Instead, Jeremy had taught her how to collect scrapings of powder burns and other areas for bomb residue.

"Would that be enough to tell if it's Russian or not?"

He nodded. "Sure. With that new spectral analyzer, I could tell PVV-5A from C-4 clear as a thumbprint. Why?"

Andi had just said, "You'll see."

Everything Holly said had proved to be true. It was *impossible* that she was dead.

The Army had cleared the bodies, then set up a guard perimeter.

For two long days their NTSB team scoured the remains of the Senators' crash. And part of another at the Falcon 7X site.

"Elayne said she blew it up. There's not that much to know."

And there wasn't. Remains were gathered as well as possible, with samples kept for DNA matching. The Cockpit Voice Recorders had kept running right to the very end. They were...horrific.

And that was just the transcription: (laughter) (screams) (giggling) (more screams)... All with the same time mark.

Taz had taken on the burden of doing the transcription,

and even the tough Latina had looked shaken by the time she was done.

By unspoken agreement, either Andi herself or Taz had always been close by Miranda's side—though she appeared completely unaffected.

The Senate plane had been downed by a simple pressure trigger—engaging when the plane had climbed aloft into thinner air, and firing when the plane descended into higher pressure near landing.

Clarissa Reese had announced that a rogue Russian Zaslon operative was suspected of causing the Senators' plane crash. Also that "he" had been regrettably killed in turn by "his" own people before questioning.

When she'd asked Taz about the half-truths, she'd laughed harshly.

"You got lucky. Your career avoided Washington, DC. It's a nest of self-serving pit vipers. Everything has two messages, except when it has three."

Andi tried, but the only one she saw was the near-truth of what had been reported.

Taz began counting on her fingers. "She told the press that the cause was discovered, by the CIA no less, and the crisis was over. So she looks good."

Andi nodded, she understood that one.

"She told the Russians we had one of their Zaslon operatives, they don't know for how long, and then we executed them. Those people are supposed to be untouchable. It will spook the crap out of them. They have to know they lost a female agent a year ago. But that they also lost a male one to us? They'll be scrabbling around for months trying to solve that one."

"Wow! That'll be a witch hunt I want no part of. Is there a third one?"

"Yes," Taz looked grim. "She told the American people and Congress that Russia is now practicing no-holds-barred covert tactics against us with the 'execution' of the Senate investigation committee. And the only answer to counter that is..."

"The CIA," Andi almost choked on the initials.

If US-Russia relations had been souring before, they were now worse.

That must have been Clarissa's intent. The CIA was supposed to help keep the peace, but they would have no role in a peaceful world.

She suspected that a lot more answers had died along with Holly.

77

THE INVESTIGATIONS WERE DONE.

Jeremy was, of course, taking a few final photographs that were sure to be duplicated by other images he'd already taken. Taz walked with him, not really looking at anything, but the Taser, with a fresh cartridge, was still jammed in her back pocket.

Miranda liked that they were doing it together. Jeremy had lost none of his drive, but he was...

"He's better around her, isn't he?" She asked Andi, who stood beside her on a slight rise overlooking the wreckage.

"I didn't know him before. But they do seem to fit together well."

"Like..." she decided to try for a metaphor, "...two pieces of wreckage finally fitting together?"

Andi laughed softly. "No, Miranda. That implies they're both broken like wreckage—destroyed beyond use. No, they fit together like a parts of an airplane in manufacture, becoming whole. Though I don't think they're that far along yet."

"I'll never understand metaphors."

Mike was still wandering around the site as if he'd find something gone astray.

"What's he looking for? I told him we were done."

"I don't think he even knows. I suspect that each piece he turns over, some part of him hopes that he'll find Holly."

"Oh, is that a metaphor?"

"No, just a sad truth."

The sun was going down and the scorching heat of the day was cooling, almost pleasant.

"Three days," Andi's voice was soft.

"What?"

"Sorry, I didn't mean to say anything."

"But you did. What was three days?"

Andi sighed. "It was three days ago, at just this time of day, that I saw Holly...uh...fly away."

"I didn't dream it, did I?"

"I was hoping you weren't awake," Andi's voice was impossibly soft.

"I wasn't sure." Even though it was medically unlikely, she could still feel the drug lurking deep inside her, making her doubt each experience, as if she didn't doubt them enough herself to begin with.

"I told Taz, but not Mike or Jeremy." She waved toward Mike as he nudged over a seat cushion with his toe, "but I think he knows. Or at least some part of him does."

"Oh."

"Do you think I should tell them? Him and Jeremy?"

"Tell them what?"

"That Holly sacrificed herself to save us from that crazy Zaslon operative. She also stopped a war. If Elayne had gotten back to the Russians, terrible things would have come out."

Miranda actually looked at Andi's face in surprise. "Is that what she did?"

"You don't think she stopped a war?"

"Oh, that? Knowing Holly, it wouldn't surprise me. I always let her take care of that sort of thing. I only care about the planes."

"You don't think she sacrificed herself? We both saw it."

Miranda thought back to the transcript of Mike's interview with Quint Dermott, the copilot on the Airbus crash. *The way I figured it, if anyone knew how to survive, it's Holly Harper. So, I told Dani we needed to get on the ground fast. Seems Holly had the right of it as usual. Crikey! Her parents buried her when she was sixteen, yet she just saved my life and a whole mess of others' on that plane. How many times has that woman survived being dead?*

Miranda merely shrugged at Andi's look as she turned to the M-ATV waiting to take them back to camp.

"But—"

Miranda turned to look at her.

"I try not to worry about what I can't change. I learned that from an incredibly wise person."

"Who?" Andi followed her to the vehicle.

"You." Miranda climbed aboard and waited for the others to catch up with her.

78

Night. Only at night.

Daylight had too many eyes.

Too much heat.

The secret to crossing the desert. Move at night.

Walk heavy to spook the snakes away.

What snakes? Not her desert. Don't know.

Finding food in the desert. Hunt at dawn and twilight.

Raw lizard, no head.

Scorpion, cut off stinger and poison sacs.

Finding water... No water.

Flecks of dew licked from a slit-open and laid-out plastic water bottle.

Now. Mirages?

Elayne flying aloft.

No. That was before. Three days. Yesterday. Last week. Some timeless time ago.

The Mi-28 Havoc.

Landing.

SASR training—she'd loved the rotorcraft.

Punch in the commands.

Especially the weapons systems.

A salvo of missiles, striking into the evening sky.

Then setting the autopilot. Hanging onto the hull, leaning into the cockpit, and pressing "Initiate."

Elayne on some rant. Jacking herself off on death.

So fast. It had happened so fast.

By the time she'd let go, she'd been lucky not to break an ankle from the long fall—or worse.

Nothing to salvage from the helo but a small bottle of water.

Nursed, but long gone.

A gun. Not hers. Two knives that were. And a hat.

No water.

Digging into the gritty dirt. Buried. Hidden. Hidden while the Russian helicopters killed the Russian Havoc flown by an autopilot with only a screaming maniac for a passenger.

The Russians. So close.

She'd laid buried long into the night. Wasting the night, but the Russians had been hunting. Hunting for...her.

At night.

No water.

Crossing that first ridge. Out of sight of the Russians. It had taken her until dawn.

Somewhere in that long first night...her phone battery had run out. Last charged...at Quint's?

Quint. Dear Quint.

The little boy who had interrupted more than a few good tussles when she was a teen seeking...

Relief.

From family.

From the madness of Elayne.

But Elayne's spirit had gone walkabout with her, following her across the parched desert. Chortling over details about the diverse, even unique ways she was going to screw each and every one of them—to death.

No, none of that was her.

Was Quint right? Was she in a relationship with someone? Mike? A real one?

She remembered Mike's first words to her a year ago, right after she'd faced down a one-star general to protect Miranda.

What is wrong with you two? Are you trying *to get shot?*

Clear as if it just happened.

In the desert.

Different desert.

Long ago.

Didn't matter.

Other than Mike, everyone she'd ever slept with was military (or close, in Quint's case). Mike was always a surprise and seemed to care about her despite how many times she'd pushed him away. Maybe despite himself. His background remained as murky as her own, but he'd found a way to move past it, and she'd always admired that about him.

Yes, the sex was good.

But even just watching Mike's care for the rest of the team had slowly taught her that there were ways to do that without killing to protect.

"Tricky," she croaked at the dawn light.

He'd definitely out-maneuvered her.

Maybe himself, too.

Like she'd told...someone.

The thought made her smile against cracked lips.

Quint was right—poor Quint.

She and Mike. Against everything they'd ever said. Or denied. Or not said.

She and Mike.

And now...mirages.

A great jet climbing into the sky above a whirlwind of brown dust. Pretty vortices of brown behind its twin engines.

So close.

She reached out a hand, but couldn't seem to touch it.

79

"WE NEED TO TURN BACK," THE C-40A CLIPPER JET continued to roar aloft.

"Why, Miranda?" Mike leaned close to her.

"Because," she pointed back out the window, "I just saw the same hat I forgot to take."

"I can get you a new hat, Miranda."

"You don't need to. My hat is on my mantle at home. I forgot it there."

"Then we don't need to turn back."

Miranda opened her mouth, then closed it again. It was one of those strange circular conversations she always had such a challenging time finding her way out of.

She tried again.

"Mike, we need to turn back."

"For a hat?"

"Yes, for Holly's hat."

"But you said it's on your mantle at home."

"Mine is."

"Then why—"

"Because I just saw Holly's hat down there."

"You mean like this one?" Mike tapped the bill of his own hat.

"No. That's *your* hat. I just saw Holly's. Down there."

Mike's eyes were slowly widening.

Andi leaned in. "Okay, Miranda. What did you say to him this time?"

"I said—"

Mike grabbed her arm hard but didn't appear to be able to speak.

"All I said was, 'I just saw Holly's hat. Down there.' It's bright yellow. It's quite easy to spot. That's all I said. Honestly," she turned to Andi. "I was being most careful."

Mike's jaw was down and now Jeremy and Taz were listening in as well.

"Miranda," Andi asked calmly. "Was Holly wearing it?"

"All I saw was the hat. They do all look alike. Unless you get close enough to inspect the individual size selections or staining, of course. I wasn't able to do that as we took off. But if Holly wasn't wearing it, then it wouldn't be hers. Or would it?"

In the frenzy that followed, no one answered her question.

———

Keep reading for an excerpt from
Miranda Chase #8: White Top

WHITE TOP (EXCERPT)

IF YOU ENJOYED THAT, BE SURE YOU DON'T MISS THE NEXT TITLE IN THE MIRANDA CHASE SERIES!

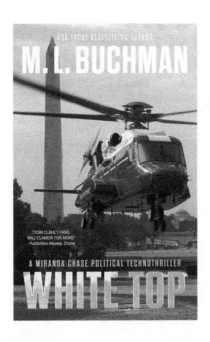

WHITE TOP (EXCERPT)

Naval Air Station Anacostia
Elevation: unlisted for security reasons
Washington, DC
6 days ago

MAJOR TAMATHA JONES DID HER BEST TO REMEMBER HOW TO breathe. Marine Corps helicopter pilots were not supposed to have trouble breathing under any conditions, but today was proving to be the exception to the rule.

She worked her way through the preflight walkaround—a wholly redundant activity here at HMX-1. The mechanics here were the best in the world and the squadrons birds reflected it; they had to. And none more so than her helo. When the President of the United States stepped aboard and it became Marine One, it had to be perfect.

But she still did a full preflight inspection every time.

Then she took one more circle around her brand-new VH-92A Superhawk just...because. Sixty-eight feet and six inches of executive transport muscle. Marine green below, white top above, and down the sides, block-lettered in white, "United States of America." The only bright colors were also the ones that mattered most—the blue-and-yellow Presidential seals affixed below both pilots' side windows.

Inside for her passengers was luxury seating, including a full armchair for the President and a guest, couches alongside, and more seating to the rear. Less obvious were the armor, attack evasion gear (both passive and active), a fully isolatable air system, and a communications suite that could run a war.

During the last two years of testing and certification of the VH-92A, she'd made the landing on the White House's South Lawn over a hundred times in the simulator. She'd also made it in the real world seven times—always when the President was *not* in residence so that he wouldn't be disturbed.

But today was the first transport of President Roy Cole aboard the Marine's newest bird. And unexpectedly, the first Presidential "lift" had fallen to her—carrying him from the White House for the ten-mile flight to Air Force One waiting at Andrews Air Force Base.

Normally, HMX-1 commander Colonel McGrady was the President's pilot. But he was already prepositioned at Tel Nof Airbase in Israel, the first stop of the President's whirlwind global tour. The colonel would fly over twenty-seven hours —and many more without the President aboard—over the next six days. She'd be aloft for approximately six minutes and a half minutes.

It didn't matter. McGrady had tapped her for the Number Two slot, and she would be the first to fly the Commander-in-Chief aboard his new Marine One helo—

which just might stop her heart along with her breathing at this rate.

She trailed a hand over the shining paint job, after wiping her fingertips on the leg of her dress slacks to make sure she wouldn't leave any smudges. The dark green paint was mirror-bright enough for her to check the set of her short-sleeved Service C—or more commonly Service Charlie—tan uniform shirt. Even the hubs of the wheels shone. Not a spec of grease would dare blemish a Marine One helo, not when it was prepared by the Marines.

At the nose of the bird, Tamatha turned to face her helo directly and saluted sharply.

"Seriously, Major?" Her copilot strolled over from the ready room. Vance Brown was from Texas, so there was no accounting for him. They'd flown together back in the VMM-265 out of Okinawa, and he knew full well that she always saluted any aircraft she was about to fly. She liked thanking her bird in advance for a safe ride.

"Dragons rule!" he declared.

"No longer a Dragon, Captain Brown. You're a Nighthawk."

"Once a Dragon, always a Dragon," Vance insisted. The emblem of the VMM-265 was *very* cool and she'd worn it with great pride—a green dragon wound through the heart of the Japanese kanji *for* dragon. But now she wore the crossed rotor blades of HMX-1 and there was no prouder patch in the Corps except for the Presidential Pilot patch she'd be cleared to wear after this flight.

She ignored Vance and circled to the right forward stair. Unlike the VH-3D Sea King, the entry door was on the pilot's side. Whenever one of the sixty-year-old Sea Kings landed on the White House lawn, the newsies were always photographing the copilot. Her big Superhawk would land facing the other way and she would be the one in the photographs.

Because of that, she double-checked that the Presidential Seal below her window was perfectly clean. Crew Chief Mathieson caught her at it and just grinned. Not a chance he would have missed that. There was an entire special protocol for cleaning and maintenance of the right front corner of the VH-92A. It, along with Sergeant Mathieson, would be the two most photographed Marine Corps assets for the years to come. Times ten, as this was the first flight.

It was only fitting that he was the one photographed as he awaited to salute the President at the base of the stairs. It was really his bird, she simply was allowed to fly it.

They'd pre-staged at Joint Base Anacostia-Bolling at the juncture of the Anacostia and Potomac Rivers early this morning. A sea fog was rolling into their main base at Quantico near the mouth of the Potomac, and she hadn't wanted to risk being grounded.

Most of the old Flying Field at Anacostia had long since been consumed by office buildings, primarily the headquarters of the Defense Intelligence Agency. The HMX-1 hangar and the sixty-thousand square feet that made up the squadron's seven helipads were all that had withstood the tide of "improvements." Give her a helo cockpit over a desk any day of the week.

Once in and seated, she took that crucial moment to switch her brain over. The thousand worries from overseeing her section of the squadron, training new pilots, making sure every action and decision was properly logged—all of it went away.

For the next hour or so, she was just a pilot and nothing else mattered.

They buckled in and started down the checklists. She and Vance could do it by rote, but they followed every step in the standard call-and-response that had kept pilots alive since the beginning of flight.

To her left and right, two identical birds were doing the same. HMX-1 always flew in flights of two or three—one designated primary and the others as decoy birds. In flight, the three of them would shuffle about the sky so that no one could guess which carried the President.

"Package ready?" she keyed the mic.

The two decoys acknowledged, then the two Night Stalkers' gunships that were already aloft in guard position. The black helos of the 160th SOAR typically flew overwatch of the official "lift package" as the Marine Corps flight was known.

Tiny wisps of fog that had wandered this far up the Potomac were blasted aside as the three big VH-92A's took to the sky for their first-ever Presidential lift.

Her world condensed even further. The key to flying at this level was to be completely present. And she was.

Two hundred feet above Anacostia, she sliced over the golf course that divided the Anacostia and Potomac Rivers and turned upriver.

The route was the most highly guarded air route in the world. Nothing and no one was allowed to fly it except the helicopters of HMX-1. Tucked underneath the incredibly restrictive approach to Reagan National Airport and the outright prohibited air space around the National Mall.

Hard right past the Jefferson Memorial. Maintain altitude across the National Mall, well below the top of the

Washington Monument. That perfect instant when everything lined up. The Washington Monument and the Capitol building to the right; the World War II Memorial, the Reflecting Pool, and Lincoln to the left.

She always allowed herself a three-second glance to either side—to check that the airspace remained clear. Unable to take her hands from the controls to salute the marble President, she gave Lincoln a respectful nod.

No one except an HMX-1 pilot, not even the President, was privileged to have such a view of the nation's capital as she had from her high-visibility cockpit. She resisted the urge to whoop out a cheer—stay in the moment. She could cheer later when she watched herself on the news tonight; she'd been careful to set record to CNN for the next two hours and the nightly news.

She and Vance did trade grins.

Mathieson had left his seat directly behind her own to stand between the seats to watch the city with them. It wasn't regulation, but no one deserved it more.

One of the decoys slid in front of her and headed for the South Lawn. At the fifty-foot treetop level, he peeled up and to the right. The other decoy was close on her tail this time, until she began the final descent. He too peeled off to take up an overhead station. The two decoys and the two overwatch birds hung back far enough that rotor noise wouldn't disturb the President's departure.

Ducking down between the trees, the approach always looked impossibly small. But practice had taught her that the helo fit, as long as the pilot was perfect. A deep breath prepared her for the final move.

At twenty-five feet, she hovered over the three six-foot aluminum disks. The White House ground crew had preplaced them in the proper layout for her bird, all she had to do was hit the marks.

No ground crew, because HMX-1 Marine pilots didn't need them.

Instead, all she had were two six-inch-wide, twenty-foot-long strips of canvas tacked to the lawn.

"L marks the spot," Tamatha muttered to herself as she lined up the two strips, one dead ahead of her nose and the other at ninety degrees to the tip of the nose.

If she twisted around, she'd be able to see some of the disk that had to end up beneath her right wheel, but practice had taught her that was a distraction.

Head up, face front when flying. Colonel McGrady had made it clear what he expected of his Marine Corps pilots and she'd given everything she had to getting it right by the McGrady Bible.

Must have worked; she was here.

The wheels kissed down.

Engines to idle, disengage and brake the rotors to a stop.

She was *here.*

On the White House South Lawn. She glanced right as Sergeant Mathieson lowered the door, descended, and moved to guard the stair.

Tamatha checked the clock, precisely five minutes early.

Exactly where she wanted to be.

Though she could do without the news pool photographers who, for the next five minutes would have nothing to photograph except her aircraft, her crew chief, and herself.

———

"YOU'RE WITH ME, DRAKE."

"Are you sure it's not too late to resign, Mr. President?"

President Roy Cole laughed, which had been the point. "Between you and Marian, I've got to find myself some better help."

"Hey, I'm Jewish," National Security Adviser Marian Feldman protested, "whining is part of the heritage. I have no idea what his problem is."

The three of them had practically been in each other's pockets all week in preparation for this trip; most vestiges of formality hadn't survived such an effort. Drake Nason was actually looking forward to the trip. As a four-star general and the Chairman of the Joint Chiefs of Staff, he rarely left the circuit of the Pentagon and the White House anymore. A chance to spend a week aloft aboard Air Force One was a welcome break—and possibly even fix some problems. The Middle East was always a nightmare. Hopefully this trip would dial it back some...maybe...not likely. But they had to try.

"How did this become my life?" He teased the President as he picked up the Berluti leather satchel that Lizzy had bought him for their one-year anniversary—which had probably cost almost as much as the pearl necklace he'd bought for her. Both of them had been relieved from fears of extravagance. She'd married late in life, and he'd had a long gap since Patty's death, which meant they had to make up for lost time.

"You both made the same damn mistake, you said 'Yes' when I asked you to serve."

"Damn it! I knew it was something," Marian gathered the final files off the Situation Room table and slipped them into her own briefcase. "How do I look?"

"Like you're about to be on national television..."

"But what?" she glanced up at him as they followed the President up the stairs, then headed toward the Oval Office for the President to get his coat.

"But don't worry, all they're going to care about is the new helicopter and him."

Roy glanced back. "The new one? About time. I was afraid they wouldn't even be ready for the *next* President."

"The Marines seem to think that being careful means four years of testing."

"Well," Marian commented, "I for one am in favor of that. Helicopters make me crazy."

Through the Oval Office's bulletproof glass—so thick that everything outside looked like a watercolor that had been caught in the rain—Drake saw the VH-92A Superhawk sitting on the South Lawn. He loved helos. As a 75th Army Ranger, he'd ridden in a lot of them. Even some flown by Marines, God help him.

The VH-92A had been a long time coming.

It couldn't have any real relation to this trip, but it gave him hope anyway. Hope that maybe they could turn some things around in the Middle East.

Major Tamatha Jones kept her focus.

President Cole was a creature of habit, which wasn't always a good thing for security, but the Marine in her appreciated it.

He exited the White House at precisely two minutes before scheduled departure. He took four questions from the gathered newsies. At thirty seconds to go, he waved goodbye. It was only after he turned his back on the newsies that she could see the deep exhaustion he'd been hiding from them. Seven years in office had definitely taken their toll. Yet he saluted Mathieson neatly before boarding. And was ready to lift precisely on schedule.

She almost yelped when a fist thumped on her shoulder.

"Damn sharp helo you've got here."

"Brand-new just for you, Mr. President."

"I see that you finally shoved McGrady aside. Well done, Major Jones."

"Thank you, sir." She'd never actually met the President before and was shocked that he knew her name. She covered her own nerves, "He fought against it but it had to be done. I hope you won't miss him too much, sir."

To the President's left, Vance's eyes went wide.

"Not so's I'd notice. Going to get me to the airport in one piece?"

"That's the plan, sir. Unless you had something else in mind."

He squinted at her. "What? Like in two pieces, delivered separately for later reassembly?"

Vance rolled his eyes in what appeared to be panic.

She should have kept her damn mouth shut.

"I was thinking more along the lines of a sunny day on the Chincoteague shore."

"That suggestion, Major, just might get you made a colonel. You're on...next time."

"Yes, sir."

"Go Marine," he held out a hand and she shook it. That he also shook Vance's was decent and would probably be the highlight of his Texan existence.

"*Semper Fi*, Mr. President. Now, if you'll sit down and

buckle up, I'll see what I can do about the in-one-piece part of that deal."

He chuckled as he turned for his seat.

The rest of the flight went precisely to plan.

White House to Andrews, she departed twenty-eight seconds late, but made sure that she landed exactly on schedule.

After the President had exited her helo and Air Force One was aloft, she lifted and turned for Quantico. The fog had burned off enough that she was able to land without needing her instruments. Once down, she and Vance headed for the mission debrief.

Sergeant Mathieson was already changing out of his dress blues. Even after so short a flight, the VH-92A would now undergo a full inspection that would take several hours.

"You're a crazy person, Jones."

"Gee, and I don't even have being from Texas as an excuse."

"Offering to cut the President into pieces...Go Marine indeed."

They were both laughing as they entered the debrief room. Every step from the foggy morning to the final touchdown would be reviewed in detail—this was HMX-1 after all.

HMX-1 had a perfect record of never *once* since its founding, having an incident while delivering the President and other VIPs. That's all she cared about. Their record was still intact on her watch.

———

Today

"HOW DID ONE LITTLE PLANE CAUSE SO MUCH DAMAGE?"

"That's what we're here to learn, Mike." Miranda thought that question was a little obvious for a seasoned NTSB investigator.

"I understand that. I simply never thought about a commuter plane creating an airliner's worth of damage."

"It did crash into an opera house," Holly commented. "Tragic and ridiculous at the same time."

Coming soon: White Top

ABOUT THE AUTHOR

USA Today and Amazon #1 Bestseller M. L. "Matt" Buchman started writing on a flight from Japan to ride his bicycle across the Australian Outback. Just part of a solo around-the-world trip that ultimately launched his writing career.

From the very beginning, his powerful female heroines insisted on putting character first, *then* a great adventure. He's since written over 70 action-adventure thrillers and military romantic suspense novels. And just for the fun of it: 100 short stories, and a fast-growing pile of read-by-author audiobooks.

Booklist says: "3X Top 10 of the Year." PW says: "Tom Clancy fans open to a strong female lead will clamor for more." His fans say: "I want more now...of everything." That his characters are even more insistent than his fans is a hoot.

As a 30-year project manager with a geophysics degree who has designed and built houses, flown and jumped out of planes, and solo-sailed a 50' ketch, he is awed by what is possible. More at: www.mlbuchman.com.

Other works by M. L. Buchman: *(* - also in audio)*

Action-Adventure Thrillers

Dead Chef
One Chef!
Two Chef!

Miranda Chase
Drone*
Thunderbolt*
Condor*
Ghostrider*
Raider*
Chinook*
Havoc*
White Top*

Romantic Suspense

Delta Force
Target Engaged*
Heart Strike*
Wild Justice*
Midnight Trust*

Firehawks
MAIN FLIGHT
Pure Heat
Full Blaze
Hot Point*
Flash of Fire*
Wild Fire

SMOKEJUMPERS
Wildfire at Dawn*
Wildfire at Larch Creek*
Wildfire on the Skagit*

The Night Stalkers
MAIN FLIGHT
The Night Is Mine
I Own the Dawn
Wait Until Dark
Take Over at Midnight

Light Up the Night
Bring On the Dusk
By Break of Day
AND THE NAVY
Christmas at Steel Beach
Christmas at Peleliu Cove
WHITE HOUSE HOLIDAY
Daniel's Christmas*
Frank's Independence Day*
Peter's Christmas*
Zachary's Christmas*
Roy's Independence Day*
Damien's Christmas*
5E
Target of the Heart
Target Lock on Love
Target of Mine
Target of One's Own

Shadow Force: Psi
At the Slightest Sound*
At the Quietest Word*
At the Merest Glance*
At the Clearest Sensation*

White House Protection Force
Off the Leash*
On Your Mark*
In the Weeds*

Contemporary Romance

Eagle Cove
Return to Eagle Cove
Recipe for Eagle Cove
Longing for Eagle Cove
Keepsake for Eagle Cove

Henderson's Ranch
Nathan's Big Sky*
Big Sky, Loyal Heart*
Big Sky Dog Whisperer*

Other works by M. L. Buchman:

Contemporary Romance (cont)

Love Abroad
Heart of the Cotswolds: England
Path of Love: Cinque Terre, Italy

Where Dreams
Where Dreams are Born
Where Dreams Reside
*Where Dreams Are of Christmas**
Where Dreams Unfold
Where Dreams Are Written

Science Fiction / Fantasy

Deities Anonymous
Cookbook from Hell: Reheated
Saviors 101

Single Titles
The Nara Reaction
Monk's Maze
the Me and Elsie Chronicles

Non-Fiction

Strategies for Success
Managing Your Inner Artist/Writer
*Estate Planning for Authors**
Character Voice
Narrate and Record Your Own
*Audiobook**

Short Story Series by M. L. Buchman:

Romantic Suspense

Delta Force
Th Delta Force Shooters
The Delta Force Warriors

Firehawks
The Firehawks Lookouts
The Firehawks Hotshots
The Firebirds

The Night Stalkers
The Night Stalkers 5D Stories
The Night Stalkers 5E Stories
The Night Stalkers CSAR
The Night Stalkers Wedding Stories

US Coast Guard

White House Protection Force

Contemporary Romance

Eagle Cove

Henderson's Ranch*

Where Dreams

Action-Adventure Thrillers

Dead Chef

Miranda Chase Origin Stories

Science Fiction / Fantasy

Deities Anonymous

Other
The Future Night Stalkers
Single Titles

SIGN UP FOR M. L. BUCHMAN'S NEWSLETTER TODAY

and receive:
Release News
Free Short Stories
a Free Book

Get your free book today. Do it now.
free-book.mlbuchman.com